Murder,
She Edited

Books by Kaitlyn Dunnett

Deadly Edits Mysteries:

Crime & Punctuation

Clause & Effect

A Fatal Fiction

Liss MacCrimmon Mysteries:

Kilt Dead

Scone Cold Dead

A Wee Christmas Homicide

The Corpse Wore Tartan

Scotched

Bagpipes, Brides, and Homicides

Vampires, Bones, and Treacle Scones

Ho-Ho-Homicide

The Scottie Barked at Midnight

Kilt at the Highland Games

X Marks the Scot

Overkilt

A View to a Kilt

Published by Kensington Publishing Corp.

Murder, She Edited

Kaitlyn Dunnett

KENSINGTON
PUBLISHING CORP.

www.kensingtonbooks.com

KENSINGTON BOOKS are published by

Kensington Publishing Corp.
119 West 40th Street
New York, NY 10018

Copyright © 2021 by Kathy Lynn Emerson

All Kensington titles, imprints and distributed lines are available at special quantity discounts for bulk purchases for sales promotion, premiums, fund-raising, educational or institutional use. Special book excerpts or customized printings can also be created to fit specific needs. For details, write or phone the office of the Kensington Special Sales Manager: Kensington Publishing Corp., 119 West 40th Street, New York, NY, 10018. Attn. Special Sales Department. Phone: 1-800-221-2647.

The K logo is a trademark of Kensington Publishing Corp.

Library of Congress Control Number: 2021931627

ISBN-13: 978-1-4967-2689-6
ISBN-10: 1-4967-2689-8
First Kensington Hardcover Edition: August 2021

ISBN-13: 978-1-4967-2691-9 (ebook)
ISBN-10: 1-4967-2961-X (ebook)

10 9 8 7 6 5 4 3 2 1

Printed in the United States of America

Murder,
She Edited

Chapter One

"Featherstone, De Vane, Doherty, Sanchez, and Schiller." I read the return address aloud as I carried the day's mail inside. "Now *there's* a mouthful for you, Cal."

The sheer number of names embossed on the flap were enough to identify the sender as a law firm. I tossed the rest of what I'd collected from the mailbox on my front porch—a flyer from the local grocery store and a postcard from my nephew, currently on vacation in Hawaii—onto the hall table and took the letter with me into the living room.

My faithful feline companion, Calpurnia, made no comment. She padded silently after me to hop up onto the loveseat and watch intently from the adjoining cushion as I extracted a thick, expensive-looking sheet of stationery from the envelope and skimmed its contents.

I could almost feel frown lines etching themselves into my forehead as I read. I started over from the top but there was no mistake. That I was the intended recipient was made abundantly clear by the fact that I was not only identified as Michelle Greenleigh Lincoln, widow of James Lincoln, but also as the daughter of Alfred and Catherine (Kitty) Coburg Greenleigh. What the letter did *not* explain was why I'd apparently inherited a "parcel of land" from a woman I'd last seen nearly two decades ago.

To be completely truthful, it took me a few minutes to remember who Tessa Swarthout *was*. When I did, and considered what little I knew of her, I still couldn't come up with any explanation for the unexpected inheritance.

Tessa and my late mother grew up together. Although they didn't see a lot of each other once they reached adulthood, Mom always referred to Tessa as her best friend. In other words, they were BFFs long before that term became popular.

I did remember the last time I'd seen Tessa. It was when I took my widowed mother, then in her eighties, to visit her old friend in a retirement community in Connecticut. I did some quick mental calculations. If Tessa had only just died, she must have been over a hundred years old. Remarkable! I turned seventy-one last December and I'm in pretty good shape for an old broad, but I have no expectation of surviving for a full century. I'm not sure I'd want to.

Calpurnia put her front paws on my thigh and nuzzled my hand, reminding me that I'd neglected to pet her for at least fifteen minutes. I remedied that situation at once, rhythmically stroking her multicolored fur while I read the letter a third time.

It was singularly lacking in details, but did suggest that I call "at my earliest convenience" to make an appointment with Leland Featherstone, senior partner in the law firm. I ran my finger over the embossed letterhead. If this was a scam, the perpetrators had spared no expense.

Gently shifting Cal out of the way, I abandoned the living room for the kitchen. I'd left my laptop on the table in the dining alcove, what my mother always called the "dinette."

I was born and raised in Lenape Hollow, New York, a

small town in the foothills of the Catskill Mountains. At eighteen, I left to attend college in Maine. Fifty years passed before I gave any thought to returning. By then, I'd been retired from teaching for some time and had recently been widowed. I was debating the wisdom of trying to go it alone in the rural location where my husband and I had long made our home. I *could* have managed, but I was ready for a change. When I received word of an approaching high school reunion, I was curious enough to look up Lenape Hollow online and, lo and behold, there was a real estate ad for the house I grew up in, the one my parents sold the same year I moved away. To make a long story short, I gave in to an impulse and bought it back.

That was just over three years ago. I won't say everything has gone smoothly since, but I'm happy with my decision. Thanks to my new career as a freelance editor—a book doctor, if you will—I've been able to pay for necessary repairs on the place and Calpurnia and I have settled in quite comfortably.

I'd been using the laptop to edit a chapter in a textbook for a client when I heard the mailman on the porch and decided it was time for a break. Now, settling into the dinette chair once more, I saved my work, made a backup copy, exited the word processing program, connected to a search engine, and typed in the name of the law firm. What came up on the screen reassured me that they were legitimate. Venerable, even. I took a few moments to study the vita and photo of Leland Featherstone, Esquire, before I reached for the phone.

A quarter of an hour later, I had an appointment for the next day at ten. I was a little surprised he could fit me in so quickly, and more curious than ever as to why Tessa Swarthout had left me a bequest.

Chapter Two

I had plans that evening. After an early supper, I changed out of my summer working clothes—baggy shorts and a T-shirt—and made myself slightly more presentable in lightweight slacks and a sleeveless top. I took a sweater, since even in mid-July it can get chilly once the sun goes down. I debated briefly whether to drive or walk before deciding in favor of stretching my legs. Lenape Hollow Memorial Library isn't all that far from my house, and I felt certain someone would offer to give me a lift home after the Friends of the Library meeting.

In less than ten minutes I'd descended the hill between Wedemeyer Terrace and Main Street and was halfway to my destination. The library, a new building since my teen years, is situated between a grocery store and the old redbrick elementary school—the same building that housed K–12 until I was in eleventh grade. That was when our brand-new high school opened. A half century later, that structure is in a sorry state while the "old" school seems likely to hold up for another hundred years. As the saying goes, "they just don't build 'em like they used to."

Most of the meeting, held in a medium-size multifunction room, was so routine as to be boring. We heard the treasurer's report and approved the cost of a field trip for the kids in the summer reading program. Then we discussed various fundraising activities, including the annual used book sale. I'd let my mind wander, wondering about my appointment with the lawyer the next day, when I suddenly realized that someone had just suggested that we increase the number of pages in the library newsletter.

I made haste to speak up. "Let's not get carried away. Copies may be printed as well as posted online, but we're not publishing a book. If the newsletter is too long, no one will read it. Important information will be lost in a sea of trivia."

My argument against expansion had an ulterior motive. At a previous Friends of the Library meeting, I'd made the mistake of letting myself be "volunteered" to edit this monthly publication. Make that write, edit, and produce. It's not an onerous task, but it can be time-consuming, and time is one thing I try not to waste. My work as a freelance editor already keeps me a bit busier than I want to be.

One of my post-retirement goals was to "stop and smell the roses." Everyone benefits from pausing now and again to enjoy the scenery. Writers call it "refilling the well" and expand the definition to include finding opportunities, every once in a while, to try something new and adventurous.

But I digress.

Since no one else in the Friends of the Library was foolish enough to want to take over as newsletter editor, my preference prevailed. I wondered if I should have taken advantage of the moment to lobby for *fewer* pages, but the moderator quickly moved on to the next item of business and I lost my chance.

In short order, the meeting came to a close and we descended on an array of desserts and drinks set out on a side table. Once I'd carried a plate overflowing with goodies back to my chair, my good friend Darlene Uberman rolled to a stop beside me. A quick glance at her lap assured me that she'd had no difficulty raiding the buffet.

"You want to avoid the gingersnaps," she warned me,

making a face. "They're tasty, but you could break a tooth biting into one."

"Figures." I'd taken three, passing up a delicious-looking slice of lemon pound cake.

Darlene and I are the same age. We were friends in high school, but lost touch once I moved away from Lenape Hollow. I was shocked when I first saw her again. The usual changes made by getting older weren't particularly unexpected—she was, to use her own words, "twice the woman she used to be" in the weight department and her hair had gone entirely white, while I was no longer the skinny kid I'd been during my teen years either, and my hair, once an ordinary medium brown, had turned that odd shade of gray that looks blond in the right lighting.

What I didn't expect were the deep lines chronic pain had etched in Darlene's face. She suffers from osteoarthritis in just about every joint in her body. It was so bad that by the time she turned sixty-two she had to take early retirement, giving up her post as head librarian, a job she loved. How well she functions from day to day depends, to a great extent, on the weather and on whether or not her meds are working. Sometimes she can walk unassisted and even do light housework like vacuuming and dusting. At others she needs what she refers to as "motorized transport," a battery-powered scooter, to get from one room to the next. She was using it this evening, but despite her mobility issues, she was in an upbeat mood. When she gave me the side-eye, her facial expression put me in mind of a mischievous elf.

"What's up?" she asked. "I was watching you during the meeting. You looked as if you were a million miles away."

"Not nearly so far. I have to go to Monticello tomorrow to talk to a lawyer." It would take me less than thirty minutes to drive there.

"A lawyer? Why?" She narrowed her eyes even more,

until I could barely make out the cornflower blue of her irises. "What have you done *now*?"

I pretended to be offended. "Me? I'll have you know I'm a paragon of virtue and rectitude."

"Ooh! Big words! Now you've put me in my place."

We grinned at each other. If we hadn't been out in public, we might very well have giggled like a couple of schoolgirls. Old friends can get away with that.

The thought sobered me. Without thinking, I bit into a gingersnap and instantly regretted it.

Darlene was watching me closely. She could tell my grimace wasn't entirely due to the texture of the cookie. "Seriously—are you in some kind of trouble?"

"Not at all. It might even be good news."

I shrugged off my sudden sense of unease and scanned our surroundings. The crowd, if you could call two dozen people a crowd, was beginning to thin out. Pam Ingram, the current head librarian, a sturdily built thirty-something brunette notable for her organizational skills, her endless patience with library patrons, and her peaches-and-cream complexion, was starting the cleanup, assisted by one of her library aides.

"Give me a lift home and I'll tell you what little I know."

"Done," Darlene agreed.

Since she's had plenty of practice, it didn't take her long to collapse the scooter and stash it in the back of her van. She heaved herself into the driver's seat with the help of the grab handle above the door and started the engine while I settled myself in the passenger seat. Before she put the vehicle in motion, she sent me the kind of look librarians reserve for disruptive patrons and teachers bestow on recalcitrant students.

"Okay, Mikki. Spill."

I gave her the gist of the letter I'd received from the lawyer.

"Tessa Swarthout? That name doesn't ring any bells." She pulled out of the library parking lot.

"I doubt you'd have met her. She didn't live in Lenape Hollow."

"How did you know her?"

"She used to come to the house to see my mother from time to time." Now that I thought about it, I realized that Tessa had been a fixture in my very early childhood. "I have a vague memory of going to see her once, too."

"Where?"

I shook my head. "I'm not sure. Somewhere out in the countryside. I remember that she lived in an old farmhouse with creaky floorboards, and that it seemed to take a long time to drive there. Of course, I was just a kid at the time. In reality it may not have been all that far away."

"If she was close to your mother, wouldn't they have grown up in the same town?"

"Probably, but that doesn't help pinpoint the location. Mom never talked much about her childhood, except to say that her family moved to Monticello in time for her to play against Lenape Hollow in high school basketball tournaments."

Darlene pulled into my driveway and put the van in park. "Well, I guess you'll find out more tomorrow."

I started to gather up my sweater and tote bag.

"You really don't remember anything else?"

"I was pretty young when we visited Tessa. Under ten." I frowned. "I think there may have been one or two other women living there with her. A sister, maybe? And their mother?" I shook my head. "I can't be sure. I mean, think about it—how much does anyone remember of events that took place more than sixty years ago?"

Chapter Three

The following morning I drove to Monticello, the county seat, for my meeting at the law offices of Featherstone, De Vane, Doherty, Sanchez, and Schiller. They were located in one of the oldest buildings in town, a brick edifice near the courthouse.

Leland Featherstone was every bit as dignified as his surroundings. He wore an exquisitely tailored, pin-striped suit accessorized with a burgundy tie and a matching silk handkerchief in his breast pocket. I put his age at around eighty, based on a shock of snowy white hair and hands that pulsed with big blue veins, but his carriage remained erect and he refused to resume his seat until I sat down. Only after I'd done so did he lower himself, a bit stiffly, into the plush chair behind his enormous desk.

Old school, I thought, *and a bit of a dandy.* A whiff of expensive aftershave tickled my nose.

The entire office was stuffed with mementoes of a long and illustrious career in the law. Framed degrees and certificates shared wall space with photos that showed him in the company of an assortment of politicians, celebrities, and local movers and shakers. There was even one of him posing with my old high school nemesis, Veronica North. That didn't surprise me. Ronnie is quite well-to-do, thanks to outliving three wealthy husbands, and has a finger in many civic pies.

Outside, the mid-July day was hot and humid and predicted to become more so. Inside, Mr. Featherstone had the air-conditioning turned up full blast. I have to admit I'd rather be chilly than overheated, but the temperature was a bit on the cold side even for me. I was glad I'd decided to wear slacks instead of a skirt, and that the sleeves of my cotton blouse were three-quarter length.

"Well, now, Ms. Lincoln," Featherstone began, "if you don't mind, I'd like to see some identification."

I fished in my tote bag for my wallet and produced my driver's license. The photo was unflattering but eminently recognizable. He scrutinized it carefully before returning it.

"I understand you're a retired schoolteacher."

"That's correct." I wondered what my former profession had to do with being one of Tessa's heirs, but I assumed he'd explain in his own good time.

"And that you currently edit manuscripts on a freelance basis?"

"Also correct."

He consulted notes made on a legal pad. "Are you settled permanently in Lenape Hollow?"

"I bought my house there three years ago," I told him. "I have no plans to move again."

He nodded in what appeared to be approval. "Excellent. Well, as I said in my letter, you are one of the beneficiaries named in the will of Tessa Swarthout. I assume you know who she was."

"More or less. She was one of my mother's oldest friends, but I never had much to do with her."

This seemed to confuse him. "She didn't keep in touch with you?"

"As I said, she was my mother's friend, not mine, and

even with Mom there were years during which their only contact came from an exchange of Christmas cards."

A snippet of conversation with my mother on the day I'd driven her to visit Tessa had come back to me the previous night. Mom had complained that Tessa never bothered to scribble a note on those cards, let alone enclose a newsy annual letter. She just scrawled her name beneath a generic holiday greeting.

"To be honest," I continued, "I didn't realize Ms. Swarthout was still alive. My mother's been gone since 2004."

"Tessa Swarthout was one hundred and two when she died. She updated her will just last year."

Since I didn't know what to say to that, I kept my mouth shut. *Patience,* I told myself. *He'll get around to explaining everything eventually.*

After a long, thoughtful pause, Featherstone finally got down to the nitty-gritty. "The property you're to inherit was Ms. Swarthout's family home just outside Swan's Crossing."

I nodded to signify that I'd heard of the place. At a guess, the hamlet of Swan's Crossing was no more than a forty-minute drive from Lenape Hollow. My inheritance appeared to be the same house I'd visited with my mother all those years ago.

"I understand it was once operated as a small dairy farm," Featherstone continued, "and that the family took in boarders during the Season."

Having grown up in Sullivan County, I didn't need further explanation. The Season—make that *tourist* season— ran from Memorial Day until Labor Day. When I was a kid, our little corner of the world was known as the Borscht Belt. Huge luxury resort hotels catered to a clientele, mostly Jewish, from the City. That's New York City, of course. Is there any other? Supposedly the movie *Dirty*

Dancing gets the details right. I don't know. I've only seen snippets, and as a "townie" who never worked at any of the resorts, I was never part of that milieu.

I knew more about the bungalow colonies that catered to the less affluent overflow and sometimes housed the singers and comedians hired to perform at the big hotels. The heyday of those accommodations ran from the 1930s all the way to the early 1970s, when societal changes and the increased availability of air travel had prompted tourists to move on to other locales.

Prior to that era, and continuing through some of it, the countryside had also been littered with smaller hotels, some of which blatantly excluded guests on the basis of religion, color, and country of origin. In addition, there had been hundreds of farm-boardinghouses. Their owners augmented the income they earned raising dairy cows or chickens by taking in boarders during the summer months. In some ways, I suppose they were the rough equivalent of the modern-day B and B, except that they supplied lunch and dinner, too, and sometimes even offered entertainment. Farm stock ponds provided places to swim, fish, and boat. The way I understand it, just the chance to breathe fresh air was a big draw for city folk back in the day.

"The house and some outbuildings are still standing," Featherstone continued, "but no one has lived there for some time and there are no near neighbors."

From his failure to meet my eyes and the way he kept fiddling with an antique fountain pen, turning it over and over in his knobby-knuckled fingers, I had a feeling the lawyer was leading up to something, most likely something I wouldn't enjoy hearing.

He cleared his throat. "There *is* a condition attached to the bequest."

When he glanced up I sent a polite smile his way but said nothing. *Wait for it,* I thought.

"Within a month of being notified of your inheritance, in other words, by the fifteenth of August, you are required to edit any diaries you find in the farmhouse. Further, you are to arrange to have the completed transcripts posted at a number of sites on the Internet. Ms. Swarthout made a list of the ones she had in mind."

He handed over a printout that named several prominent social media outlets and specified that there was also to be an e-book, although I had an additional two weeks to put that into production. I don't know which surprised me more, the condition itself or the fact that a hundred-and-two-year-old woman was sufficiently computer savvy to know where her legacy would best be preserved.

"How many diaries?" I asked.

"She never said."

"Do you know who wrote them?"

"I know nothing about them."

Somehow I didn't think we were talking about the kind of diary I received as a Christmas present when I was eleven, a fat little volume with a bright pink cover and a lock so flimsy a two-year-old could have broken it. It contained one page for each day of the year—not enough space for much reflection; too much if all you were going to do was record the weather. I'd ended up filling the pages with clippings from *TV Guide*. I have no idea what happened to that record of my pre-teen viewing preferences. I expect it was tossed out when my parents moved away from Lenape Hollow.

"Can you make a guess at how old these diaries are?" I asked.

If the pained expression on Mr. Featherstone's face was anything to go by, my question put him in an uncomfortable position. Some men just hate having to admit that they don't have all the answers.

"I've never seen them," was his tight-lipped reply. After a brief hesitation, he reluctantly added, "It's likely they were written more than sixty years ago."

That meant I'd undoubtedly have to decipher someone's handwriting. Once upon a time, every schoolchild was taught to write in cursive. Youngsters were forced to produce perfectly formed letters that were easy to read. Unfortunately, as individuals age, their handwriting evolves and becomes more distinctive. In far too many cases it ends up as scrawls and squiggles that not even the writer can interpret after a few weeks have passed. It was probably too much to hope that these diaries were written in a clearly legible hand, let alone in a lovely, flowing script that would be a delight to read.

"I've never edited a diary before," I said. Memoirs, yes. Diaries, no.

"How hard can it be?" Featherstone's forehead creased with worry in direct contrast to his jovial tone of voice.

"Have you ever looked at nineteenth-century census records?" I'd seen a few at a meeting of the local historical society. "Not only are they difficult to interpret, they're also extremely . . . creative when it comes to spelling."

"I don't believe these diaries are *that* old. Perhaps from the late nineteen fifties?"

I had a sneaking suspicion there was still something he wasn't telling me. I bestowed what I call my "sweet but dithery little old lady smile" on him, the one I usually save for security officers at the airport and policemen who think I'm meddling where I shouldn't.

"In that case," I said, "there could be some legal issues surrounding their publication."

His bushy white eyebrows, a perfect match for his hair, shot up a good inch.

"Suppose the author made an unsubstantiated claim about a neighbor. Even if that person is long dead, his descendants might not like having their family's dirty linen aired online."

His smile was ever-so-slightly condescending. "I see what you mean, but let's take it on a case-by-case basis, shall we? Do you feel you are you equal to the task? If not, there's no point in proceeding further."

"What happens to the farm if I fail to meet Tessa's condition?"

"I'm not at liberty to say."

He didn't look happy about that, either, and I decided not to press the issue. I didn't have to think about my answer for more than a few seconds. I love a good challenge.

"I'm good at my job," I said. "I imagine that's why Tessa chose to leave her property to me. When can I see my inheritance?"

He consulted his watch, thought for a moment, and seemed to come to a decision. "Are you free this afternoon?"

"One of the advantages of working for myself is that I make my own hours. I'm at your disposal, Mr. Featherstone."

"Excellent. If you'll allow me to treat you to an early lunch first, we can visit the farm immediately afterward."

I had no objection to this plan. In fact, I hoped to be able to worm further details out of him in the more relaxed atmosphere of a shared meal. In that, I was disappointed. Professing a great interest in what I do for a living, he kept me too busy answering his questions to ask any of my own.

We took separate vehicles for the drive to Swan's Crossing. It made sense for me to follow him there. Otherwise, when I was ready to go home, I'd have to return to Monticello first—some twenty miles out of my way—to pick up my car.

I spent the trip wondering what I'd find at the end of the journey. I was more certain than ever that there was more to this unexpected inheritance than the lawyer was telling me.

Chapter Four

We hadn't seen any signs of habitation for at least a mile when Mr. Featherstone signaled a turn and pulled off the two-lane country road into an overgrown driveway. I'd never have noticed it if I'd been driving past on my own. The house was well hidden by a screen of trees. Maples and birches predominated, but there were enough evergreens to assure year-round privacy.

In the early afternoon sunshine, Tessa's former home appeared to be in good repair, but it had the unmistakable aura of an abandoned building. When I got out of my car, I took a moment to study the house.

It sat on a low rise facing the road. From the driveway, I was looking up at one side and the front of the structure. Large and plain, two stories high with an attic, the whole thing was sided with white clapboards and roofed with green shingles. A deep porch with a waist-high railing wrapped itself across the front and disappeared around the far side. The main entrance was there, but another was closer to where we'd parked our cars. A flagstone path led from the driveway to a section of the building that looked as if it had been built as an afterthought. Unlike the rest of the farmhouse, it was only one story high and had a flat roof. A flight of steps ended at a landing and a side door.

"Ready for a tour of your inheritance?" Mr. Feather-stone asked.

"As ready as I'll ever be," I replied.

He steered me across the overgrown lawn to the front entrance. He was spry for such an elderly man, but he walked slowly. By the time he'd mounted the one step to the porch, resting his hand on the railing for support, his face was flushed and he was noticeably short of breath. He removed the silk handkerchief from his pocket and wiped his face.

"Are you okay?" I asked.

He waved aside my concern and produced a key. When he'd unlocked the door, he stepped back and let me enter first.

The interior of Tessa's farmhouse looked like a time capsule.

In fact, that's exactly what it was.

"Everything has been left just as it was on the day Tessa went away," Mr. Featherstone said. "That was in the late nineteen fifties. If you'll follow me, I'll give you the ten-cent tour."

"It's awfully clean for so many decades of neglect." I trailed after him into a small living room full of large furniture, decor that struck me as vaguely familiar. "I take it someone's been in to dust and vacuum?"

"Tessa hired a service to take care of that, handle any necessary upkeep on the building, and clear away the worst of the underbrush in the yard. She also employed a security company to keep an eye on the place and make sure it wasn't burglarized or invaded by squatters."

As most people do, I looked to my right first. My gaze fell on an ornately framed fashion print hanging on the wall between the two windows that faced the road. An old-fashioned radiator—the same kind I have in my first-decade-of-the-twentieth-century house—stood beneath it, flanked in the corners of the room by an enormous radio of 1940s vintage on one side and an early television set on the other.

An oversize sofa sat at a right angle to the radio. I stared at it while my mind conjured up a surprisingly vivid recollection of myself seated next to my mother on that very piece of furniture. Tessa had occupied the matching armchair.

I reached out to touch the sofa cushion. Oh, yes. I could still remember how that prickly fabric had abraded the backs of my legs. As was proper for little girls in those days, I'd worn a dress to go visiting. I had a strong suspicion that there had been crinolines under the skirt. What I was certain of was that it had taken a great deal of willpower not to squirm. I'd been told I had to behave like a "proper little lady" and sit still while the grown-ups talked.

Frowning, I struggled to bring back that day in more detail, but my memory of Tessa's appearance had blurred with time. It was probably fanciful to imagine that her posture had been unnaturally upright and her expression grim. Had the atmosphere been fraught with tension? I just didn't know. I couldn't remember anything specific that had been said that day. Shaking off a frisson of unease, I decided that in all likelihood we'd had a pleasant visit during which nothing out of the ordinary had occurred.

Two large head-and-shoulders portraits hung above the sofa. On closer inspection, they proved to be enlarged photographs tinted to resemble paintings. I couldn't begin to guess when they'd been taken. The clothing the couple wore was typical of what country people wore from the late 1930s right through the early 1950s. Neither subject was smiling. Prune-faced was the description that came to mind. The only other detail of note was that the woman looked much younger than the man.

"Who were they?" I asked.

"Tessa's father and stepmother, I presume," Mr. Featherstone said.

"Did you know them?"

"I did not. I barely knew Tessa. Her father died a number of years before his wife and she left the area after her stepmother's death. As far as I know, Tessa never set foot inside her family home again."

"Why not?" I asked.

"Who can say?"

Even for a lawyer, that answer seemed evasive.

"Surely you can make a guess."

Featherstone shrugged. "I imagine she and her sister were simply ready to move on. It can't have been much of a life for two young women, stuck out here in the country."

"So there *was* a sister. I thought I remembered one."

"Estelle," he said.

"Younger or older?"

"Younger."

"And where did she end up? I know Tessa eventually moved to Connecticut."

"I've no idea. Tessa never said much about her, other than that she died some years ago."

He gestured for me to follow him back into the front hall. "As is often the case in nineteenth-century houses, many of the rooms are connected. We'll circle around and I'll show you the kitchen on our way out."

As we stood in the hallway, the porch was to my left. I opened the door directly opposite it, to my right, to reveal a narrow stairwell and steps leading steeply upward. Since the door at the top was closed, they were in darkness. I looked for a light switch, but before I could find one, the lawyer took my arm to steer me away.

"There are bedrooms and a bath on the second floor," Featherstone said. "Nothing out of the ordinary. Those are the rooms the Swarthouts rented out every summer."

He opened another door, this one facing the entrance to

the living room. The corner room was furnished with a double bed and a dresser. There wasn't room for more furniture. In fact, there was barely enough space for those two pieces.

I circled the bed, thinking as I did so that changing the bedding must have been a real challenge. Although I'm not tiny, neither am I huge, and I could barely squeeze into the few inches of space between the bed and the wall. In order to look out the side window, I had to sit down. The mattress gave under my weight, making the springs beneath it squeak. At least I hoped it was the springs. If the cleaners had done their job properly, there shouldn't be any mice in residence.

My view across the side section of the wraparound porch consisted of an overgrown field and a sprinkling of apple trees interspersed with large boulders, rocks of the type left behind by ancient glaciers. At the edge of this more-or-less open area what looked like a mini-forest had sprung up, forming a barrier much like the one between the front of the house and the road. If there were neighboring houses in that direction, I couldn't catch so much as a glimpse of them.

"Does that line of trees mark the boundary of Tessa's property?" I asked, pointing.

Featherstone braced his hands on the coverlet, leaned forward, and squinted through the window. I shifted position so he could see better.

"That's right, and Swarthout land extends an equal distance from the other side of the house. As I'm sure you've already noticed, it was built on high ground. At the back, the land dips down to a manmade pond. You can't see that from here, or the hill that rises up behind it, but when you walk in that direction, both gradually come into view. If you were to climb to the top of that hill, you'd have an excellent view of downtown Swan's Crossing."

I twisted my head around to look at him as he straightened. "Have you walked the property?"

I'm certain I sounded skeptical. I was recalling how short of breath he was after doing no more than crossing the uneven surface of the front lawn and climbing that single step to the porch.

He squared his shoulders, as if daring me to challenge his ability to make such a trek if he wanted to. "At my request, my young assistant came out to inspect the property last week. He's very thorough. The back boundary of Swarthout property runs along the top of the hill."

I edged out from behind the bed. As I passed the bureau, I stopped to pick up a picture frame. People often keep likenesses of those nearest and dearest to them where they can see them when they first get up in the morning. At least that's the reason why I have a favorite photo of my late husband in *my* bedroom. This photograph showed two young girls and an older woman. Tessa, Estelle, and their mother? Since it was not the woman from the portrait in the living room, that seemed likely.

It was only after I put the picture back where I'd found it that it occurred to me to wonder why Tessa hadn't taken it with her. Idly, I opened the top drawer of the bureau, expecting to find it empty. Instead, it was filled with neatly folded clothing. The same was true of all the other drawers.

Everything has been left just as it was on the day Tessa went away.

Featherstone's words were suddenly heavy with meaning. Something very peculiar had happened in this house.

"Why did they leave so much behind?" I asked.

The lawyer was already moving on toward the back of the house. "Perhaps the diaries will tell you. All I know is that Tessa and Estelle walked out and never came back."

I trotted after him. "And where, exactly, *are* these diaries?"

A narrow hallway took us past a small bath with a claw-foot tub. We didn't go in. Instead we continued on, passing through the door at the end of the hall to enter yet another small room crammed with furniture.

"The diaries are somewhere in the house. That's all I know." The admission came with a grimace, making it clear he didn't like being as much in the dark as I was.

Looking around, I saw that a single bed was tucked in beneath the room's only window. A desk and a tall, free-standing wardrobe took up most of the rest of the available space. As my gaze fell on the latter, I realized that there hadn't been any closet in the other bedroom, either.

"Where did they hang their clothes?"

"In wardrobes like that one and on bars and hooks." Featherstone shrugged. "What else can you expect in a place this old? The original building dates from the early eighteen hundreds. The Swarthouts added a second floor and an addition to the kitchen around the beginning of the last century, in order to take in summer boarders."

Another door led from the back bedroom into a closet-size space that contained two more doors. The one to my right was the entrance to the cellar.

"The furnace, an electric water heater, and the pump that brings water up from the well are all in working order," Featherstone assured me.

Since neither of us had any inclination to descend the stairs and explore the dank, dimly lit reaches below, we went on to door number two and found ourselves in a room situated between the living room and the kitchen. The sideboard that took up most of one wall provided a clue to its use. At one time, this must have been the dining room. When Tessa abandoned her home, however, it was clearly in use as a second living room. In addition to the sideboard, the furnishings included a sewing machine tucked into one corner and two overstuffed chairs.

As yet, I'd seen no sign of any diaries. In fact, I hadn't noticed books of any sort. That realization made me frown. If Tessa and Estelle had left clothing behind, it stood to reason that they wouldn't have bothered taking reading material with them, yet there wasn't so much as an old newspaper or a magazine in evidence.

Mr. Featherstone cleared his throat. He was waiting, somewhat impatiently, for me to enter the sunlit kitchen ahead of him. When I had done so, I glanced back over my shoulder and caught him giving his surroundings an uneasy look.

I didn't think much of it at the time. My attention was diverted by the kitchen appliances. They came from a variety of eras. The stove was built on the same lines as an old-fashioned woodstove, except that it ran on propane. The sink was a deep utility model. Even the refrigerator appeared to predate the 1950s—at least I assumed so, since it was plain white instead of avocado green or some other trendy '50s shade. I was relieved to see that it had been emptied out, turned off, and left open to prevent mold and mildew from establishing a stronghold.

The countertops and cabinets were made of pine. One of the latter had a built-in flour sifter. Although I knew what it was, I'd always associated this labor-saving device with the nineteenth century, not the twentieth. A table and four ladderback chairs occupied most of the space at the center of the room. A ceramic bowl filled with plastic fruit sat in the center of a flowered linen tablecloth.

Tessa's farmhouse had all the basic amenities.

Very basic.

Given the temperature on this particularly steamy July day, I was acutely aware that the place lacked air-conditioning. I sincerely hoped I wouldn't need to spend a great deal of time on the premises in order to locate the diaries. Once I'd found them, I fully intended to take them home with me and transcribe the contents in comfort.

The chirp of a cell phone made me jump. I knew it wasn't mine. I never leave it turned on unless I'm expecting a call. Since I have a landline at the house, my cell sometimes lies forgotten in the bottom of my tote bag for weeks on end.

Mr. Featherstone, looking faintly apologetic, extracted his phone from an inside pocket and answered with a brusque, "Featherstone here."

I have to admit that knowing there was cell service at the farmhouse came as a pleasant surprise. The property could just as easily have been located in a "dead zone." There are still plenty of those in rural areas, no matter what the phone companies tell their customers.

To give the lawyer privacy, and because I hadn't had time on the way through to give it more than a cursory glance, I returned to what I'd mentally dubbed "the middle room." I smiled when I noticed a vintage telephone sitting on the narrow end table between one of the overstuffed easy chairs and a window. Wanting to take a better look at it, I sat down, but I was immediately distracted by the view.

From my new vantage point I could see past the driveway where we'd parked our cars and into the field beyond. It must have been a pleasant vista back in the day. Now there was little in sight beyond a mass of weeds and underbrush. The arrangements Tessa had made to maintain the property clearly hadn't included more than the front lawn, and even that looked as if no one had mowed it for some time.

Shaking my head, I settled back in what proved to be a remarkably comfortable chair and once again contemplated the telephone. It was even older than I'd thought.

Instead of the standard black, rotary-dial model I remembered from my childhood, this one had no dial at all. That dated it to a time when an operator was necessary to place a call. The phone number showing beneath a clear circle on the front of the instrument told me that the Swarthouts had been on a party line. I wondered if Tessa and her sister, and maybe their stepmother, too, had made a habit of listening in on their neighbors' conversations.

My idle speculations were interrupted by Mr. Featherstone's abrupt appearance in the kitchen doorway. "I do apologize, Ms. Lincoln, but that call was to remind me that I need to be back in Monticello within the hour. That said, I'm sure you can manage on your own here going forward. You have the key to the house and I've given you my contact information, should any questions arise."

He began to retreat even as he spoke. I followed more slowly. By the time I reached the side door, he had already descended the outside steps and reached the weed-infested dirt driveway. He slid behind the wheel of his BMW without looking back. Within seconds, he was gone, his tires squealing just a bit in his rush to leave the farm behind.

I am not normally a superstitious person, but in that moment, in spite of the sultry weather, I could swear I felt a chill run up my spine.

Chapter Five

When I turned away from the door and glanced at my watch, I was surprised to discover that I'd been at the farm for only a little more than an hour. In that time, I'd taken a cursory look at the downstairs rooms, although I hadn't investigated any of them very thoroughly, and I hadn't gone upstairs at all. Now I had a decision to make—start again, give the second floor a once-over, or call it a day and come back in the morning when I'd be fresh, well-rested, and more appropriately dressed for serious searching.

Dusty, sweaty, and tired as I was, the choice was a no-brainer. The afternoon wasn't likely to get any cooler or less humid. The interior of the house wasn't as hot as the great outdoors, but it had been closed up for a long time. The air wasn't just stifling, it was stagnant.

I'd seen enough to suspect that the diaries I was supposed to edit were not lying out in plain sight. I wondered if they were still in the house at all. What if they'd been stolen? Anything could have happened to them in the course of sixty-plus years. If it was true that Tessa had never once returned to her old home, she'd never have known they were missing.

I shook off that depressing thought. I'm an optimist by

nature. The diaries had probably been tucked away somewhere safe by the person who'd kept them. If that someone had been worried about other people reading what
she'd written, she might even have taken pains to stash
them where no one else would think to look.

"Thanks a bunch, Tessa," I said out loud. Mom's BFF
seemed the most likely diarist. Would it have killed her to
leave behind directions to her hiding place?

I turned the deadbolt on the kitchen exit and made my
way through the house to the front door. Once that was
secured, I lost no time getting into my car and driving
away.

I didn't go straight home. Instead, I went to Darlene's
house.

I knew she'd be interested to hear how I'd spent my day,
but that wasn't the only reason for the detour. Most of the
time, Calpurnia makes a great sounding board, but this
was one occasion when I needed to talk to someone who
could answer back with something other than "meow."

Darlene's husband, Frank, was out playing golf. He's almost always out playing golf on summer afternoons. I es-
timated that we'd have a couple of uninterrupted hours
and I meant to take advantage of them.

"I need your research skills," I said as we adjourned to
her lovely air-conditioned kitchen and I foraged in her refrigerator for the pitcher of lemonade I knew I'd find
there.

Darlene was considerably more mobile than she had
been the last time I'd seen her. She loaded a plate with
freshly baked homemade chocolate chip cookies while I
filled two tall glasses with the sweetened thirst-quencher.
Her dog, Simon, of the breed known as "purebred mutt,"
sat in the middle of the floor, his shaggy head moving back
and forth as he attempted to watch both of us at the same
time.

"Does this have something to do with your meeting with that lawyer?" she asked.

I sat down at the kitchen table and took a long swallow of lemonade before I answered. "Indeed it does."

"What did your mother's friend leave you?"

"Would you believe the very same farmhouse I told you I visited as a kid? But there's a catch. I have to do a small editing job in order to inherit."

"That shouldn't be too hard."

"So you'd think . . . except that the diaries I'm supposed to edit haven't turned up yet. After the meeting in Mr. Featherstone's office, he took me out to visit to the property. It's just outside of Swan's Crossing." I took another sip of lemonade.

Darlene made a "hurry up and get to the point" gesture with one hand.

"Here's the really weird part. That house looks exactly the way it did on the day Tessa and her sister moved out back in the late nineteen fifties. According to the lawyer, they left everything they owned behind and never went back for any of it. Not once. From what little I saw while I was there today, I believe it. They didn't even take their clothing."

I frowned as I bit into a cookie. Weird didn't begin to describe the situation. I was about to go on when I caught sight of Darlene's expression. I'd have expected to see curiosity, or mild surprise, or even amusement in her face. Instead, she looked deadly serious.

"What am I missing?"

She shrugged. "I couldn't help myself. While you were exploring the house, I went web-crawling to see what I could find out about Tessa Swarthout. Fortunately, all the local newspapers from the nineteen fifties have been scanned, and since I can access them from here, I did."

"Of course you did." There were advantages to being a librarian, even a retired one.

"So sue me," she joked.

I held up both hands in mock surrender. "I'm not complaining. Research is your superpower!"

"You better believe it, but with a name as distinctive as Tessa's, it wasn't hard to find information online. The only thing that surprises me is that you haven't already Googled her for yourself."

"Some of us still have to work for a living, you know. And, to be honest, I didn't think of it. Well? Don't keep me in suspense. What did you discover?" Responding to a cold-nosed nuzzle, I reached down and absently began to stroke Simon's silky black fur.

"I printed out the relevant articles so you can read them for yourself, but I think I can guess why Tessa could never bear to return home. Brace yourself—her stepmother was murdered in the house you just inherited."

I doubt my jaw literally dropped, but that would have been an appropriate response to Darlene's announcement. What I actually did was rear back to stare at her. It's entirely possible that stare was "goggle-eyed." Reactions become clichés precisely because they are so common.

"No way," I said, my words providing yet another shining example of a trite response.

"Way." She forced a smile. "You said you were ten, or maybe younger, when your mother took you to the farm to visit Tessa, right?" At my nod, she continued. "It must have been just a few months later when Rosanna Swarthout was killed."

I drained my glass and poured a refill. "Mr. Featherstone did not mention that little detail. He didn't even give me Rosanna's name, although he did say that the sisters moved out after their stepmother died. Now that I think about it, he was downright evasive every time I showed an interest in *why* they left. Can you summarize what you discovered?"

Without thinking, I reached for another cookie. My appetite was unimpaired by the topic of conversation. Besides, I figured I'd need my strength to withstand any further bombshells Darlene lobbed at me.

"There were three adult females living in the farmhouse at the time: Tessa; her younger sister, Estelle; and their stepmother. In addition, a young couple named Roth lived in an apartment above a detached garage. The Swarthouts rented it out year-round for extra income."

I nodded, calling up a vague mental picture of that particular outbuilding. A flight of outside steps led up to the second story above a one-bay garage. The whole thing was more dilapidated-looking than the farmhouse, but had appeared to be in better repair than the barn. I hadn't really paid much attention to any of the structures scattered around the property, except to notice that there were quite a few of them.

"The Roths were at home when the murder took place," Darlene continued, "but they claimed they didn't hear or see anything. Tessa and Estelle had gone to a movie. They came home to find Rosanna's body in one of the downstairs rooms."

The penny dropped. "He knew," I whispered.

I'd bet money that Rosanna had been killed in that middle room where the phone was. When we reached that part of the house, Featherstone had been quick to find an excuse to leave. I'd thought at the time that there was something odd about his behavior.

"He who?" Darlene asked. "The lawyer?"

Simon shifted his attention to her, plunking his bottom down next to her chair and staring up at her with adoring eyes. When she broke off a tiny bit of cookie, one without any chocolate in it, and fed it to him, his tail thumped against the floor in canine delight.

I was in a far less happy frame of mind. "Who else? From the first, he was reluctant to answer specific questions. He *must* have known about the murder."

Darlene was watching me closely. "He didn't even hint at what happened there?"

"He didn't say a word about it, and I have to wonder why. What else did you find in the newspapers? Did they catch the person who killed her?"

"Apparently not. The police concluded that Rosanna interrupted a burglary, although it doesn't appear that they ever made an arrest. I'm sure it would have been a major story if they had, and there would have been follow-up articles about the trial."

"Was anything missing from the house?"

"Your guess is as good as mine. None of the stories said. Take the printouts with you. You can read the articles for yourself. It's a pity the case wasn't sensational enough to attract the scandal sheets of the day." She grinned at me as she snagged the last cookie on the plate. "The *Daily News* didn't give it so much as a paragraph."

I smiled back. When we were growing up, most households relied on magazines and Huntley and Brinkley to keep them informed and only subscribed to the local biweekly newspaper—one of the ones Darlene had consulted on-line—and the slightly more far-reaching Middletown *Times Herald-Record*. For reports from the City, a few people probably read the *New York Times*, but the majority preferred the racier, much more interestingly written and illustrated *Daily News*.

To be honest, I still do.

Chapter Six

When Frank returned from his golf game and Darlene started preparations for their evening meal, I remembered that I hadn't done any food shopping for a while. My pantry wasn't exactly bare, but if I wanted something more appetizing for supper than plain pasta or an omelet containing nothing but eggs, I needed to restock.

Sitting in the car in the parking lot at the grocery store, I fished a notebook and pen out of my tote and started a list. Spaghetti sauce and grated cheese were the top two items, but I quickly added more. Cat food, of course. Soup. Nuts. Chocolate. Milk. Coffee. Apples—I've eaten an apple a day for years. It may not "keep the doctor away," as the old adage claims, but to borrow another oft-used phrase, "it couldn't hurt."

When I couldn't think of anything else to include, I stopped writing and reached into the back seat for the reusable grocery bags I keep there. I took all four into the store with me. I was going to need them. I might even have to buy a fifth one.

I really should get better organized, I thought as I moved from aisle to aisle. If I could only remember to pick up a few items every time I went out, I wouldn't end up with an overflowing cart when I did get around to visiting the grocery store. I didn't even want to think about what a massive unloading job I'd have when I finally got home.

In the checkout line, I braced myself for sticker shock. I haven't yet reached the point where I shop for the cheapest brands and clip every coupon in sight, and I'm certainly not reduced to sharing the cat's dinner, but I am very aware of how much food prices have risen since my retirement from teaching. It was while the checker was running the last few items through the scanner that I heard a loud, sibilant whisper behind me.

"Is that she?" a woman asked.

I smiled to myself. "Is that her?" is the far more common way to phrase that question, even if it is grammatically incorrect.

If someone answered her query, I missed it. I was too busy writing out a check for the absurdly high total cost of my purchases. Yes, I still write checks. I keep my financial records on paper, too, and I don't bank online. That may be old-fashioned, but the axiom "if it ain't broke, don't fix it" has always made a lot of sense to me.

I wheeled my cart out to the parking lot and off-loaded my grocery bags into the trunk of my bright green Ford Taurus. When that task was complete, I shoved the empty cart into the nearest carrel. I'd just turned to head back to the car when I once again heard the whispering woman's voice. This time it came from directly in front of me and she didn't trouble to lower it.

"Two typos."

I blinked. Caught off guard, I was at a loss as to what she meant.

I didn't think I'd ever seen her before, although I'm not always good at recognizing faces, especially when they're out of context. She stood a little shorter than I do. Once I was five foot seven, but I've shrunk a bit with age, so make that five foot five or so. Although I wasn't quite eye to eye with the woman, there was no way I could miss the glare she was sending my way.

It had been a long day. The best response I could manage was a befuddled "Excuse me?"

"You let two typos get past you in the new Illyria Dubonnet novel."

I continued to stare at her. My mind was no longer blank, but I honestly didn't know how to reply to her accusation.

"Well?" The belligerence in her voice was reflected in her stance. She went up on the balls of her feet like a boxer ready to throw the first punch—a boxer dressed in off-white cotton slacks and a sleeveless red-and-blue-striped blouse.

I said the first thing that popped into my mind: "What typos?"

"On page twenty-five, *then* should have been *them*."

Can you say "nit-picking"? I bit back the sarcastic comment and waited for her to tell me what else she'd found to complain about.

"And on page three hundred and twelve, the name of the heroine was misspelled. It's *Eliza* all the way through the book and then, suddenly, it's *Elissa*."

I had an explanation for that error, but it was not one I was prepared to share with a total stranger. Elissa was the name my friend and fellow teacher, Lenora Barton, originally chose for her protagonist. I was a little surprised that the "find and replace" function on Lenora's computer hadn't dealt with the problem, but it was entirely possible that the old name had slipped back into the four-hundred-page manuscript during one of Lenora's many revisions. It might even have been inserted, accidentally, of course, at the copyediting stage.

I would not have been in a position to catch the mistake, or the typo, or any other errors that *everyone* had so far missed. Lenora, better known to readers by her romance-writing pseudonym, is published by one of the big New York conglomerates. I don't even do a final proofread of her manuscript before it goes to her editor. I'm what's called a beta reader. I give her feedback at a much earlier stage in the writing process.

After I hung out my shingle as a professional freelance editor, Lenora offered to pay me for my time. I refused to charge her so much as a penny. Together with my decades as a junior high school language arts teacher, it had been the experience I gained from reading her early drafts that persuaded me I was qualified to pursue my present career in the first place.

"Well?" the irate Illyria Dubonnet fan in front of me repeated. "What do you have to say for yourself?"

If I'd wanted to deliver a lecture, I could have said plenty. I doubted she had any idea of the process a book goes through on its way to publication. Most readers don't. After all the revisions the author makes before submitting a manuscript, there's a line edit. That's done by Lenora's primary editor, the one who bought the book in the first place. Sometimes that editor asks for revisions, but once the manuscript has been officially accepted, it's sent on to a copy editor. After that it goes back to Lenora. If she disagrees with something the copy editor changed, she can change it back. Later, she gets one more chance to catch typos, continuity errors, repetitious words, and the like when she receives her page proofs.

Unfortunately, the author of a work is the absolute worst person to proofread her own writing. She knows what it's *supposed* to say. That means she has a tendency to skim right over a wrong word because she's mentally substituted what *ought* to be there. Despite other eyes searching for them, one or two errors always seem to slip through and appear in the published book. There, inevitably, some sharp reader immediately spots them, but at that point it's far too late to make any corrections.

I was not inclined to explain any of that to an irritated, argumentative stranger in a steamy parking lot while my ice cream melted in the overheated trunk of my car. I cut to the chase: "You're complaining to the wrong person."

"You're Michelle Lincoln, aren't you? The one who calls herself the Write Right Wright? Illyria thanked you on her acknowledgments page."

I sighed. I'd forgotten about that. "Illyria" had meant to do me a favor by plugging my fledgling post-retirement business.

"I take it you're a fan?" My question was meant to be rhetorical.

"I *love* her."

Her. Not her writing. Not her books. Her. Oh, boy! It's no coincidence that the word *fan* derives from *fanatic.*

"I'm fond of her, too," I said. "She's a friend, and because we're friends, she lets me read early drafts of her work. I sometimes point out places where she needs to add more detail, or explain something better, but I'm not the one who checks the final copy."

"You would it you were a *real* friend."

"I would if she *asked* me to. She doesn't."

When I tried to get past the woman, she shifted position to block the path to my car. Eyes narrowed in suspicion, she got right in my face.

"I think you're lying. And I think you're a fraud. She paid you to find mistakes and you failed." She jabbed an accusatory finger into my chest every time she used the word *you.*

I was hot, I was tired, and I don't have a lot of patience with fools in the best of times. "Listen, lady," I said with my best snarl. "There's not a book out there that doesn't have at least one typo in it. Get over yourself."

With that, I pushed past her, got into my car, and started the engine.

A moment later she was banging on my driver's-side window.

I refused to lower it by so much as an inch.

"You ruined Illyria's book!" she shouted through the glass. "You need to accept responsibility!"

"Fine," I muttered. "I ruined her book. *Mea culpa*. Now get out of my way!" I shouted the last few words and put the car in reverse, backing slowly out of the parking space and forcing her to step back or lose a few toes.

I caught one last glimpse of her in my side mirror as I drove off. Her face was set in a ferocious scowl and she was shaking a raised fist in my direction.

Some people need to get a life.

Ordinarily, I'd have taken my usual shortcut, a steep semiprivate road located almost directly across Main Street from the supermarket exit. The other end comes out on Wedemeyer Terrace, just opposite my house. Someone standing in the right place in the parking lot would be able to follow my progress all the way to my home. With the image of Illyria Dubonnet's biggest fan fresh in my mind, I decided it would be best to take an alternate route.

The effort was probably a waste of time. Lenape Hollow is a small town. Anyone who wanted to find out where I lived would have no difficulty discovering my address. Not for the first time, I was glad I'd installed a first-rate security system soon after I bought the place.

Chapter Seven

A few hours later, after I'd put away the groceries, fed Calpurnia, and fixed myself a light supper, I settled in to read through the printouts Darlene had made for me. She'd been right about one thing. The date strongly suggested that Rosanna Swarthout's murder took place not long after my childhood visit to Tessa's house.

That September over sixty years ago, I'd been seven. No wonder my memory of that day was so vague. I wasn't surprised that I hadn't heard anything about the crime at the time. At that age, I didn't read newspapers or listen to local news on the radio and my parents, who were always a bit overprotective of their only child, would have taken care not to discuss the subject in my hearing.

One of the printouts included a detail Darlene had failed to mention during our conversation at her house. Assuming that the reporter for the *Sullivan County Record* wasn't exaggerating for effect, it sounded as if the police had entertained serious suspicions about the alibi of the young couple renting the apartment above the Swarthout garage.

"Listen to this, Cal," I said to my furry sounding board.

Curled up next to me on the loveseat in the living room, she opened one eye. As soon as I reached out a hand to scratch her behind the ear, she closed it again.

I cleared my throat and read aloud from the printout: "Charles and Nina Roth told this reporter that they went to bed early and slept soundly until they were awakened by the wail of sirens. Their garage apartment is situated only some thirty yards distant from the main house and since it was a warm autumn night, the windows in both residences were open in the hope of catching a breeze. A source in the sheriff's office has confirmed that the Roths were taken to Monticello this afternoon for further questioning."

To the jail, I wondered, or just to the sheriff's office?

"This doesn't say they were arrested," I mused aloud. "Just questioned."

A small movement next to my hip made me glance down at Calpurnia. She wasn't just asleep. She was actively dreaming. All four paws twitched as she chased imaginary prey.

Smiling, I went back to reading. The official theory seemed to be that Rosanna had surprised a burglar. I assumed that meant the Roths had been cleared of suspicion. I wondered what had become of them. It seemed doubtful they remained in their apartment on the Swarthout farm.

If no one saw or heard anything, I asked myself, then what led the police to the conclusion that Rosanna interrupted a burglar? None of the news stories listed any items that had been stolen from the house. Was that because the police had kept that information to themselves, or because nothing, in fact, had been taken?

One headline read, MURDER AT SWAN'S CROSSING. I've always heard that the first paragraph of a news article is supposed to tell readers the who, what, when, where, and why of the story, but this one seemed more bent on sensationalism. Or maybe melodrama.

Just after the summer season drew to a close, murder and possible rape and robbery darkened the scene at

Swan's Crossing, where on Wednesday the body of a woman in her early seventies was discovered in a farm-boardinghouse on Columbine Road. The woman, Mrs. George Swarthout, died of multiple stab wounds. She was found dead in a first-floor room of the summer boarding-house the Swarthout family has operated for several decades. Clues to the murderer and the motives of the cul-prit are not yet clear as we go to press.

The suspicion of rape appeared to have been unfounded. At least it was never mentioned again in the articles Dar-lene had found for me. Neither was there any mention of the house being ransacked. If the killer was looking for something to steal when Rosanna confronted him, it was possible he'd fled without taking any loot with him.

Tessa and Estelle were nowhere mentioned by name, al-though the newspaper stories did say that the body was discovered by the victim's stepdaughters. They'd returned from seeing a movie at the Rialto in Monticello and walked in on what must have been a truly horrific scene.

My heart filled with compassion for the two sisters. How terrible it must have been for them to discover Ro-sanna's body. It's bad enough encountering murder when the dead person is a stranger, a situation with which, un-fortunately, I've had personal experience. The shock of finding a loved one murdered in their own home must have been traumatic in the extreme.

Traumatic enough to make them leave everything they owned behind? Apparently. I could certainly understand why they hadn't wanted to live in that house anymore.

Calpurnia, awake again, nuzzled my hand.

"They took only the clothes on their backs," I told her. "Where did they get the money to buy everything new? How did they survive?"

That question and others continued to nag at me as I reread the articles Darlene had found.

Despite the wealth of extraneous detail, there were several very large gaps in the coverage. No one had followed up on what happened to the Roths, and no further mention was made of Rosanna's stepdaughters. In fact, when no one was arrested in a timely manner, the press seemed to lose interest in the story.

As I skimmed through the accounts of the crime and the investigation that followed, I took notes. In particular, I wrote down every name that was mentioned. Aside from the Roths, Charles and Nina, these included the officer investigating the case, Robert L. Lenman from the Sidney office of the state police BCI, and the county sheriff, Louis Ratner. The sheriff had been the one who'd issued statements to the press. The coroner called in to examine the body at the scene was Dr. Ralph S. Breakey. He, along with Margaret Baker, the pathologist on staff at Liberty Loomis Hospital, had done the autopsy. The district attorney, Benjamin Newberg, had been "on the scene early." No doubt he would have prosecuted the accused killer, had the police been able to make an arrest.

I didn't recognize any of those names. In all probability, they'd been mature adults at the time of the murder. Until I did some quick mental calculations, I thought it extremely unlikely any of them would still be alive. After I added up the numbers, I realized I couldn't assume they were all dead. Many people live well into their nineties. And just look at Tessa! Of course, *alive* doesn't necessarily mean *in command of their faculties*. I still thought finding someone who'd been part of the investigation was a long shot, but I resolved to ask Darlene to undertake a search for survivors.

More promising was the possibility of written records. Unsolved murder cases are never closed. At least, that's what I've always heard. Forensic science has come a long way since the 1950s, but surely, even then, the police would have dusted for fingerprints and gathered other evidence.

I sighed, wondering if I was right about that. The entire sum of my knowledge of police procedure at the time of Rosanna's murder came from watching *Dragnet* and *Perry Mason* on television when I was a kid. *Real life is not a TV show*, I reminded myself, although Joe Friday's catch phrase—"Just the facts, ma'am."—still has merit.

How thoroughly *had* the police searched Tessa's house? Had they gone through all the rooms at least once to make certain their hypothetical burglar wasn't still hiding on the premises? Had they inventoried the contents to determine if anything was missing? And had they, perhaps, taken something away with them . . . like those diaries I was supposed to edit?

I couldn't think why they would have. The books were probably in one of the upstairs rooms, just waiting for me to find them when I returned to the farmhouse. Maybe, I thought, it was Rosanna who had written them and Tessa had set this task for me because she thought I might be able to solve a decades-old murder.

"More questions than answers," I grumbled.

It was time to call it a night. I gathered up the printouts and my notepad and got to my feet, dislodging Calpurnia in the process.

"Come on, cat," I said, trying but failing to sound cheerful. "Let's go to bed. All of this will make much more sense after we've had a good night's rest."

Chapter Eight

As soon as I let myself into the farmhouse the next morning, I started opening windows. It was early, not yet eight, and the day hadn't had time to heat up. A refreshing breeze brought cool air into the living room and stirred the light coating of dust that had accumulated since the last visit from Tessa's cleaning service. I sneezed twice on my way to the kitchen.

I wondered if the murder had occurred there rather than in the middle room. My overactive imagination conjured up a grisly image of an intruder entering through the side door and surprising Rosanna over an evening cup of cocoa.

There was little sense in speculating about what might have happened. With any luck, either Darlene or I would unearth a more detailed account of the crime. If I was right in thinking that cold cases are never closed, the sheriff's department would still have a file on Rosanna's murder. Whether they'd let me take a look at it or not remained to be seen, but that was a problem for another day. My immediate goal was to find the diaries.

It would have been helpful to know how many of them there were, and useful, too, to have been told who had written them. There had been three people living here at the time of Rosanna's death. Any one of them might have been in the habit of jotting down her thoughts. I grimaced, struck by another possibility. What if all three Swarthout women had been diligent about recording what went on in their lives? I could be looking at dozens of volumes and a proportionate amount of work before they were in any shape to be posted online.

Mr. Featherstone had been no help at all when it came to narrowing the search. I couldn't help but feel he knew more than he was saying, but I'd believed him when he told me he didn't know where the diaries were kept.

It was eerily quiet in the old farmhouse kitchen. Only the sound of my shoes on the linoleum disturbed the silence as I strode to the nearest window, the one at a right angle to the door to the porch. I opened it wide and peered out at a view almost identical to what I'd seen the day before from the middle room—a rather depressing vista comprised of the winding dirt driveway, some trees, and an overgrown field.

As I straightened and went to see what was visible from the back window, I wondered why Mr. Featherstone had insisted on feeding me and escorting me to Swan's Crossing in person. He could have had that young assistant he'd mentioned show me the way to the farm. Easier still would have been to give me the key to the front door and a set of directions.

The simple answer was that elderly lawyers are as prone to curiosity as the next person, but he hadn't seemed all that interested in the place once we arrived, and he certainly hadn't provided me with any more information about my inheritance than was absolutely necessary.

Why *hadn't* he told me about Rosanna's murder? He must have known I'd hear about it eventually. He had to be aware of the pertinent details. Why else would he have been so jumpy when we were in the middle room and the kitchen? Given what I'd learned since, it seemed likely he'd been recalling some of the gorier details of the crime, but instead of coming clean about Rosanna's death, he'd seized upon a convenient excuse to return to Monticello. Had he arranged for someone to phone him after a set amount of time had passed, giving him an out if he decided he needed one?

As blind dates went, I'd had better.

Once I had the back window propped open, I took a moment to inhale the faint, pleasant scent of wildflowers. Don't ask me what kind. I've never been any good at identifying flora or fauna.

This vantage point offered a good view of the farm's outbuildings. The detached garage with the apartment on its second floor was closest to the farmhouse. A little farther along stood a dilapidated barn and beyond that were some smaller, equally weather-beaten structures that might have been used as anything from chicken coops to storage sheds.

Mr. Featherstone had been right when he'd said that I wouldn't be able to see the man-made pond from the house. I could barely make out the hint of a hill, the one he'd described as rising up on the far side of the water. The field in between the house and the hill was horribly overgrown with tall grass and weeds. There were scraggly bushes and stunted trees, as well.

I thought it likely there were snakes living in the underbrush. Like Indiana Jones, I'm not fond of reptiles. I hadn't cared for the varieties in my old stomping grounds in Maine, but at least none of them were venomous. New York State can't make the same claim. The very thought of encountering a copperhead or a rattlesnake was enough to give me the willies.

Supposedly there are no water moccasins this far north, but my mother used to claim she'd seen them in swampy areas near her childhood home. The odds were good that she'd been talking about the Swarthout farm. Thank goodness I wouldn't have to go into the field to find the diaries! Wherever they were, it was surely *inside* the house.

I turned away from the window to give Tessa's kitchen my full attention. It was a large, square room. About a third of it jutted out from the rest of the building to connect to the small side porch.

Going through the cabinets held little appeal. It wasn't likely they'd conceal anything interesting anyway. Certainly no one would have chosen to hide a diary there. I headed for the door to the middle room, but to reach it I had to pass the sink.

A sudden flash of memory from that long ago visit to Tessa's farm stopped me in my tracks. The Swarthouts had kept chickens. There had been one in the sink, newly beheaded and bloody. To a child accustomed to neat grocery store packaging, it had been a ghastly sight. Someone had taken great delight in informing me that the dead bird was slated for scalding and plucking, following which the carcass would be cleaned and cut up so that it could be cooked and eaten. I remember feeling relieved that we hadn't been invited to stay for supper.

Had it been Rosanna who'd told me that? Or Estelle? The woman's identity was obscured by time. I wish I could say the same about the appearance of the chicken carcass. That image returned in living color, as vivid as if I'd encountered it only yesterday.

Repressing a shudder, I relegated the disturbing picture to a back corner of my mind, where I devoutly hoped it would remain. I left the kitchen and walked rapidly through the middle room, pausing only long enough to open the window.

When I came to stop in the living room, I hesitated. For about a minute, I seriously considered abandoning the search and leaving. Legally, I had that option, but I couldn't bring myself to take it. If I backed out now, without even trying to find the dairies, it wouldn't be just Tessa who'd haunt me. My mother would get into the act as well.

Then, too, I was a victim of my own curiosity. That alone would have compelled me to continue what I'd started. I had dozens of questions that needed answers, starting with why Tessa Swarthout had chosen me to carry out her wishes.

I turned in a circle, studying my surroundings. The living room and what I could see of the middle room through the wide archway that separated the two were crowded with furnishings. There were chairs and tables and knick-knack shelves, but nary a book of any kind. Should I search under and inside every piece of furniture first, or start elsewhere in the house?

The choice wasn't hard to make. I reasoned that since diaries are meant to be private, they would most likely be found in one of the bedrooms. I started with the one across the entry hall. I was thorough, even looking under the mattress and behind the bureau. In the bureau itself, I found handkerchiefs embroidered with Tessa's initials, confirming that this had been her room.

She appeared to have left everything she owned behind *except* a diary. A pretty tortoiseshell grooming set, consisting of comb, brush, nail file, hand mirror, and hair receiver, sat on top of the bureau next to the photograph I'd examined on my earlier visit. There was also a bottle of My Sin perfume. In the adjacent bathroom, I found soap, toothpaste, and toothbrushes right where they'd been left on the day Tessa and Estelle walked out.

I explored the back room next, finding similar evidence of occupation but no diaries. I felt fairly certain it had been used by Estelle, but she'd done little to personalize it. The clothes were neatly stored, as were a variety of cosmetics, but as I'd already noticed, there wasn't so much as a fashion magazine or a copy of *Reader's Digest* in sight, let alone a diary or any letters.

How do people exist without reading? The very idea boggled my mind.

I retraced my steps and opened the door to the stairwell. The steps leading up to the second floor were as narrow and steep as I remembered and the single bare lightbulb overhead didn't do much to dispel the shadows. It was a relief to reach the top.

The number of upstairs bedrooms surprised me, until I remembered that the Swarthouts had taken in summer boarders. I started at the front of the house, following a narrow stretch of hallway until it opened out into a duplicate of the entryway directly below.

The bedroom situated above the living room had been used by Tessa's stepmother. There was a pendant with an *R* on it in her jewelry box. She'd owned plain but expensive clothing, preferred using a powder puff to more modern makeup, and didn't have a single photograph on display, not even one of her late husband. A quick but thorough search of the dresser drawers and an ornately carved hope chest turned up nothing of interest.

Stymied, I stood with my hands on my hips and glared at the four-poster bed. Either none of the Swarthout women had been inclined to keep souvenirs, or they had managed, after all, to carry away some of their personal belongings. If they'd returned or sent someone else in to retrieve certain items, it seemed odd that they'd leave clothes and toiletries behind, but the only other explanation I could come up with was that the police had confiscated every letter and paper in the house. I thought I might be able to find out, since I'm friendly with several people who work in local law enforcement.

In the meantime, I had more rooms to search.

There was a door to my right as I left the master bedroom, opposite a window that looked out over the roof of the front porch. I opened it and took one step up a flight of stairs that clearly led to an attic before retreating in haste. Even though it wasn't yet noon, the day had already begun to heat up. It was too darned hot to contemplate exploring under the eaves. I'd leave that project for the next time I visited, assuming I didn't find the diaries this time around. If the weather didn't break before then, I'd have to remember to bring along a portable fan and a couple of bottles of water, too. Heat prostration is no joke.

The corner room across from the master bedroom contained more of Estelle's belongings. After a moment's thought, I remembered that Rosanna's murder had taken place at the end of the tourist season. If family members had moved downstairs for the summer, to make more rooms available to boarders, September would have been the time they reclaimed those they used during the rest of the year. Estelle must have been in the process of moving from one to the other.

Unfortunately, there was nothing resembling a diary in this bedroom either. I was beginning to be discouraged.

I headed back along the narrow hallway, stopping to investigate another room that opened off that short stretch. It was furnished, but otherwise empty, cleaned out at the end of the season. Where the hall opened out onto the second floor landing, I found two more bedrooms in the same condition and a bathroom well stocked with towels but little else.

By the time I went back downstairs, I was ready to call it a day. I was also, to be truthful, a little spooked. It wasn't that I'd been expecting the bogeyman to jump out at me, and I certainly didn't think Rosanna's murderer would return to claim another victim after sixty-odd years, but being alone in an empty farmhouse was creepy. My old home in rural Maine was off the beaten path, but this remote location was even more isolated.

It didn't help that so much mystery surrounded the place. I could understand why Tessa and her sister never wanted to live in their home again, but it still didn't make sense to me that they'd leave all their possessions behind. That's the sort of thing you expect to encounter in a horror novel, where the characters flee from a ghostly encounter and fear they'll be driven mad if they ever return.

I chuckled at my own flight of fancy. I wasn't worried about ghosts or madmen or even snakes—not really—but it did bother me that I couldn't figure out why Tessa had been so insistent on having those diaries published.

There was something *off* about this whole scenario. If the diaries were hidden, why hadn't Tessa left directions on how to find them? If she'd left them someplace obvious, then what had happened to them? Had they disappeared early on, perhaps confiscated by the police? Or had someone else, for some unknown reason, taken them away at a later date?

That thought brought me back to one of the questions Mr. Featherstone had refused to answer: Who inherited the farm if I failed to fulfill the conditions set by Tessa's will? The person she'd named as residuary heir might have a pretty compelling motive to make off with the diaries before I could find them.

I drove home in a contemplative frame of mind.

Chapter Nine

That evening I settled in at the desk in my upstairs office for what I hoped would be a long, uninterrupted stretch spent editing a new short story from a repeat client. He'd sold an earlier story I helped him with and was hoping lightning would strike twice. Before I could get started, someone knocked on my front door. I have a doorbell, but whoever was there ignored it in favor of furious pounding.

My first thought was that one of my neighbors had an emergency. I was halfway down the stairs before it occurred to me that if that were the case, they'd be calling my name, or perhaps shouting for help, as well as knocking. They'd probably be ringing the doorbell, as well. When the hammering abruptly ceased, only to be resumed with greater force a moment later, I continued my descent at a much slower pace.

Perhaps it was my imagination, but the sound seemed more angry than frantic. I took the precaution of double-checking to make sure my security system was engaged before I peeked through the peephole.

It was nearly eight o'clock. It was also July, so it wasn't yet dark. Unfortunately, my house faces east and my porch light wasn't turned on. The figure on the other side of the door was partially obscured by evening shadows, but there was something familiar about her.

My visitor was definitely a woman. From what little I could make out in the gloaming, she was of middling height and average weight. Her hair, color indeterminate but not white, gray, or blond, was mid-length. It floated out from her face every time she threw herself against the door panels. She was using both fists to beat on them.

Instinctively, I drew back. She could launch such assaults all night long and that door wouldn't give, but what if she tried to gain entry by some other means? It was obvious she wasn't in a rational state of mind. If she broke a window, it would set off alarms, but she'd have a few minutes' grace period before anyone had time to respond. Unwilling to take chances, I headed for the nearest phone and called the police.

A patrol car pulled up in front of my house a few minutes later. The woman didn't notice. She kept banging on my door right up until the moment Ellen Blume, a Lenape Hollow police officer I happen to know quite well, tapped her on the shoulder and asked her what she thought she was doing.

I didn't plan on joining them outside, but I decided it was safe to turn on the porch light. Besides, I was curious about the woman's identity.

As soon as I flicked the switch, I recognized her as the person who'd accosted me in the grocery store parking lot, the woman who'd been upset because she'd found two typographical errors in the latest Illyria Dubonnet romance and blamed me for not catching them before the novel was published.

"Oh, for Heaven's sake," I muttered under my breath. I keyed in the code to deactivate my security system and opened the door.

"You!" she shrieked the moment she caught sight of me. "You were here all along!"

"Yes, I was," I admitted from my relatively safe position on the other side of the screen door. "And if you'd rung the doorbell like a civilized human being and been willing to engage in a rational conversation, I'd have been happy to talk to you."

Yes, I was exaggerating just a bit. I wouldn't have been happy about it, but I would have listened to what she had to say. Probably. On the other hand, if she'd had the same look in her eyes that she did now, one that suggested she'd just as soon slit my throat as chat with me, I might have been even quicker to call the cops.

"Do you know this woman, Ms. Lincoln?" Since she was on duty, Ellen was excessively formal in addressing me.

I summarized my earlier encounter with my irate visitor. Had it only been the previous day? A lot had happened since then.

Ellen stopped scribbling in her notebook. "All this fuss is over a *novel*?"

"This woman is under the mistaken impression that I'm to blame for making her idol's book less than perfect." I faced my detractor directly. "I'm only going to say this once more. I'm a beta reader for Ms. Dubonnet. I read *early* drafts of her work because she's a personal friend. I'll willingly take the blame for errors that slip through in any material I'm paid to edit, but I read *her* books as a favor. They go through many more drafts before they're published and I have nothing to do with those. You're blaming the wrong person."

If I'd thought it would make any impression, I'd have tried to convince her that, really, no one was to blame. I could understand a reader being upset if there were obvious mistakes on every page, but two little typos? The odds of human error being as high as they are, I'd call that pretty darned good.

To my surprise, a crafty look came over her face. "You said that before. That you're her friend. Do you really know her? Would she do you a favor?"

Oh, boy! I had a feeling I knew what was coming next, but I didn't see any way out of asking for clarification. Maybe she just wanted an autographed copy of one of Lenora's novels.

"What kind of favor?"

"I want to meet her. I'm her biggest fan!"

Over the woman's shoulder I caught sight of the grin on Ellen's face. I wanted to tell her this was nothing to smile about. Hadn't she ever read Stephen King's *Misery*?

Sometimes an outright lie is the only appropriate response: "She's out of the country right now. Her next book is set in Europe so she's doing research."

The truth of the matter is that Lenora hates to travel by air and I don't think she's ever applied for a passport. That said, she does do a great deal of research to make sure she gets the details of her foreign settings right. She just does all of it online and in books.

"Will you introduce us when she comes back?"

The eagerness in her voice was my undoing. I couldn't bring myself to dash *all* her hopes.

"I'll think about it." That was another lie, but when Ellen took the woman's arm to escort her back to her car, she looked happy.

Nope, I thought. *Never going to happen.*

No way would I subject my old friend to that kind of over-the-top adoration. Lenora is excellent with children, but she's shy and retiring in social situations involving adults. She doesn't even go to writers' conferences or do signings, and I'm one of only a handful of people who know her secret identity as a bestselling romance author.

She chose to write under a pseudonym years ago for a good reason. Until her recent retirement, she was an elementary school teacher in rural Maine. The school board would have been appalled had they ever read any of the more graphic sex scenes in her novels, and very likely would have asked her to resign. It would have been easier for her to choose to keep one of her children and disinherit the other.

When Ellen and my obsessed visitor reached the other side of Wedemeyer Terrace, they stood under the street-lamp and conversed for a few minutes longer. Ellen seemed to be lecturing Illyria's biggest fan on the folly of showing up unannounced and attempting to beat down a stranger's door. All she got for her trouble was a shrug.

Ellen watched the woman get into her car and drive away before glancing in my direction again. Seeing me watching her, she mimed wiping sweat from her brow and mouthed the word "whew!" Then, with a cheery wave, she climbed back into her police cruiser and drove away.

I waved back, went inside, and reset the alarm system, but by then my concentration was shot. There was no point in trying to get any more work done. Instead I opted to microwave a bag of popcorn and curl up in front of the television with the cat. That old Katharine Hepburn/ Spencer Tracy classic *Desk Set* was on TCM, followed by Rosalind Russell in *His Girl Friday*.

Do I know how to have a good time or what?

Chapter Ten

The next morning, although I had work to do—the editing I hadn't finished the previous evening—I still had trouble concentrating. I'd managed to banish Illyria Dubonnet's biggest fan from my mind, but my thoughts kept drifting away from my client's short story to dwell on Tessa's bequest. Truthfully, it was not a very gripping tale, but that's no excuse for shirking. I'm supposed to be a professional.

Despite repeatedly telling myself that, I couldn't focus. I was distracted by thoughts of the mysteries surrounding Rosanna's murder, her stepdaughters' reaction, and the fate of those missing diaries. I'd already left a half dozen messages at Featherstone, De Vane, Doherty, Sanchez, and Schiller. I'd called the first time as soon as I got home from my second visit to the farmhouse. Mr. Featherstone had yet to return any of my calls. It was almost as if he was trying to avoid me.

The weather did nothing to improve my concentration or lift my sagging spirits. It was pouring rain, sheets of it obscuring everything more than a couple of feet beyond the window.

You should be grateful you don't have arthritis like Darlene, I told myself. Muggy weather, with or without rain, is hell on inflamed joints.

That thought plunged me even deeper into melancholy. Darlene had offered to do more research into the Swarthouts by visiting both the public library and the local historical society, but I doubted she'd feel up to leaving the house until this deluge let up. If the weather report I'd listened to while eating breakfast was accurate, that wasn't going to happen anytime soon. If I didn't want to wait to learn more about the events of sixty-plus years ago, I'd have to do the legwork myself.

"Not today," I told myself in a firm voice. "Today you have a living to earn." Besides, it was way too dismal outside to make spending any time at the Swarthout farm appealing.

Since editing using track changes to make comments on the electronic document hadn't been working well, I printed a copy of the story and took the pages downstairs with me. I'd just settled in at the dinette table with a red felt-tip pen and a fresh cup of coffee and was actually beginning to make progress when the doorbell rang.

I said a very bad word.

It buzzed again. A glance at the clock told me it could be the mailman. He usually rang if he was leaving a package, and even in a nice, quiet town like this one, parcels are occasionally stolen off porches. I headed for the front door.

Calpurnia met me in the entryway.

"The postman always rings twice," I told her, although I was well aware that, being a cat, she couldn't appreciate the fact that I was making a play on words with the title of a classic Lana Turner film.

I opened the door without checking through the peephole first and let out a little squeak of surprise when I saw who was standing there. He just shook his head at me, and asked if he could come in.

Let me pause a moment to describe Detective Jonathan

Hazlett of the Lenape Hollow Police Department. He's in his late thirties with thick, rust-colored hair, dark, piercing eyes, and craggy features that include a beak of a nose and a cleft in the chin. He stands a little over six feet tall and is in good physical shape. If I were thirty-five years younger and he wasn't married, I'd have even more reason to be delighted to find him on my doorstep.

We had been on moderately good terms for some time. He'd once gone so far as to admit that I'd been helpful to him in an investigation. Even so, it hadn't occurred to me until that moment that he might have some idea how I could find out more about the murder of Tessa's stepmother.

"To what do I owe the honor of this visit?" I asked as I led him back to the kitchen and provided him with coffee.

He had to step around Calpurnia to take a seat. She seemed determined to make much of him, stropping the legs of his dark blue trousers and leaving behind a fair amount of much lighter color cat hair. He took her affection in the spirit with which it was offered. Once he was settled opposite me at the dinette table, he reached down to pet her.

"I hear you had a visitor last evening." He watched my face for a reaction.

I grimaced. "Oh, yes. The crackpot fan. I appreciate how fast Ellen got here. That woman definitely has a few screws loose."

"I gather you'd met her before."

"Yes. The first time was when she came up to me in the parking lot at the grocery store to tell me I was to blame for the horrendous sin of overlooking two typos in a book by her favorite author." I frowned. "Still, it's a stretch to say we've met. I don't even know her name."

"It's Bella Trent. Ellen did a little checking into her

background and passed on what she found to me. This isn't the first time Ms. Trent has become obsessed with a cause."

"What happened the last time?"

"She was involved in a protest that got a little out of hand. You know how people are always urging others to boycott a certain business if they find out the owner backed a political candidate they don't like or did something else they disagree with?"

I nodded. There's been a lot of that sort of thing going around for the last few years and most of it is just a lot of foolishness. If someone is doing something criminal, then an arrest is in order, but if he's simply expressing an opinion, whether it be by donating to a campaign, or writing an op-ed, or exercising his freedom of speech . . . well, let's just say I wouldn't want anyone to dictate *my* thoughts or actions.

"She got a little carried away," Hazlett said. "Took a spray can of paint and expressed her feelings on the windows of the man's store."

"In grammatically correct sentences, I'm sure," I murmured. I shouldn't have been amused, but my lips didn't get the message. I felt them twitch into a tiny smile.

Hazlett sent me a repressive look. "She was arrested for vandalism, Mikki, and as soon as she was out on bail, she went right back and did it again. After that, she spent some time behind bars and was required to get counseling."

"Was this here in Lenape Hollow?"

He shook his head. "Grahamsville, and it was a few years ago, so she wasn't on our radar until you had your run-in with her last night."

"Has she been in any trouble with the law since the spray-paint incident?"

"No, but I thought you ought to be warned that she

might come back. She appears to be fixated on your connection to this author, and not in a healthy way. If she
shows up again, don't hesitate to call us. And whatever you
do, don't go feeling sorry for her or try to befriend her!"

"I think you're safe on that score." I took a sip of my
coffee. "Does she live in Grahamsville?"

"No. Fallsburgh."

That wasn't reassuring. Fallsburgh isn't much farther
away from Lenape Hollow than Monticello is, and it's
considerably closer than Grahamsville. That probably explained how Bella Trent had found me. Since moving back
to Sullivan County, I've been mentioned several times in
the local papers. She must have put two and two together
when she saw my name on Lenora's acknowledgments
page.

"She may not become a problem, but you might want to
make sure your security system is active at all times."

I made the cross-my-heart gesture. "I promise to be
careful."

He rolled his eyes and started to get up.

"Since you're here, I have a question."

He sat back down, a wary look in his eyes.

"It's about a cold case."

At that, his eyebrows shot up.

Fine-looking as Hazlett is, his brain is even more im-
pressive. He has a degree in criminal justice and years of
experience with the Lenape Hollow PD. Even better, he
doesn't discount the fact that civilians *can* contribute to
solving crimes. He once compared me to Dorothy Gilman's
fictional character, Mrs. Pollifax. I *think* he intended it as a
compliment.

"*How* cold?" he asked.

I rattled off the date.

"Nineteen fif—? You've got to be kidding."

"I wish I were." I gave him the capsule version of Tessa's bequest, the condition she put on it, and Darlene's discovery of the reason Tessa and Estelle abandoned their home. "As far as we can tell, Rosanna Swarthout's killer was never caught. Is it true that unsolved homicide cases are never closed? I was hoping there might be records somewhere that contain more details about the crime."

"That long ago, police procedures weren't as stringent as they are today. I have no idea what, if anything, still exists, and I'd be surprised if anyone involved in the original investigation is still alive."

"You never know. Tessa was a hundred and two when she died. Darlene is looking into that end of things, but she can't access police archives."

"You'll have to pursue that angle with the sheriff's department. Perhaps Detective Brightwell will help."

He grinned when I made a face. The good detective and I had not exactly seen eye to eye during our encounters the previous summer.

"I don't suppose old files have been digitized."

"I doubt it. What there is, if there's anything at all, is more likely to exist only in paper format. Brightwell might let you browse, since it's a cold case, but I wouldn't count on it. That's not the kind of material that's usually made available to the general public."

"But it *is* possible records of the original investigation are still around?"

He sent me a considering look. "Seems to me you'd do better to focus on finding those diaries you're supposed to edit. Since they date from before the homicide, it's unlikely there's any connection."

"You're right," I admitted. "My only obligation is to locate and publish the diaries, but finding where Tessa hid them isn't the only mystery surrounding my inheritance, and I've never liked unanswered questions. If only to satisfy my own curiosity, I'd like to know more about what happened at the Swarthout farm that night."

"I take comfort," Hazlett said as he once again stood to leave, "in the belief, possibly misguided, that you can't get into too much trouble trying to solve a crime that took place well over half a century ago."

Chapter Eleven

It was still raining an hour and a half later when I finally finished editing that short story. I'd been interrupted only once more, by a phone call from Darlene. She'd confirmed my guess that her arthritis was acting up due to the dampness, but that hadn't stopped her from contacting the library and making arrangements to borrow some materials she hoped would prove relevant. I readily agreed to pick them up and take them to her at home.

Noting that it was just shy of noon, I considered fixing myself a sandwich, but I wasn't really hungry. What I needed more than food was to get out of the house for a bit, rain or no rain. After I checked to make sure Calpurnia had kibble and water, changed the battery in one of my hearing aids, and cleaned my glasses, I traded the lightweight sweatpants and somewhat ratty T-shirt I'd been wearing for a slightly more respectable outfit.

I'm long past the age when I feel any need to impress people with my sense of style or the cost of my wardrobe. I consider jeans and a clean T-shirt with no holes in it, this one emblazoned with the motto "Books and Cats/Life is Good," to be perfectly appropriate attire for running casual errands around town.

Given the weather, I added a windbreaker and a floppy hat. Then I drove the short distance to the library.

As soon as Pam Ingram caught sight of me, she sent me a sunny smile from behind the circulation desk. "I thought you might show up. I have those files Darlene wanted right here." She indicated a stack of manila folders crammed with what appeared to be items clipped from newspapers and magazines.

"Good grief!" I hadn't expected there would be quite so much material. "Have you got a plastic bag to put those in? I don't want them to get wet."

She produced one decorated with the logo of a local variety store and began to fill it. "I'm not too worried about what happens to them. To tell you the truth, I've been considering tossing all these old files. Now that we've finished scanning our newspaper collection, they're pretty much redundant."

"There are more than newspaper clippings in here." I could see the corner of a page from a glossy magazine sticking out of one of the folders.

Pam chuckled. "At the least, they need to be weeded. Maybe you can do that for me as you go through them. Back in the day, the library bought two copies of each newspaper. The librarian put one out for patrons to read and cut anything of local interest out of the other. What category to file the clippings under was optional, so they're a bear to search. Some files are labeled with the surnames of prominent Lenape Hollow families. Others are even more general—'Murder,' for instance. We have one of those for each town in the county."

"Is that the folder Darlene asked you to pull? For Swan's Crossing?"

"One of them. What are you two up to now?"

"Just a little research." I tried to look innocent but I suspect I failed miserably. This seemed a good time to change the subject. "You know, if you don't want to keep all this stuff, you could donate to the historical society."

"I'm sure they have their own copies."

"Individual librarians, individual choices. If they decide the donation isn't worth keeping, then *they* can toss it."

"That's not a bad idea." Pam pushed the bag of file folders in my direction but didn't let go when I tried to pick it up. "How is the library newsletter coming along?"

"I'm working on it."

"Don't forget to save space for pictures of the summer reading program's field trip."

"I've set aside an entire page for that, but someone will have to be sure to send me the files as soon as the kids get back from their outing." The field trip to a nearby living history center would take place near the end of the month, way too close to my deadline for peace of mind.

"That won't be a problem. Darlene has promised to take care of it."

I tugged the parcel free and clutched it to my chest, but it would have been impolite to cut and run. I resigned myself to lingering a bit longer to reassure Pam that the newsletter was in good hands and would be ready on time.

"Have you received any announcements from outside groups?" she asked.

To increase interest in the newsletter and therefore, hopefully, encourage more patrons to use the library's services, the Friends of the Library had voted to solicit information on events sponsored by other community organizations. The offer of free publicity had been sent to the Rotary Club, the Elks, assorted churches, and a sprinkling of local nonprofits.

"I've received copies of several notices via e-mail," I said.

Apparently hearing the lack of enthusiasm in my voice, Pam cocked her head. "That's good, isn't it? I mean, we told them that was the method of communication we preferred."

"Oh, the method is fine." All I had to do was use "select

all," "cut," and "paste" to transfer the information to a file in my word processing program. "It's just that no one seems to proofread what they send. Every time I make a correction, I have to get approval for the change."

"I don't see the problem. Obviously a newsletter needs an editor. That's why we were so grateful that you volunteered."

Volunteered? Roped into it would be a more accurate description. If I'd known at the start how time-consuming the job would be, I'd have risked losing a few friends and declined the honor.

"Let me give you an example," I said. "The very first submission I received was a classic, an announcement for the annual rummage sale put on by the women of the Methodist church. Anyone can donate items for sale, so the text read, *Here's your chance to get rid of the things in your house that are not worth keeping. Bring your husbands.*"

She chuckled.

"The husbands, or so I assume, were to come along to help carry the unwanted items, but the very next line made the ad seem even more absurd."

At home, encountering it for the first time, I'd given a snort of laughter loud enough to startle the cat. To better illustrate for Pam, I set the files on the circulation desk and held up both hands to represent a banner. Then I pretended to read from it.

"We have cast off clothing. Come see us in the church basement every Saturday in August from ten to five."

Pam blinked at me in confusion.

"There was no hyphen in cast off, meaning the invitation was to come see naked church ladies."

Never try to explain why something is funny. It always falls flat.

"I trust you fixed the problem." Pam's tone was dry.

"Yes, I did. The thing is, there's a lot more involved in this editing job than finding the odd typo to correct. It took me nearly twenty minutes on the phone to convince the person who submitted the ad that it needed to be revised."

"I can see why it would be much simpler to explain punctuation when you can see it written down."

"I tried that, by return e-mail, but instead of giving me the okay to make the correction, the church secretary insisted on trying to talk me out of it. I suppose I should be grateful she didn't insist on confronting me in person. She was certain, you see, that there was nothing wrong with the ad because she'd written it herself."

"I'm sure you were very tactful."

"Don't look so worried. I *can* be subtle, you know." I hadn't been, but Pam didn't need to know that. "The thing is, I was perfectly able to verbalize the difference in meaning. She just wouldn't listen to what I was saying."

Hearing my own words reminded me of an example of a comma error I'd frequently used when I was teaching. I smiled at the memory.

Pam's eyes narrowed. "What?"

"I was just remembering the classic example of how misplaced punctuation can change meaning, only in this case the difference is impossible to misunderstand."

"Go on. You're dying to share." Pam looked resigned.

I obliged. "Let's eat, Grandma!" I said, and then, in an entirely different tone of voice, added, "Let's eat Grandma."

Pam groaned. Handing over the package of files once more, she made little shooing motions. "Not everyone is as picky about such things as you are."

No, I thought. *Some are pickier.* Bella Trent came to mind.

Ducking raindrops as I headed for my car, I wondered what would happen if I *didn't* correct all those silly errors.

Would the Friends of the Library vote to replace me as editor?

I doubted it. No one else wanted the job.

Besides, I didn't think I had it in me to spot a grammar, punctuation, or usage error and *not* fix it.

Chapter Twelve

I'd intended to head straight back home, postponing my visit to Darlene until later in the day. I didn't want to impose on her so close to lunchtime when she wasn't feeling well. She'd insist on feeding me, and since my stomach had just given an insistent growl, I knew I'd be weak and selfish enough to accept.

There *was* an alternative. Harriet's, a café-style restaurant that served breakfast and lunch, was just a bit farther along Main Street, past the gas station and right across from the police department. After I secured the bag full of files in my trunk, I left the car where it was and scurried to the crosswalk. I didn't bother putting up my umbrella. The windbreaker I was wearing was waterproof and my hat had a brim wide enough to keep raindrops off my glasses.

I expected to find the place packed. Instead, only a few customers occupied the small two- and four-person tables. I'd barely seated myself before Ada Patel popped out of the kitchen to take my order. After a quick look around to make sure no one needed her, she plopped herself down in the chair opposite me.

"Haven't seen you for a while," she said in an accent that clearly identified her as a native of New Jersey. Her family might originally have come to the US from India, but there was no trace of that heritage in her voice.

Distinctions in regional speech are subtle, but since I've been back in New York State, I've been forcibly reminded that people in Sullivan County have their own way of speaking, and that it's as different from other regional dialects as Bronx is from Brooklyn. The main thing all these speech patterns have in common, in both New York and New Jersey, is an annoying tendency to end sentences with an interrogatory *y'know*.

Ada didn't mean her greeting as an accusation, but I felt an instant stab of guilt all the same. For the last couple of years, I've fallen into the habit of having lunch at Harriet's two or three times a week, but for the past month, with the weather so uncomfortably hot and humid, I'd avoided going outside the house during the hottest part of the day. It was both easier and more comfortable to grab a cold drink from my own refrigerator and slap together a sandwich.

From the look of things, Ada's business was in a slump. I thought that was a bit peculiar. None of the downtown shops, what there were of them, had recently closed its doors, and office workers, as a general rule, like to go out for lunch. If ageing baby boomers could be said to have a hangout in Lenape Hollow, Harriet's was it, and cops from the police station frequented the place, too, given how conveniently located it was.

As if she'd read my mind, Ada sighed. "New competition just down the street." She looked glum. "Salad bar and all-you-can-eat buffet for five bucks."

"Cheer up. A deal like that won't last long. Either the prices will go up or the business will go bankrupt."

She didn't look convinced and wasn't inclined to continue the conversation. She heaved herself to her feet, using the table for support, and removed the order pad she carried tucked in her apron pocket. "So what'll it be?"

I'm attempting to break myself of the habit of always ordering the same thing—a cheeseburger and fries. I glanced at the chalkboard behind the cash register and decided to live a little. "I'll try the special."

That's all it said—TODAY'S SPECIAL, $4.99. It could be absolutely anything. Ada doesn't go in for fancy cuisine, but she does like to experiment. Fortunately, the results are always tasty.

"Coming right up," she promised.

Before she could dash off, I asked, "Are you on your own today?"

"Today and just about every day. Young Spring took a job for the summer at some fancy resort on Cape Cod. Her father's not too happy about that." Her lips twitched as she added, "He doesn't like not knowing what his baby girl is up to."

"I expect she can take care of herself."

Joe Ramirez would have made sure of it. I have only a slight acquaintance with Spring, but I've been friends with her father for some time. He owns the gas station across from the elementary school and sits on the village of Lenape Hollow's board of trustees. He's also active in the chamber of commerce and an all-around nice guy.

While Ada was dishing up my mystery meal in the kitchen, I found myself remembering what I'd been like at Spring's age. *Pitifully naïve* pretty much sums it up. It's probably a good thing that I attended a college that still had all sorts of rules and regulations in place to prevent students, especially young women from sheltered backgrounds, from running wild.

A few minutes later, Ada plunked a plate down in front of me. The aroma rising from hot, shredded meat generously piled on a kaiser roll was enough by itself to send me into a state of bliss. I hesitated for a moment, wondering if it would be neater to eat the sandwich with a knife and fork, before deciding that would take all the fun out of it. Seizing Ada's creation with both hands, I bit into it. The first delectable tidbit of what turned out to be pork all but melted in my mouth.

"You've outdone yourself this time," I said as soon as I'd swallowed. "I don't suppose you'd be willing to share the recipe?"

Ada laughed. "Not on your life. I want to keep you coming back for more. Besides, I mostly make it up as I go along. I don't write anything down."

Why didn't that surprise me?

She left me alone long enough to make change for two departing customers. When she returned, she sat down opposite me again and leaned across the small table, her eyes bright with anticipation. "So? When's the wedding?"

I stopped eating to stare at her. "What wedding? I mean, *whose* wedding?"

It certainly wasn't mine. I have no desire to marry again. I wed my best friend right after we both graduated from college. After so many excellent years with James, I'm convinced there's no way I could win the marital lottery a second time. Besides, I have better things to do with my time than plunge back into the dating pool.

"Have you *seen* your cousin and his lady friend lately?" Ada asked. "They can't take their eyes off each other."

She looked ready for a good gossip, but I had nothing to offer. Luke Darbee is my second cousin thrice removed. We met when he decided to climb the Greenleigh family tree and came to Lenape Hollow in pursuit of our mutual ancestors. To my surprise, he decided to settle down in my hometown. For the last year and more, he'd been dating Ellen Blume, the Lenape Hollow police officer who came to my rescue and dealt with Bella Trent. I'd suspected for some time that they were in an intimate relationship, but as far as I knew, they weren't living together, let alone talking about marriage.

"If you think there's a wedding in the offing," I told

Ada, "then you know more than I do, and I see Luke at least once a week."

"Pity," she said. "It would have livened things up, especially if they hired me to do the catering. This summer is the slowest I can remember in years. Whatever happened to that boost in tourism we were supposed to get from all those businesses that opened up near the new casino?"

She didn't expect an answer and before I could mount an attempt to cheer her up by regaling her with some of my recent adventures, the couple seated at a table in front of the plate-glass window facing Main Street got up to leave. By the time they paid their bill and Ada returned, I'd decided against making her my confidante. She isn't precisely a gossip, but I'm not the only person with whom she shares juicy stories she's picked up while waiting on customers.

People talk about all sorts of things when they're out in public, even intimate matters that would be better discussed in private, and Ada has excellent hearing. It's a good thing she only repeats what she overhears to a select few. While I polished off my lunch, she shared a story she knew I'd appreciate.

"Had a bunch of Lenape Hollow's movers and shakers in here yesterday," she informed me. "Mrs. North was one of them. Dressed all in white. Pretty suit. Probably cost her a fortune."

I pasted a polite smile on my face at the mention of my high school nemesis. All these years later, Ronnie North and I have declared a truce, but it would be stretching the truth to call us friends.

"Must have been some sort of emergency," Ada continued, her dark eyes twinkling. "Police car took off from across the street, siren blaring. Startled everyone in here, but she was the only one holding a cup of coffee at the time. Spilled the entire thing right down the front of that fancy white suit."

It was a good thing I wasn't taking a sip of my own drink just then! I tried not to laugh. I really did. But the mental image of Ronnie drenched in coffee, wet brown liquid staining her pricey outfit from collar to crotch, struck me as hilarious.

"How embarrassing," I sputtered. "I wish I'd been here to see it."

It wouldn't have made up for all the mean tricks she played on me when we were girls, but I'd have enjoyed the spectacle. Petty of me, I know, but everyone is entitled to a few flaws.

After lunch, I drove to Darlene's house. Frank was home, since the intermittent downpours had spoiled his plan to spend yet another day playing golf. He took the files I'd picked up at the library and promised to give them to Darlene as soon as she woke up from a nap.

"Her knees were really bothering her last night," he said in a quiet voice. "She doesn't like to sleep during the day, but sometimes she just has to catch up on lost sleep."

"The new pills aren't helping?"

"She won't take them. She says there's too much risk of becoming addicted."

I couldn't argue with that, but my heart went out to her, and to her husband. Getting older isn't for wimps. I thanked my lucky stars that, so far, I haven't had to deal with any debilitating or, worse, life-threatening, diseases. Even losing a husband was easier on me than on many of my acquaintances. I missed James every day, but we'd both been spared the agony of a lingering illness. I rather hope that when my time comes, I'll go just as quickly.

Enough of that! I told myself as I said goodbye to Frank and headed home. It does no one any good to dwell on their own mortality.

Focusing on someone else's death, especially one classified as an unsolved murder, is another matter altogether. That thought brought me back to the diaries and as I traveled the short distance between the Uberman house and my own, I considered what my next step should be in my search for them. I intended to resume the hunt first thing in the morning.

Maybe, I thought, *if I can't locate them on my own, I should recruit Luke and Ellen to help me.*

Aside from a desire to satisfy my curiosity about the current state of their relationship, I was motivated by a very practical reason. Physically, I may not be as bad off as Darlene, and I can kneel without much difficulty, say to peer under a bed, but getting up again is a bit of a struggle. Luke is barely thirty and Ellen is a couple of years younger. They're clever and resourceful, but most of all they are considerably more agile than I am.

I resolved to get in touch with my cousin within the next day or two, whether I'd found the diaries by then or not.

Chapter Thirteen

Later that day, I caught myself staring out my office window at the rain instead of concentrating on my work. Really, it was most annoying, and most unlike me to be so distracted. My late husband would have joked that I was experiencing early senility. Unfortunately, that quip becomes much less amusing as the years go by!

With a sigh, I focused on the words on the screen and typed a note into the comments section: *"The earthy smell of dirt" is redundant. Find a better sensory image.*

Five minutes later, my mind had gone wandering again. *It's just that I hate unfinished business,* I told myself. I wanted to find those diaries and get on with the task of transcribing and editing them. If I happened to discover more about the mystery of Rosanna Swarthout's death in the process, that would just be icing on the cake.

Despite that morning's visit from Jonathan Hazlett, I don't often have visitors drop by during the week. My friends know I work at home and are good about not disturbing me. UPS and FedEx have my okay to leave packages on the porch, out of sight behind the wicker sofa. That's why it came as something of a surprise to hear my doorbell ring again around three in the afternoon. Given how little progress I'd made, I can't say I minded the interruption.

I saved my work, closed the laptop, and trotted downstairs. By the time I turned off my security system and opened the door, the young man who'd come calling had given up. Sheltering under a large black umbrella, he was halfway down the porch steps when I hailed him.

"Hello! Did you want to speak to me?"

Startled, he tripped over his own feet. For a moment, I thought he was going to take a tumble, but by dropping the umbrella, he was able to regain his balance. He retrieved it and returned to the porch, somewhat wetter for the interlude.

"Ms. Lincoln? Ms. Michelle Lincoln?"

"That's right. And you are?"

"Jason Coleman. I'm Mr. Featherstone's assistant." He stood a little straighter as he identified himself, squaring his narrow shoulders and meeting my eyes. The business suit he wore supported his claim, as did the expensive leather briefcase he carried.

That being said, Leland Featherstone's "young" assistant was a good deal older than I'd been led to expect, somewhere between thirty and forty with a lean build, dark brown hair, mild gray eyes, and the pale complexion of someone who doesn't get out of the office much. His face was long and thin, narrowing even more toward the chin. He had thin lips, too, and if laugh lines or the lack of them are anything to go by, he didn't smile much.

"I've been trying to reach your boss," I said. "He hasn't returned any of my calls."

"He's a very busy man. He doesn't have time to mess around with—that is, he—" He colored slightly, but soldiered on. "What I mean to say is that he has a very heavy caseload, being the head of the firm and all. But he hasn't forgotten about you. In fact, he sent me here to deliver some documents he hopes you'll find useful."

"To do with Tessa Swarthout's estate?" I opened the

screen door. "You'd better come in, then. Would you like a cup of coffee?"

My invitation seemed to surprise him. "If it's all the same to you, I'll just leave the packet Mr. Featherstone sent and be on my way."

"But you *are* the one who walked around the Swarthout property at Mr. Featherstone's request, are you not? You took note of the pond and other features?"

"Yes, ma'am. I did that."

He couldn't quite control a moue of distaste at the memory. Tromping through underbrush and weeds had clearly been an unpleasant experience for him. I wondered if he'd neglected to change into more suitable clothing beforehand. Such an expedition would have been ruinous to a nice suit and a pair of highly polished, undoubtedly expensive shoes.

Despite his protests, I hustled him down the hall, through the kitchen, and into the dinette. "Sit," I ordered. "At least take the time to dry off. And if you'd like something to drink, it's no trouble at all to fix you something. I was about to take a coffee break myself."

He sat. I busied myself filling two mugs. By the time I brought them to the table, he'd opened his briefcase and removed the "packet" he'd spoken of. I'd been expecting legal documents of some sort, perhaps even a copy of Tessa's will. Instead he presented me with a thick stack of letters tied together with a faded green ribbon.

I didn't need to remove it to read the return address on the top one. A single glance was sufficient to recognize the loops and flourishes of my mother's handwriting.

"Where did Mr. Featherstone find these?"

"They were with Ms. Swarthout's papers."

A cursory examination of the postmarks revealed that the earliest letter was written shortly after Rosanna's murder. The most recent dated from the year of my mother's death. All were addressed to Tessa and all had been sent to her by her BFF. I opened the oldest first and started reading, too intrigued to be concerned about being rude to a guest.

"I should go," Mr. Coleman murmured.

I barely noticed when he left and didn't realize until much later that he hadn't taken so much as a sip of his coffee. That first letter, with its oblique reference to a "recent tragedy," riveted my attention despite the fact that it gave no specific details. The next few were completely unhelpful when it came to learning more about the crime, but I found them fascinating all the same.

What my mother wrote to Tessa reflected Mom's optimistic outlook on life. She was obviously trying to cheer up her oldest friend. She did so, in large part, by relating a string of silly stories about me. She recounted several of my youthful escapades, some of which I'd completely forgotten and a few of which I wished I could forget. One or two, in retrospect, made me nostalgic, but most just embarrassed me.

To my frustration, nowhere after that first letter did Mom come close to touching upon the reason Tessa no longer lived on the farm. She never mentioned Rosanna by name and in the course of dozens of letters made only one vague reference to Estelle.

After I'd read them all, I studied the addresses on the envelopes. Tessa had moved around a lot before she settled into that apartment complex in Connecticut. I didn't suppose that fact was particularly significant, although it did interest me to see that her earliest abode after leaving Swan's Crossing was in Los Angeles, California. Clearly, she'd wanted to get as far away from her old home as possible.

I got up, dumped Mr. Coleman's untouched coffee down the sink, and poured myself a fresh cup. On the way back to the dinette, I collected a lined tablet and a pen from my kitchen junk drawer. While I sipped at my drink, I made a list of the places Tessa had lived. I stared at it when it was complete, wondering what on earth I thought I was going to do with it. It was highly unlikely that anyone who'd known Tessa was still living near any of her old addresses. Besides, the mysterious diaries weren't in California or Connecticut or anywhere in between. If they still existed at all, they were in that farmhouse in Swan's Crossing.

Tearing off the top page of the tablet, I crumpled it up and tossed it onto the floor for Calpurnia to play with. That was all it was good for. I scooped up the letters, putting them back in order. When they'd once again been collected into a neat stack, I tapped the bottoms and sides on the tabletop to even up the edges and retied the green ribbon.

This was worse than one of those jigsaw puzzles that came with no illustration on the outside of the box. How was I supposed to figure anything out with so few clues?

I wandered into the dining room. Or rather, what had been used, occasionally, as a dining room when my parents owned the house. Then and now it was furnished as a family room. My television set held pride of place against one wall, and I'd recently set up the purpose-built jigsaw puzzle table I acquired from a local craftsman shortly before I moved to New York from Maine. It's a cleverly designed piece of furniture with legs raising the surface to a comfortable height, a tilt-top feature to make all of the puzzle easier to reach, two drawers on each side for sorting pieces, and a cover specifically intended to keep cats and small children from wreaking havoc on the work in progress.

The current puzzle was titled "Lighthouses of the World" and it, unlike the mysteries surrounding the Swarthout farm, offered me plenty of hints on how to proceed. I removed the cover, sat down, and resumed my search for pieces that contained parts of place names. I already had the border together. Continuing on, I'd look for distinguishing features on each piece. I like to be challenged . . . but not to the point of frustration.

Successfully putting together parts of a dozen little pictures of lighthouses provided an excellent antidote to my inability to find answers to any real-life puzzles. I kept at it until Calpurnia appeared in the doorway and demanded, in loud and strident tones, that I feed her. I was surprised by how late it was, but I felt considerably more relaxed than I had been after reading those letters.

"Yes," I said to the cat, "it *is* time for supper. And after we eat, we're going to continue to ignore problems we can't solve and spend the entire evening watching a movie, preferably something with no redeeming social importance or literary value whatsoever. How about *Tremors*? You'll like that one."

Mentally reviewing the collection of DVDs James and I had acquired over the years, I decided that one of Mel Brooks's comedies might be even more appropriate. Or perhaps *Erik the Viking*.

Chapter Fourteen

I was all set to leave for the farm the next morning when Luke turned up on my doorstep.

"Speak of the devil," I greeted him.

My cousin sent me a questioning look. "I can go away again if you like."

"On the contrary, since fate seems to have sent you my way, I intend to make use of you. Unless you have other plans for the morning, that is."

"Free as a bird," he assured me. "It's Saturday, in case you hadn't noticed."

I hadn't. Retired people and those who work at home have the same problem—no regular schedule to help them keep track of the date. A lot of folks my age have daily pill keepers to remind them if it's Monday or Friday. I swallow a multivitamin every morning with my toast and coffee, but I'm fortunate in that I don't have to take statins to lower my cholesterol or medicine for high blood pressure. Unless I've turned on the news or have been reading the local rag on my iPad, I don't necessarily register what day of the week it is.

Over a second cup of coffee I hadn't planned on drinking, I filled Luke in on the details of my unexpected inheritance. He made short work of the contents of his mug and listened to the rest of my account while doling out affection to my cat. Calpurnia can be extremely persistent when she wants to be stroked.

I often refer to Luke as my *young* cousin, in much the way Mr. Featherstone called Mr. Coleman his young assistant. Now that he's passed his thirtieth birthday, I really have to stop doing that. Tall and slender, with light brown hair and blue eyes, he'd be rated as handsome if it weren't for the one hereditary appendage we share. The "Greenleigh nose" is . . . distinctive. On me, its size is notable but not unduly so. In Luke's case, it's too big for his face and tends to be remarked upon. For all that, we are among the luckier ones in the family. Seen in profile, the nose gives some of our relatives a distinctly ratlike appearance.

It could be worse. Literally dozens of my distant relatives on my mother's side of the family are afflicted with abnormally large, square front teeth. Most of those teeth are crooked, since they're way too big for the average mouth and singularly resistant to realignment. Wearing braces fails to have a lasting effect.

"So," Luke summarized when I came to the end of my tale, "you only get to keep the place if you find and edit these diaries?"

I nodded over the rim of my coffee mug and took a last swallow to polish off the contents.

"Have you considered *not* looking for them? From the way you've described the property it sounds like a real white elephant."

"It's not *that* bad."

Or was it? I hadn't been thinking in terms of what would happen after I met Tessa's conditions, but once the deed was transferred to me, I'd be responsible for upkeep and taxes and deciding what, ultimately, to do with the house and land.

"I'll sell it, of course," I said aloud.

"That might be easier said than done. I wouldn't presume to tell you what to do—"

"Better not!" I gave him a little kick under the table to reinforce the warning.

"But it could be a very big mistake, financially, to saddle yourself with an old house and undeveloped land."

"Speaking as my accountant?" Luke works part-time as a tax preparer.

"Speaking as your friend. You know as well as I do that the promised improvements in the economic prospects of this area didn't materialize. Our part of Sullivan County isn't considered prime real estate. It might be years before you can unload your inheritance. In the meantime, it'll be nothing but a money pit."

"Maybe I can rent it out."

"How's the wiring?" Luke asked. Calpurnia was now in his lap, purring loudly.

Following his line of thought, I stared at him in dismay. "Pre–nineteen fifties."

"So it's not just old, it's probably too dangerous for continuous use. I'll bet the outlets don't even have an extra hole for a three-pronged plug."

My hands hurt from clenching them so tightly around my empty coffee mug. Tessa's family farm was a relic out of another century. Fixing it up to the point where someone could actually live there would not be cheap. At the very least, all the wiring and plumbing would have to be brought up to code.

I have the best of reasons for knowing how expensive such upgrades are. Paying to have similar work done on my house was the reason I'd had to start a second career during what was supposed to be my retirement.

But *not* look for the diaries? *Ignore* the mysteries Tessa had left behind? Impossible!

I caught myself worrying my lower lip, stopped, and

frowned instead. "You're right, of course, but I feel a sense of obligation to Tessa. She and my mother were such close friends that Mom used to say Tessa was the sister she never had. How can I ignore the dying wish of someone who, for all intents and purposes, was my honorary aunt?"

Luke sent me a rueful smile. "I get it. It's a *family* thing."

"Pretty much," I agreed.

He stood, dislodging Calpurnia from his lap, and carried his mug to the sink to rinse it out. "In that case," he said, "we'd better get going. Do you want to drive or shall I?"

Chapter Fifteen

An hour later, Luke and I stood in the middle of the kitchen of Tessa's farmhouse. We'd spent the drive going over a list of places I'd already searched and trying to decide where to begin looking this time around. We were still debating the issue.

"You said you skipped the cabinets," Luke said, eyeing them. "Maybe I should start there."

"Be my guest, but I doubt you'll discover anything but dust and mouse droppings. If the cleaning crew Tessa hired did their job, you won't even find that much."

"Did they also clear away the foodstuffs the Swarthouts left behind?"

"I suppose they must have. Someone emptied the refrigerator and turned it off. And before you ask, I think it's highly unlikely that the diaries were wrapped in plastic and stored in the freezer compartment."

"Toilet tank?" he suggested.

I laughed. "Obviously, despite the difference in our ages, we were both brought up on a similar diet of low-budget TV detective shows."

"True," he agreed. "This whole setup could have come straight out of an episode of *Murder, She Wrote*."

"Are you comparing me to Jessica Fletcher? I'm not sure if I should be flattered or insulted."

"Why insulted?" He sound genuinely curious.

"Because there's a theory out there about why there were so many murders in Cabot Cove and other places Mrs. Fletcher visited. Some think she was a serial killer who covered her tracks by manufacturing evidence to convict other people of her crimes."

He laughed.

"And don't even get me started on how many things that series got wrong about Maine!"

"Easy there." Still chuckling, Luke put one hand on my shoulder. "Let's stick to the business at hand. One murder is quite enough for this scenario, and you can model yourself after whatever great detective you choose."

"I'd prefer to be myself, thank you very much."

"Done." Luke started going through the cabinets. As I'd predicted, they were as bare as Old Mother Hubbard's cupboard.

"I'm not sure Rosanna Swarthout's death had any connection to the diaries," I said after a moment. "Other than that they were left behind because Tessa and her sister refused to return to the scene of the crime."

"But that's peculiar in itself, isn't it? Why not ask someone else to retrieve them? They were obviously important to her. Why else would she leave such detailed instructions about them in her will . . . unless she was senile by the time she wrote it and forgot what she'd done with them."

"Bite your tongue!"

"Do you think Tessa is the one who wrote the diaries?" he asked.

"I've been wondering about that myself." I opened the oven door and peered inside, then moved on to the cabinet next to the sink. "There were three women in the house. Any or all of them could have been in the habit of writing down their thoughts and recording their daily activities."

The prospect of dozens of diary books, all needing to be

transcribed and published, was almost enough to have me turning around, getting back into the car, and driving straight to Monticello to tell Mr. Featherstone I wanted no part of Tessa's strange bequest.

"We need to be methodical about this," Luke said, closing the last of the overhead cabinet doors. "Diaries are where you record your most personal thoughts, right?"

"They can be, especially for young women. If you don't want someone else to read what you've written, you don't leave it out in the open. I'm not sure the person who wrote the diaries actually hid them, but she'd certainly have kept them in a place where no one else would be likely to stumble upon them by accident."

"So, she'd probably have tucked them away out of sight, but it would still have been in a location that was easy for her to access. Maybe we need to start tapping on walls and listening for hollow sounds, rather than looking in cabinets and drawers."

"Shades of Nancy Drew," I murmured.

"And the Hardy Boys," he said with a grin. He gestured for me to precede him into the middle room. "Do you want to start in here or take the living room?"

"You can have the pleasure of checking for a safe hidden behind one of those ugly portraits, but don't overlook that drawer in the table under the radio."

"How big a book are we looking for?"

"There's more than one diary," I reminded him, "and I don't know what size they are." I described the fat little page-a-day diaries I'd had as a teen. "Some people prefer to write in a journal, and that could be the size of a small ledger, or we might be looking for a composition book."

I'd seen one of the latter, from 1910, in the Lenape Hollow Historical Society's museum. The green paper cover had been torn and faded but the writing inside had still been bright and easy to read.

"Got it," Luke said. "Anything big enough to scribble in."

He left me in the middle room and went directly to the portrait of George Swarthout. I watched him through the archway as he gently edged it aside . . . and found nothing more exciting than wallpaper printed with vines and cabbage roses.

In addition to chairs and end tables, the Singer sewing machine tucked into the corner, and the sideboard, the room I was searching also contained a large drop-leaf dinner table collapsed to its smallest size and shoved out of the way against an interior wall. Its presence confirmed my earlier assumption that the Swarthouts had used this space as a dining room when they had boarders to feed. During the off-season, with only the three of them living in the house, they'd undoubtedly taken their meals in the kitchen and treated this space as a second living room.

The sideboard had been designed to store china, linens, and silverware. It took up an inordinate amount of space against the wall the middle room shared with the kitchen. In the drawers and cabinet on the right-hand side, I found almost exactly what I expected, including a complete set of hand-painted china. The storage space on the left side of the sideboard was devoid of diaries, too, but it did yield the most interesting find of the day.

The Swarthout family Bible was a heavy old thing, ornately bound. I stood up with it cradled in my arms and placed it on top of the sideboard before I opened it. It didn't take me long to find the pages where the Swarthouts had recorded marriages, births, and deaths. Different hands had inscribed the details. The earliest entry was from the 1860s; the latest was dated 1951.

At my fingertips, I now had a treasure trove of information about the Swarthout family, including records of George Swarthout's two marriages and the births of his daughters. Struck by an anomaly, I went back to take another look at the dates of his marriages. I hadn't misread the information. George Swarthout and Nellie Perry were wed a scant five months before the birth of their first child, Tessa May Swarthout.

I jumped when Luke came up behind me.

"Find something?" he asked.

"Yes, but not what I was looking for." The family Bible was interesting, but it was also a distraction. "Will you put this in the car for me? Then I can get back to searching for the diaries."

We should have quit while we were ahead. We'd had all the luck we were going to for one day. Although we looked in every drawer and cabinet we could find, even those I'd already been through, peered under beds, rapped on walls, and looked behind picture frames, there was no sign of any diaries. We even ventured into the musty reaches of the attic to open old trunks full of mothballs and seriously outdated clothing. The most exciting thing we found was a campaign button that said "I Like Ike." At midafternoon, tired, dirty, and hungry, since I'd neglected to pack a lunch, we headed home to Lenape Hollow.

"What are you planning to do next?" Luke asked from the passenger seat.

"I wish I knew. Those diaries have to be *somewhere* in the house."

"No, they don't," Luke reminded me. "You said yourself that they may have been there when Tessa left, but they could well have disappeared at any time in the years since. If the police didn't take them, maybe someone else did. You should talk to that cleaning service Tessa hired."

"Interview sixty years' worth of housekeepers? Oh, there's a fun task!"

"Start small, then. Talk to someone at the sheriff's department. Maybe you'll get lucky and they'll find the diaries in some dusty corner of an evidence room."

I'm ninety-percent certain Luke was trying to be helpful, as opposed to facetious, but with each suggestion he made, I felt more discouraged.

"We should also search the outbuildings," he added.

I glanced his way. He *looked* serious.

"Tessa's instructions said I'd find the diaries in the house." I found it difficult to work up much enthusiasm for looking elsewhere. I hadn't inspected any of the other structures close up, but from a distance they all had a distinctly derelict appearance.

"Tessa was over a hundred years old. Maybe she wasn't senile, but are you sure her memory was all that great? Maybe she took the diaries with her when she left and just forgot she had them."

"In that case, Mr. Featherstone would have found them in her effects, the way he found my mother's letters, and would already have passed them on to me."

"Would he?"

"You are way too good at playing devil's advocate."

"Do you want me to stop?"

"No. Why do you question the lawyer's motives?"

"I was remembering what you told me about his refusal to tell you who inherits if you *don't* fulfill the conditions of Tessa's bequest. Could she have left the property to him? Maybe he'd like to own the house, or the land, himself."

I sent Luke a narrow-eyed look. "Are we still talking about that 'white elephant' you were afraid I'd be stuck with?"

He laughed. "That's the one. Hey, here's another thought: The old lady was totally gaga and the diaries never existed at all."

"So many wonderful possibilities." I didn't bother to hide my sarcasm.

"Giving up?"

"Not on your life. Are you game for another go after I have the chance to check into a few things? Maybe you could ask Ellen to join us."

"Why not? I have to admit I'm intrigued in spite of myself, and Ellen loves a good mystery as much as you do. Do you want us to bring along a crowbar? Maybe one of the Swarthouts had a hidey-hole under the floorboards."

That comment coaxed a reluctant smile out of me. "Keep in mind that I don't own the place yet. Wholesale demolition may be a little drastic."

All the same, checking for loose floorboards in the bedrooms went to the top of the list of things to look into on my next visit to the farm.

Chapter Sixteen

By the time Luke and I returned to Lenape Hollow, we had our plans in place for the next phase of the search. He phoned Ellen from the car and secured her enthusiastic agreement to help us look for the diaries. The only downside was that she wouldn't be available until Tuesday. Her hours as a police officer involve shiftwork, which in turn means her days off tend to be in the middle of the week.

I wasn't averse to waiting until then to go back to the farm. I had other strings I could pull in the interim, not to mention the work I had pending for clients and on the library newsletter.

I knew I wouldn't be able to get hold of Leland Featherstone until Monday at the earliest, when the law firm reopened for business, but I had quite a few questions for Tessa's lawyer. Even if he wanted to keep me in the dark about who would inherit if I failed to meet Tessa's condition, he could have no reason to hold back the names of the companies who'd kept the house clean and in good repair over the years. I also wanted to know more about the security company he'd mentioned. There was no alarm system at the farm, and I hadn't noticed any security cameras. There weren't even any "this house is protected by" decals in the windows.

After Luke drove away, I let myself into the house and reset *my* security system. I was heading for the kitchen to make myself a late lunch when I noticed the madly flashing light on my answering machine. I detoured into the living room to listen to the messages. What I heard left me with plenty of food for thought while I fixed myself a peanut butter and jelly sandwich.

Every single message had been left by Bella Trent—a series of long, rambling monologues that didn't make a lot of sense. The gist of each, however, was the same. Bella wanted to meet her favorite romance writer in person and had apparently convinced herself that Illyria Dubonnet would immediately make herself available for such an encounter if her *friend*—that would be me—made the arrangements. I was to do so *at once!*

"If only Bella had believed me when I'd told her 'Illyria' was out of the country on a research trip," I lamented to the cat. "I should have been more specific."

Calpurnia looked from me to her empty bowl and back again. I abandoned my sandwich to pick it up, put it in the sink, and run hot water into it to soak off the crusted remains. Then I opened a fresh can of cat food.

"I could have said she was in Australia at a romance writers' conference, or on a river cruise somewhere in Europe," I continued as I scooped Seafood Surprise into a clean bowl. I had to wrinkle my nose against the strong fishy smell. "Maybe a more detailed lie would have convinced her to leave me alone."

Calpurnia was far more interested in eating than answering. I left her to it and carried the sandwich and a glass of milk to the dinette table. As I ate, I considered what to do about Bella Trent.

Introducing Bella to Lenora was out of the question. It wasn't that my old friend wouldn't come for a visit if I asked. She'd spent several days as my houseguest the previous August. But it was precisely because of the things we'd talked about during that visit that I knew such a request would be a terrible imposition. She'd gone back to Maine afterward in order to teach for one more year before she retired. Her plans for this summer included writing another of her literate but steamy novels, grubbing in her flower garden, catching up on her recreational reading, and going fishing.

Since I wasn't about to agree to Bella's request, I thought it best that I simply ignore her phone calls. At least she didn't also have my cell phone number. No one did but close friends and family.

Reminded that it probably needed a charge, I popped the last bite of my sandwich into my mouth, chewed and swallowed, and washed it down with the remaining milk. Then I fished the cell phone out of the bottom of my tote bag, hunted up the charger, and plugged it in. The screen lit up, showing me it was still a long way from dead, even though I hadn't used it in ages.

I have a love-hate relationship with my cell phone. I take it with me when I go out, and have been glad, once or twice, to be able to call for a tow truck or let someone know that I was running late. I do, occasionally, use it to take a picture, but most of its functions are beyond my level of technical expertise. I don't know how to text and have no interest in learning.

For phone calls, my preference will always be a landline. As soon as my chores in the kitchen were done, I settled myself on the loveseat in the living room and picked up the receiver on the extension that sits on the end table, attached to the answering machine. I punched in the number written on the back of a business card I'd been given over a year earlier. When Calpurnia hopped up beside me, I stroked her absently with one hand while I waited, a bit nervously, for someone to answer.

I heard the click as he picked up. A moment later, Detective Arthur Brightwell of the Sullivan County Sheriff's Department snapped out his name in a harsh, impatient voice.

Should I respond in a bright and cheery tone of voice or hope that sounding apologetic would elicit more sympathy? I had only a second to decide. What came out of my mouth was somewhere in between.

"Good afternoon, Detective Brightwell. This is Michelle Lincoln. I hope you won't think it presumptuous of me, but I have a favor to ask."

Dead silence greeted this conversational foray. I was about to try another approach when he cleared his throat. "This isn't the best time, Ms. Lincoln."

"Is there a good one?"

He gave a bark of laughter. The sound wasn't particularly encouraging, but it was so in character that I could suddenly picture him with complete clarity. In my mind's eye, he appeared as a man in his late thirties and only a little taller than I am—perhaps five foot eight—with black hair and a physique that, while not flabby, wasn't exactly trim, either. In that image, he glared at me, but there was also a distinct twinkle in his eyes.

"At least you caught me when I'm in the office instead of in the field," he said in a slightly less antagonistic tone. "You've got five minutes. Make it good."

I didn't know Brightwell well, and I certainly wouldn't have called him a friend, but he *had* given me his card. I tried to focus on that, rather than on the fact that, when we first met, he considered me a viable suspect in a murder case.

My words came out in a rush. "I've inherited a house in Swan's Crossing where a murder took place back in the nineteen fifties." I gave him the exact date. "The victim was Rosanna Swarthout, and her killer was never caught.

Is it possible records from the investigation still exist? I'd like to know what the police took away as evidence. As a condition of the inheritance, I'm supposed to edit some diaries left behind in that house, but I haven't been able to locate them."

After I stopped talking, there was another moment of silence. This one had ominous overtones and seemed to stretch out for hours.

Then I heard Brightwell sigh. "You don't want much, do you?"

"Does the sheriff's department keep records that old?"

"Keep? Yeah. But they won't be in the computer."

I envisioned a stuffy basement room, crammed to the ceiling with file boxes. "What about evidence from that long ago?"

"For an open case, everything should have been kept, but I won't guarantee it was. Look, I'll see what I can find, but I'm not making any promises. Cold cases aren't exactly top priority around here, and satisfying the curiosity of civilians is even lower on the list."

"I appreciate anything you can do to help."

I was talking to empty air. He'd hung up on me.

"Well," I said to the cat, "It was worth a try."

Chapter Seventeen

Although the next day was Sunday, I skipped church to spend a little more time on material sent to me by my paying clients. When I took a break to check my e-mail, I found a message from an aspiring writer who'd just discovered my Write Right Wright website and was inquiring about hiring me to help her find ways to improve her work. I skimmed over what at first appeared to be fairly typical wording for such a request: "I am in need of an editor for the novel I have just completed."

A moment later, I blinked and went back to reread that sentence. What I saw the second time through had me laughing out loud. My prospective client had clearly meant to type the word *editor*, and that's what my mind had substituted on the initial read, but what she'd actually written was *ediotor*. I couldn't help but wonder if that had been a Freudian slip as well as a typographical error. Perhaps she'd just coined a new word to express her true feelings toward those in my profession. Bella Trent would certainly agree that there was such a thing as an idiot editor.

It was more likely, of course, that she'd inserted an extra letter by accident. That can happen easily enough, especially when someone is typing rapidly.

It also makes a good case for proofreading e-mails before hitting SEND.

After I'd composed, proofread, and sent a reply, I took a break for lunch. I was just fixing myself a sandwich with some leftover pot roast, and reminding Calpurnia that she'd already been fed, when I heard Darlene call to me through the screen door. As it was a lovely summer day, not too hot and not too cool and not raining, I'd left my front door, and most of the windows in the house, wide open. Abandoning the food on the counter, I went to let her in.

"How come you had the screen locked?" she asked as she followed me into the kitchen. She was walking well, with only a cane to help her balance, and had a large tote bag slung over one shoulder.

"I've been upstairs. Working."

That was the truth, although not all of it. Illyria Dubonnet's biggest fan had left another message on my answering machine late the previous evening, just as I was about to go to bed. Needless to say, I didn't return her call, but it had alerted me to the possibility that she might drop by in person.

"Have you had lunch?" I asked.

"*One* of us has been in church until a few minutes ago."

Darlene's voice was suitably prim and her tone was annoyingly superior, but she was just giving me a hard time. I don't doubt my friend's faith, but I also know it's mostly force of habit that keeps her attending services week after week. For her part, Darlene knows how boring I find our minister's sermons, and that I can't stand his wife's aggressiveness. Every time I show up for services, she buttonholes me and tries to badger me into volunteering for one of her pet projects.

"I was just making something to eat," I said. "It's nothing fancy, but you're welcome to join me."

Darlene snickered. "Are you sure you have enough?"

"Of course I—" I broke off when I saw what she'd already spotted. A loaf of bread and a tub of margarine were where I'd left them, but the meat I'd been slicing and had left on the cutting board was nowhere in sight. Neither was my cat. "Calpurnia! Where are you?"

"If you're expecting her to bring it back, you'll have a long wait."

I sighed. "How does grilled cheese and canned soup sound?"

It wasn't much to offer someone who cooks and bakes as well as Darlene Uberman, but she's not a food snob. Working side by side we put a meal together and carried the result into the dinette.

"I want you to see something in one of the files you picked up for me at the library the other day," Darlene announced after she'd taken a few bites and a sip of her drink.

"What is it?"

"I'll show you after we finish eating. First tell me what *you've* been up to. Have you been back to the farm?"

It took the rest of lunch to bring her up to date, not that I'd found all that much. To date, the family Bible was the biggest discovery I'd made.

"I brought it home with me so I could make a copy of the entries, but I'll have to take it back on Tuesday."

"Isn't it part of your inheritance?"

"Only if I locate the missing diaries." I collected plates and glasses and carried them to the sink. "So far, I've come up empty. Do you have any idea how frustrating it is to keep finding more questions and no answers? Those three women lived in that house for decades. Wouldn't you think they'd have left more of themselves behind?"

"I may be able to help with that." Darlene reached into the bag she'd brought with her and extracted a manila folder.

Abandoning the dishes to deal with later, I sat down

again, watching with interest as she spilled newspaper clippings of reviews of plays and programs from dozens of amateur productions onto the tabletop. I took the empty folder from her and looked at the label.

"Little Theater of Sullivan County," I read. "I've never heard of them."

"That's because they'd disbanded by the time we were old enough to take an interest in such things. Take a look at this." She opened one of the programs and pointed to the cast list.

Estelle Swarthout had played the title role in a production of *My Sister Eileen*. I checked the date. The six performances given by the company had taken place a couple of months before Rosanna's murder.

"She was in other shows, too, always with good parts. She appears to have been a regular with the troupe, and the reviews she got are generally pretty good. One of the earliest said she ought to consider a career on the stage."

"I wonder why she didn't." I thought about that for a moment. "Or maybe she did, after she and Tessa left Swan's Crossing." I already knew, from the address on one of the letters my mother had written, that Tessa had lived for a short time in Los Angeles.

"I don't think so," Darlene said. "I couldn't find much about Estelle online, and certainly nothing to suggest she became a professional actress. I've been checking all sorts of places for both sisters and the only other thing I turned up on Estelle is this." She fished in her bag a second time and came out with a one-page printout. "That's a page from her high school yearbook."

"They have old yearbooks online?"

Darlene chuckled. "Oh, yeah. Ours is there, too. Every single page of it."

I groaned. We'd both been on the yearbook staff. Some of the photo selections we'd made had been a tad insensitive. Back in the day, so that it could include pictures of our graduation ceremonies, the Lenape Hollow yearbook didn't come out until late August. By the time it was published, I was already halfway through Freshman Week at college in Maine. I remembered hearing, much later, that our old history teacher, a woman we never much cared for, flew into a rage when she saw the unflattering photo of her we'd included. That hadn't surprised me. To add insult to injury, we'd captioned it with the word "Duh!"

Estelle Swarthout's yearbook photo showed a serious-looking girl with short hair worn in a style typical of the late 1930s. None of the other girls on the page looked any more cheerful or better coiffed. They were all smiling, but no one showed any teeth.

I glanced at the year. "She was older than I thought, not much younger than Tessa and my mother." For some reason, her birth date in the family Bible hadn't registered with me in the same way this photograph did.

According to the scant information given in the yearbook, Estelle had been enrolled in a "Commercial" program rather than "College Entrance" or "Academic." She'd played basketball, soccer, and hockey, been a member of the Commercial Club, had acted in the junior and senior plays, and had performed in an operetta.

"So she was interested in the theater even then," I mused. "I wonder why she didn't try for an acting career right out of high school? She wouldn't have been the first girl to head for the bright lights of Broadway or Hollywood with nothing but dreams to sustain her."

"You've been watching that PBS video of *Forty-Second Street* again, haven't you?"

I ignored the jibe. Had Estelle tried and failed? Or had she stayed in Swan's Crossing all her life, living at home with her older sister and her stepmother until she was in her late thirties and, quite possibly, too old to make a go of it on the legitimate stage?

"I wonder," I mused aloud, "who inherited the farm

when Tessa and Estelle's father died? Do you suppose he left everything to the wicked stepmother, maybe for her lifetime, with reversion to his daughters after Rosanna's death?"

Darlene gave a low whistle. "Talk about your motive for murder! But if either Tessa or Estelle killed her to get the farm, why would they abandon it?"

"Maybe they wanted something else from their father's estate."

"I don't know, Mikki. If their only incentive was financial gain, why hang on to the property? Surely they'd have sold it at the first opportunity."

"A house where there had been a murder? Not an easy sell." I sighed. "All this information about Estelle is interesting, but it just raises more questions. If I wasn't such a cockeyed optimist, I might start to get discouraged."

"Cheer up. Think positive. Just keep telling yourself that when you search the house again, with help from Luke and Ellen, you'll find those danged diaries."

"Rah. Rah!" I halfheartedly pumped one fist in the air. "In case you've forgotten, there's a reason neither of us were cheerleaders."

"I was a klutz." Darlene sent me a cheeky grin. "What was your excuse? Oh, yes. You thought the cheerleaders were snooty."

I was still trying to think of an appropriate comeback when the phone rang.

I ignored it. I didn't even bother getting up to check the caller ID.

At the sound of the beep, the answering machine in the living room whirred into action. Even at a distance—the length of the front hall *and* the length of the kitchen—I recognized Bella Trent's whiny voice as she launched into another of her rambling diatribes.

Darlene cocked her head, listening with growing bemusement as Bella recounted my numerous editing sins and once again urged me to introduce her to Illyria Dubonnet.

"Who on earth was that?" she asked after Bella hung up.

I gave her the edited version. I didn't reveal Illyria Dubonnet's secret identity and I left out the fact that I'd called the cops on Bella the one time she'd come to my house.

"She sounds . . . unstable."

I shrugged off Darlene's concern. "It's no big deal. If she doesn't get a response, she'll eventually get tired of hassling me and that will be that."

Had I, as the saying goes, but known.

Chapter Eighteen

Detective Brightwell surprised me. He got back to me a little after eight on Monday morning, phoning to say that he had found a list of the items taken from the Swarthout house after the murder.

"Does it include diaries, or books of any kind?"

"No. And that's the only reason I'm giving you that information. It may be a cold case, but it isn't closed. Details aren't shared with the general public."

That was no more than I'd expected, but I tried to wheedle a little more out of him anyway. "Can you tell me how she was killed?" I already knew of course, from the newspaper articles I'd read. She'd been stabbed.

His voice over the phone sounded resigned. "No, I can't."

"You mean you won't. You know, it isn't as if her murderer is still running around loose and likely to kill again. You don't have to hold back information just so you can verify the truthfulness of a confession."

"You've been watching too much television."

I swear I could hear him smile when he said that.

"I freely admit that I have only the sketchiest idea of how police procedure works in real life. Do you know why the police back then decided it was a burglary gone wrong?"

"I couldn't tell you if I wanted to. I haven't read the investigating officer's notes. I'm not even sure we have them here, since the state police were also involved in the case. And before you ask, I don't know what suspects were interviewed and I haven't seen the coroner's report. You asked if any diaries were taken from the scene. I checked. They weren't."

"Aren't you the least bit curious? Surely it would be a feather in your cap if you solved Rosanna Swarthout's murder after all these years."

"I have plenty of current cases to keep me busy, Ms. Lincoln."

I let him hear my sigh. "Okay. Thank you. I'll keep hunting for the diaries at the farmhouse."

I was about to hang up when he cleared his throat.

"If you do find them, and there is any information relevant to the case—"

It was my turn to smile into the phone. "You'll be the first to know," I promised and hung up.

I picked up the receiver again a moment later and punched in the number for Featherstone, De Vane, Doherty, Sanchez, and Schiller, wondering as I did so if I ought to reconsider getting one of those computer programs that let you see the person you're talking to. Facial expressions and body language might help me determine if someone was telling the truth or lying to me.

Of course, the person on the other end of the line would have to have the same software—or was it hardware?—and be willing to use it. And they'd be able to judge my reactions, too. Since I've been told more than once that my face tends to give away everything I'm thinking, that probably wouldn't be a good idea.

The same pleasant-voiced receptionist I'd talked to on numerous previous occasions answered my call and put me on hold. A few minutes later, she informed me that Mr. Featherstone was not available.

"I don't need to speak with him in person," I said. "I just need the names of the companies Tessa Swarthout used for security and housekeeping."

That wasn't entirely true. I'd have loved an opportunity to question the lawyer at length. In addition to contact information for those businesses, I wanted to ask what he knew about ownership of the farm after George Swarthout's death, and again after Rosanna's murder, and if he knew where Estelle had gone when she left Swan's Crossing. Most of all, I wanted to know the rest of what was in Tessa's will. He'd already refused to tell me what would happen to the property if I failed to fulfill the conditions of her bequest, but I hoped I could change his mind. It might not matter in the least. On the other hand, if someone *had* taken the diaries before I started searching for them, that information could turn out to be vitally important.

The receptionist promised someone would get back to me. I'd heard *that* before.

After I finished some editing for a client and made myself lunch, I left a second message for the still unavailable Mr. Featherstone. That done, I was at loose ends. I could have vacuumed and dusted, or cleaned my two bathrooms, but I'm not the world's most dedicated housekeeper. Instead, I sat down at the dinette table with the folders Darlene had left, the Swarthout family Bible, and the letters my mother had written to Tessa.

Given what Darlene had discovered about Estelle's acting, I wanted a second look at Mom's single mention of Tessa's sister. It took me a while to find the reference again. It didn't turn up until a letter that was written some ten years after Rosanna's murder.

I'm sorry to hear your sister's ambitions haven't been realized, Mom had written, *but that's hardly your fault. You know where the blame belongs.*

It would have been nice if my mother had been a little

more specific, but I thought I could puzzle out what she meant. Because of that single California address, I suspected Tessa and her sister had headed straight for La-La Land after Rosanna's death. Tessa had left soon after, but Estelle might have stayed on.

From the reviews I'd seen, she'd possessed a modicum of talent as an amateur actress. It wasn't much of a stretch to suspect that she'd developed an exaggerated opinion of her abilities. Her family—rural, conservative, and probably more realistic than she was—would surely have opposed the idea of a career onstage or onscreen.

History, other than that which directly affected my ancestors, has never held a great deal of interest for me, but the date in Estelle's yearbook had reminded me that Mom, Tessa, and Estelle were young women during the Great Depression. That would not have been the best time to strike out on one's own in search of fame and fortune. Since Estelle had still been living at home twenty years later, my best guess was that she'd lacked the gumption to rebel.

If my reconstruction of events was anywhere near the mark, it was easy to imagine Estelle spending those years regretting her lost chance. She must have felt trapped on the family farm, perhaps even desperate to escape.

It was a good thing both she and Tessa had an alibi for the time of the murder.

Shaking my head, I tucked my mother's letters back into their envelopes. I felt confident in surmising that Estelle had, somewhat belatedly, gone after her dream. I was equally certain that she'd failed to achieve it. Unfortunately, my conclusions didn't bring me any closer to solving any of the mysteries surrounding the Swarthout farm. Who killed Rosanna? Was there a clue to be found in one of the diaries? And where the heck *were* those darned diaries anyway?

I got up, stretched, and walked over to the wall phone in the kitchen. Leland Featherstone still hadn't returned my calls. Muttering under my breath—I won't repeat the words I used—I tried again to get through to him.

As I'd expected, I was told he wasn't available.

"Then let me talk to Jason Coleman," I snapped.

"Oh, he's—"

"Now!"

"Hold, please."

Is there anything more annoying than what we used to call "elevator music" playing in your ear while you wonder if you might be stuck in telephone limbo for the rest of your life? Every once in a while a recorded voice chimed in to tell me my call was important and someone would be with me shortly.

Sure they would!

I was about to hang up when Coleman finally came on the line. "Ms. Lincoln. What can I do for you?"

The first answer that popped into my mind is probably illegal. Besides, a lowly assistant would never do that to the senior law partner at his firm. Instead, very glad he *couldn't* see my face, I simply asked for contact information for the companies Tessa had used.

"Is there a problem?" he asked.

"I don't think so, but I haven't yet found the diaries Tessa wanted me to edit and it's possible one of those services can give me an idea about where else to look. The people who came in to clean must know the house well."

"I suppose so." He sounded doubtful.

"As for the security company, they should be able to tell me if anyone besides the housekeepers ever went inside, or if the farmhouse was ever broken into."

"I'll look up the information and get back to you," Coleman promised.

"Sure you will," I muttered after he disconnected. I wasn't going to hold my breath.

Chapter Nineteen

I hadn't heard a peep out of Jason Coleman by the time I left Lenape Hollow on Tuesday morning to return to the farm with Luke and Ellen. That Ellen was willing to spend her day off with Luke was no surprise—I was beginning to suspect there *was* a wedding in their future—but devoting her free time to scouring an old house for diaries that might not exist went above and beyond being nice to the boyfriend's relatives.

"You don't have to do this, you know." It was not the first time I'd tried to give her an out.

"I want to, Mikki. It'll be fun." Looking up at the farmhouse from the driveway, she grinned. "I love old houses."

We started with a walk-through. As we went from room to room, I gave Ellen a brief summary of what I'd learned about the family, the murder, and the history of the farm.

"From what I gather, the Swarthouts had been taking in summer boarders since the late eighteen hundreds. A lot of people around here did that to supplement their income. Guests expected something to be offered by way of entertainment, so the Swarthouts dug a pond on the property to use for swimming, boating, and fishing."

"A pond?" Ellen interrupted. "Is it still here?"

I made a vague gesture in what I thought was the right direction. "It's back there somewhere."

By that time we were upstairs. Ellen peered out a window. "There it is! How lovely."

Luke went to stand beside her. "I bet old George Swarthout used to harvest ice in the winter."

Ellen looked puzzled. "For drinks?"

He shook his head. "To keep ice boxes cold in the days before everyone had electricity and owned refrigerators."

"Hard to imagine," I murmured.

"I'm glad we're not living back then," Ellen agreed, "but it's interesting to hear about. Were they still taking in boarders when the murder took place?"

"Yes, but the season had just ended. Rosanna was killed in September, after all their guests had gone back to New York except for a young couple who were renting the apartment over the garage."

"Have you looked for the diaries there?" she asked.

I shook my head. "They're supposed to be in the house." Frowning, I considered the source of that information. "If we don't turn up anything in the farmhouse, I guess the next logical step *would* be to search all the outbuildings."

Three hours later, we'd examined every nook and cranny we could find and come up empty. Remembering how hungry treasure hunting had made me the last time around, I'd packed a picnic basket containing plenty of food and drink. We took a break and sat at the kitchen table to eat lunch.

"Well, that was discouraging." Ellen poured coffee from my oversize thermos into one of the heavy-duty, hotel-style ceramic cups she'd found in a kitchen cabinet.

"Tell me about it." I sighed.

"So, outbuildings next?" Luke asked. "Or do we start ripping out walls and tearing up floorboards?"

I sent him a quelling look and unwrapped a ham and cheese sandwich. "I don't own the place yet. No demolition. I just wish I could work up more enthusiasm for poking around in the garage and barn."

"You don't think we'll find anything. I get it." He'd already devoured two sandwiches, making me glad I'd made plenty.

"It's not only that. Those buildings look ready to fall down around our ears and inside they must be filthy. Nice hiding places for mice, rats, spiders, and snakes." I barely repressed a shudder. "Diaries? Not so much."

"Bring those critters on," Luke said with a laugh. "We're bigger than they are."

Ellen sent me a sympathetic look. "Snakes are more likely to be outside in the tall grass than inside."

"Then thank goodness we don't have to go traipsing across any of the fields."

"Well . . ." She toyed with her napkin.

"Let me guess—you want to take a closer look at the pond."

"I thought I might stroll over that way and check out any buildings I come across. The Swarthouts probably had a boathouse at one time, and maybe a shack for their guests to use as a changing room." She turned a smile on Luke. "I might even find your hypothetical ice house."

"Just be careful," I warned her.

We were both wearing sturdy shoes, but where I had on jeans, Ellen had dressed for the warmth of the day in shorts and a sleeveless top. That left a lot of bare skin exposed, should she happen to stumble over a venomous reptile.

"I'll search the barn," I offered. "Luke can investigate the two smaller outbuildings just beyond it. I'm pretty sure one was used as a chicken coop back in the day."

He must have heard something in my voice, because he sent me a narrow-eyed look. "That's suspiciously generous of you."

Ellen giggled. "You can't blame her for wanting to hand off the chicken coop. Some smells . . . linger."

"Right. Okay." He took his assignment with good grace. "That still leaves the garage and the apartment above it."

"Why don't we meet there when we've finished the rest and do that part of the search together," I suggested. "That apartment strikes me as a pretty unlikely spot to hide anything, since it was occupied at the time Tessa left, but I suppose the garage is a possibility. They must have owned a car. How else would she and her sister have gotten to Monticello to go to the movies?"

From its derelict appearance, I didn't expect much of the barn. I couldn't think of any reason why someone would hide a diary there. If it turned out to be as unsafe up close as it appeared from a distance, I didn't intend to do more than poke my head inside.

The barn door resisted my first effort to push it open, then abruptly yielded and slid along its track with a horrendous screech. I was drenched in perspiration by the time I shoved it as far as it would go. Only then did I notice a smaller door a little farther along the same wall. Gaining access that way would have been far easier and much quieter . . . except for the fact that it was secured with a large padlock.

Weird, I thought. *Why not lock both doors?*

No, that was the wrong question. The right one was: *Why lock the barn at all?*

I had my answer as soon as I switched on the large utility flashlight I'd brought with me and took a look around the interior. Despite outward appearances, the Swarthout barn was not in any danger of collapse. The walls and roof had been reinforced, and much more recently than the 1950s, too.

At one time, the barn had contained stalls for livestock. In their place, someone had installed a half dozen prefabricated self-storage units of the sort people rent to stash their excess belongings. On *Storage Wars*, they sometimes contain unexpected treasures. In more than one mystery novel, they've been a great place to hide the body.

I approached the nearest unit with extreme caution. It had a latch, but no padlock. Drawing in a deep breath, I swung open the door and exhaled in relief when it turned out to be empty.

They were all empty. One by one, I inspected the interiors, shining my flashlight into every corner. By the time I came to the last one, I was both disappointed and puzzled. All the units were remarkably free of dust, but the beam of my flashlight had revealed numerous scratches and scuff marks on the flooring. Until quite recently, all six units had been in use.

Had Tessa had them installed and rented them out for storage? Somehow, I doubted it. Given the remote location of the property, and the fact that no one had lived in the house for more than sixty years, it seemed more likely that a person or persons unknown had made use of the barn *without* permission.

I was still standing in front of the sixth storage unit when Ellen returned from reconnoitering by the pond. She gave a low whistle, obviously reaching the same conclusion I had. The shift from Luke's girlfriend to cop took about a second and a half.

"It might be a good idea to get a drug-sniffing dog out here," she said.

I stepped back from the unit and closed the door. "It couldn't hurt."

"I thought you said Tessa hired a security company to look after the property."

"That's what the lawyer told me. Don't worry. They'll be hearing from me just as soon as the dog does its thing." And as soon as I could pry the firm's name out of Featherstone, De Vane, Doherty, Sanchez, and Schiller.

It's good to have contacts in law enforcement. After

Ellen made her call, it didn't take long for a team from the sheriff's department to show up. While they went over every inch of the barn, Luke and I stayed out of the way by belatedly conducting our search of the garage and the apartment above.

The latter had been fully furnished when it was closed up. Everything was covered with a thick layer of dust and there were cobwebs galore. I was filthy within minutes.

I avoided the overstuffed sofa and chairs, since it was obvious mice had been living in the upholstery. I suspected a few rodents might still be nesting there. I expected more of the same when I entered the bedroom and discovered a hole in the ceiling above the bed. I stepped closer and peered up into it and was only moderately alarmed to encounter a pair of beady eyes staring back at me from the darkness.

Then I took a closer look and screamed bloody murder. It wasn't a mouse. It was a snake. When it moved, I froze, watching helplessly as it emerged from its nest and slowly dropped down onto the yellowed bedspread. The thing was a good three feet in length. Tan stripes stood out among black-bordered reddish-brown patches. On a cat, the coloring would be pretty. On a reptile, not so much.

Luke ran in from the other room. Ellen and a sheriff's deputy arrived a moment later. By that time, the snake had slithered off the bed and across the carpet and taken refuge in the storage space under the eaves.

"If the diaries are in there," I said in a faint voice, "they can stay there."

"I'll look," Ellen offered. "That's a milk snake. They're harmless."

I retreated into the other room, so shaken that I was grateful to have Luke offer me his arm. I was also flushed with embarrassment. I'm not ordinarily such a wuss, but that had been a *big* snake. There wasn't enough money in the world to persuade me to voluntarily go within ten feet of any reptile. There are way too many varieties of snake that *aren't* harmless.

When Ellen joined us in the living room, she was empty-handed. "Nothing," she said, "and there was no sign of drugs in the barn. We were just coming to tell you that when we heard you shriek."

"That's good, right?" Luke asked. "If there's no evidence of illegal drugs, then Mikki doesn't have to worry about drug smugglers turning up in her backyard."

"It *is* good," I agreed, "but it begs the question. If not drugs, then what *was* stored in those units? And why?"

Chapter Twenty

There were no messages from the law firm waiting on my answering machine when I got home from the farm. I stewed about the situation for a good part of the night. In the morning, I thought about phoning Featherstone, De Vane, Doherty, Sanchez, and Schiller again but I couldn't see much point in it. Why bother when I'd only end up with a long wait on hold followed by the news—big surprise!—that Mr. Featherstone was not available? I decided it would be quicker and more efficient to drive to Monticello and beard the lion in his den. If I showed up in person, *someone* would have to talk to me.

The trip gave me time to build up a good head of steam. I stormed into the suite of offices determined to get answers. Ignoring the pleasant-voiced receptionist who'd kept putting me off when I phoned, I headed straight down the hall that led to the domain of Tessa Swarthout's legal eagle. A secretary I dimly remembered from my last visit looked up in alarm when I placed both hands flat on the surface of her desk and locked eyes with her.

"I'm here to speak with Leland Featherstone and I do not intend to leave until I have done so."

"Oh, ma'am, I don't know. Mr. Featherstone has a very busy schedule today."

I hid my sense of triumph. Her stammered response

confirmed that he was in the office. He wasn't going to elude me now!

"Tell him Ms. Lincoln is here and has urgent business to discuss about the Swarthout estate."

Ordinarily, I don't like to badger people, but I was fed up with the runaround I'd been getting. I leveled my best former teacher's glare at the young woman and waited for her to cave.

She burst into tears.

The commotion brought reinforcements, including one burly gentleman I suspected was a security guard rather than an attorney. Before he could accost me, Jason Coleman emerged from a side corridor.

"I'll handle this, Mindy," he told Featherstone's secretary.

Taking a firm grip on my elbow, he propelled me back the way he'd come. I went with him without a fuss and took the client chair he offered in the closet-size cubbyhole that was his private office, but as soon as he seated himself on the other side of the desk, I leaned forward and jabbed an accusing finger in his direction.

"You promised to get back to me, Mr. Coleman. The information I asked for is even more crucial today than it was before." In succinct sentences, I described the storage units I'd found in the barn. I was about to tell him about the drug-sniffing dog when he interrupted to sputter an apology.

"I have the information you asked for right here," he added. "I was going to call you later today."

"All right. Who *has* been handling security for the Swarthout farm?"

He fumbled among the papers littering the top of his desk, finally pulling out a legal pad with scribbles all over it. "The company is called Sure Thing Security. Their office is right here in Monticello."

Convenient, I thought, and asked for the street address.

Since in-person visits seemed to be effective, I'd make that my next stop.

"And the company that cleans the house?" I asked after I jotted down the pertinent details about Sure Thing in a small notebook of my own.

"Monticello Maids." He rattled off their address and I added it to the bottom of the same page.

"Are they also the ones who take care of the grounds?" This time his response was a blank stare.

"I realize no one's hayed the fields or cleared out underbrush, but Mr. Featherstone told me Tessa paid someone to mow the front lawn. I suppose she wanted to make it look as if the place was inhabited. An overgrown yard would have been a dead giveaway that the house was empty."

"I haven't found any records of a landscaping firm," Coleman said. "Perhaps a neighbor cut the grass."

"For fifty years?" I didn't bother to mention that there *were* no near neighbors. "Check your files again, please. A lawn service wouldn't have had access to the house, but if they had someone on the property on a regular basis, I want to talk to them."

"I'll see what I can find," Coleman promised.

I foresaw more nagging in my future, but for the moment I focused on the information he'd already given me. "Were these same two firms on the job from the beginning?"

My question brought another bewildered look to his long, thin face. "The beginning?"

"I was given to understand that it was shortly after Tessa Swarthout abandoned her property that she hired people to maintain it. Have the same two companies had the contract since the nineteen fifties?"

"I'm sorry. I don't have that information."

"Why am I not surprised?" I muttered. "All right. See if

you can find out and I'll do the same. In the meantime, I have one more question. I'd like to know who inherits the Swarthout farm if I fail to meet the conditions Tessa set up in her will."

"I'm afraid I'm not at liberty—"

"—to say," I finished for him. "The thing is, Mr. Coleman, I haven't been able to find those diaries I'm supposed to edit and publish. Given the lax security at the farm, I can't help but wonder if someone else, perhaps someone who would benefit by my failure, might have waltzed in and taken them, perhaps with the goal of preventing me from inheriting."

"I think that highly unlikely, Ms. Lincoln."

"Oh? Why is that?"

My question started him sputtering again, but the gist of his answer was clear. Why would anyone *want* that old farmhouse and the land?

He had a point. I wasn't certain why I wanted it myself. I certainly didn't plan to keep it.

When Coleman continued to insist that he couldn't tell me the name of Tessa's residuary legatee, I let the matter drop. I had other fish to fry.

Chapter Twenty-one

I took Jason Coleman with me to Sure Thing Security. After all, I wasn't yet the official owner of Tessa's farm. I assumed I'd need his authority to back me up when I asked my questions. Following a considerable wait on uncomfortable chairs in an airless waiting room, we were ushered into the manager's office.

First impressions are often wrong, but not in this case. I had Martin Meyerson pegged as a fussy little man from the get-go. Not Hercule-Poirot fussy, or fussy like that paranoid detective Tony Shalhoub played on TV, but pain-in-the-ass-with-no-redeeming-characteristics fussy.

"We're here representing Featherstone, De Vane, Doherty, Sanchez, and Schiller," Coleman said, presenting his business card. "We have questions about one of your accounts, the Swarthout farm in Swan's Crossing." He didn't bother to introduce me or clarify my reason for being there.

If Meyerson noticed the oversight, he didn't remark upon it. He was too busy staring at the pasteboard rectangle he'd just been handed. His lips flattened into a thin, hard line, making me wonder about his previous dealings with the firm's attorneys.

"The owner is a client," Coleman added.

"That doesn't entitle you to access confidential information."

"It does when we're the ones paying your bill. We are executors of the estate of Tessa Swarthout."

Meyerson's attempt to thrust out a nearly nonexistent chin only succeeded in emphasizing the scrawniness of his neck. "I am not familiar with that name."

What he was really saying was that he couldn't recall which property Coleman meant. Fortunately, we'd brought the paperwork with us. The receipts included an account number.

His memory jogged, Meyerson found the records we wanted on his computer, but his frown deepened as he skimmed the details. "This is one of our oldest contracts," he said in a prissy, disapproving voice.

I perked up at that news. If this firm had been in charge of security at the farm since the beginning, that would make my search for information much simpler.

"What, exactly," I asked, "were you contracted to do?"

He looked down his nose at me, a prim expression on his face. "Regular security checks. Nothing out of the ordinary."

"Could you be a bit more specific?"

"May I ask why you want to know? We've had this account for decades and never received a single complaint."

"That's because no one was living there to notice there was something to complain about. A barn on the property was recently renovated without the owner's knowledge or permission. How is it possible your company missed that much activity?"

He glanced at the screen. "We were hired to monitor the house. There's nothing in here that says we were to keep an eye on any other buildings."

The smug way he answered my question made me want to smack him.

"I'd have thought your people, being security experts and all, might have noticed that something a little out of the ordinary was going on."

"Not necessarily." There was that prissiness again.

I scowled at him. "Just what does a 'regular security check' involve?"

He didn't like my tone of voice any better than I liked his. With a mulish expression on his face, he clammed up. I poked Jason Coleman in the ribs, a gentle reminder that he was supposed to be there to back me up.

Coleman cleared his throat. "We're the ones paying your bills. We have a right to that information."

Meyerson glared at him. "It means that one of my operatives drives out there once a month."

"Once a *month*?"

"And there is a camera installed under the eaves of the barn. It's aimed at the house."

I didn't remember noticing one, but I hadn't been looking. "How often do you check to see if it's recorded anything?"

He tapped a few keys. "According to this, it runs on a loop."

"That's not what I asked you."

For the first time, he appeared to be slightly embarrassed. "It has not been serviced recently, but there didn't seem to be any reason to—"

I was on my feet before he could finish. "This is inexcusable!"

Sputtering indignantly, he threw himself into the faceoff. "You get what you pay for. This contract was negotiated in the nineteen fifties at a fixed rate. These days, what we're being paid doesn't even cover the cost of gas to drive out there. You can't expect—"

"I expect professionalism."

"If you aren't satisfied with our services, feel free to terminate the contract."

I glanced at Coleman. "Am I within my rights to fire him?"

"Well, er, I—"

"Yes or no?" The situation wasn't Coleman's fault, but I'd run out of patience. Neither Meyerson's equipment nor his services were worth keeping.

The lawyer stood. He looked ill at ease and awkward, but he'd heard for himself how inefficient Sure Thing Security was. "Perhaps it would be best to end our association."

"If you insist." Meyerson might look disgruntled, but there was a definite note of relief in his voice. He was delighted to be getting rid of an unprofitable account. "I'll send someone out this afternoon to remove the camera."

"I want to see what's been recorded most recently. Can you access the camera from here?"

"It's . . . not one of our newer models."

"Videotape?"

He nodded.

"That won't be a problem. My husband and I had a video camera twenty or so years ago. A mini-cassette had to be snapped into a larger frame before we could view what we'd recorded on our VHS player. I still have all that equipment." It was packed away in boxes in my attic storage room. Unlike most people who'd upgraded to newer devices, I hadn't discarded my collection of movies on videotape, or the VHS player, when I switched to buying DVDs.

Once I made arrangements to meet Meyerson's technician at the farm and get the recording from him, Coleman and I left Sure Thing Security. Even the sultry summer air felt fresh after being cooped up in that office. I drew in a deep lung full. Although I hadn't learned as much as I'd hoped, I felt much more upbeat than I had when I left the house that morning.

It took me a few moments to notice that Jason Coleman didn't share my optimism. In fact, he looked downright worried.

"What?" I asked.

"Are you sure that was a wise move? The Swarthout farm is quite remote."

"If I decide I need security, I'll call the firm that installed the alarm system in my house in Lenape Hollow. It isn't as if Sure Thing was actually doing anything to protect the place. If it wasn't for regular visits from Monticello Maids, there would probably be squatters living in the house and marijuana growing in the fields."

Chapter Twenty-two

L ater that afternoon, I drove to Swan's Crossing to wait for Sure Thing Security to show up and rip out their camera. I was also expecting Honoria Steinberg, the owner of Monticello Maids. That business had been our second stop of the morning. Ms. Steinberg had been much more cooperative, and a hundred times more pleasant to deal with, than Martin Meyerson. When she asked for a couple of hours to go through her records, I suggested that she bring them out to the farm. She'd been happy to oblige.

Meyerson's man needed only a few minutes to remove the company's equipment. Grinning, he presented me with the broken pieces of a disintegrating cassette. "Piece of junk," he said. "Hasn't worked in years."

He'd just left when a low-slung sports car pulled into the driveway and a woman I'd never seen before got out. She could have been any age from forty into her late fifties, given her artfully streaked hair and skillfully applied makeup. Her outfit, although casual, probably cost more than I spend on refurbishing my entire wardrobe in the course of a year.

"Ms. Lincoln? Michelle Lincoln?"

"Yes?"

She held out a hand. "I'm Laura Roth."

"What can I do for you, Ms. Roth?"

"My parents rented that apartment." She gestured toward the garage. "Charles and Nina Roth."

"Ah," I said, belatedly making the connection. "Won't you come in?"

She followed me up the steps to the landing and into the kitchen, looking around with a great deal of curiosity and a hint of distaste. When I sat down at the table, she followed suit.

"I'm afraid I can't offer you refreshments. There haven't been any provisions in the house since your parents lived here."

"They lived above the garage," she corrected me.

"Of course."

"And they were suspected of killing Rosanna Swarthout."

"They were questioned, certainly, but—"

"They were subjected to interrogation, their names were in the newspapers, and they were never cleared of suspicion. It haunted them for the rest of their lives. As their only child, I was also forced to bear the weight of an unjust accusation."

She didn't seem to have suffered too badly, but I bit back that observation. It was unfair of me to make assumptions. A polished exterior doesn't always reflect the inner person.

"It was a long time ago," I said, careful to keep my tone neutral and my voice gentle. "Before you were born." Seeing her up close, I readjusted my estimate of her age and put her in her mid-fifties.

"Do you think that makes a difference? How would you feel if your parents were forced to live their entire lives with the fear that they might, at any moment, be arrested for a crime they didn't commit?"

"It must have been terrible," I agreed, "but surely, after

the police announced that the murder was committed during a burglary, they were off the hook."

"Every few years, the sheriff's department would review the case. Every time, they'd come and question my parents again. It never ended!"

Since she looked as if she was about to cry, or maybe scream in frustration, I kept to myself the thought that the Roths might have been a tad paranoid. Alternatively, they might have had reason to worry . . . if they *had* killed Rosanna.

"I'm sorry they had to endure such persecution," I said, "but I'm not sure I understand why you're here today."

"I would have thought that would be obvious. You inherited the place and everything in it, including Tessa Swarthout's diaries. Have you found them yet?"

"I'm still looking, but how did you—"

"You have to find them. Find them and publish them."

"That's what Tessa wanted, and that's my intention, but how did—"

"That's the only way the lies will be exposed. The only way my parents' names will be cleared."

I struggled to follow her reasoning. The diaries, whoever had written them, dated from before the murder. I couldn't understand why Laura thought there would be anything in them to exonerate her parents.

She leaned closer, her eyes a little wild. "You have to help me. The truth was edited out of the original investigation of the case."

"A cover-up?" That seemed unlikely. "Why would anyone do such a thing?" I held up a hand to stop her from answering. "Wait. First tell me how you found out about the diaries." Their existence wasn't common knowledge.

Before she could answer, we were interrupted by the toot of a car horn. A van with the logo for Monticello Maids emblazoned on its side pulled into the driveway.

"Excuse me," I said. "I'll be right back."

Leaving Laura Roth sitting at the kitchen table, I went out to greet Ms. Steinberg and offer to help her carry the stack of printouts she'd scooped up from the passenger side of her vehicle. I steered her across the lawn to the front porch.

"Thank you for coming," I said. "Would you mind waiting in the living room while I finish up with something?"

I was trying to be considerate, assuming that Laura wouldn't appreciate a third party overhearing the questions I had for her, but by the time I returned to the kitchen, it was empty. The sound of a car starting drew me to the window just in time to see Laura back around the van and out into the road. A moment later, she'd driven out of sight.

I bit back a curse. I had no idea how to contact her. My only chance to press for answers had just disappeared in a cloud of dust.

Chapter Twenty-three

Honoria Steinberg had brought all the paperwork Monticello Maids had on Tessa's house. Her firm kept meticulous records. Unfortunately, they only went back ten years.

"It's my understanding that the previous company went out of business." She craned her neck to see into the next room.

"Would you like a tour?" I asked.

"I'd love one. I have to admit I've been curious about this place. The housekeepers who've cleaned here have come back to the office with some pretty strange tales." At my lifted eyebrows, she shook her head. "Oh, nothing sinister!"

"No ghosts?"

Missing the dryness of my voice, she forced a chuckle. "Hardly! They were just taken aback by the way the place looks. It certainly is . . . retro."

As I showed her around, I gave her a sanitized version of Tessa's abandonment of her family home. Twenty minutes later we were back downstairs again, settled at the kitchen table with her records spread out on top of it.

"Can you recall anything at all about the company that looked after the house before Monticello Maids took over?" I asked.

She remembered only that they'd gone by the name Clean-Rite.

With Darlene's help, I could try to track down their former employees, but I didn't hold out much hope that we'd find them. Clean-Rite might not even have been the first firm to care for Tessa's farmhouse, and I didn't suppose that housecleaning services in the 1950s kept much in the way of records anyway. Anything considered women's work back then didn't get much respect. Even in the seventies, when I'd been a young wife, I'd often felt like a second-class citizen. Although my income was on a par with what James made, I couldn't get a credit card in my own name. If I'd wanted to buy a house, I'd have had to find a man to cosign before I could get a mortgage. As the saying goes, "You've come a long way, baby."

"Why are you so interested in these records?" Ms. Steinberg asked.

Jerked back to the present day, it took me a moment to focus. When I did, I realized that I'd have done better to look at them in her office. I needed to talk to the women who actually did the cleaning, not their boss.

"Two or more diaries were supposed to have been left behind in this house," I said bluntly, "but I haven't been able to locate them."

She bristled with indignation. "I can assure you that none of my employees removed anything from the premises."

"I didn't think they had, but I was hoping one of the housekeepers might remember having seen them."

"My ladies come in to keep things clean and tidy. They don't snoop and they leave everything exactly where they found it." Still sounding huffy, she added, "A diary is a book. They'd see it as another object they have to dust, nothing more."

"Of course." I tried to make my voice soothing, but some

of my impatience bled through. "The thing is, if I can't find and edit those diaries, I won't inherit the house."

She frowned. "Then who will?" Clearly, she hoped whoever owned it would continue to employ Monticello Maids.

I tried to see the place through her eyes. This was a pretty cushy job—just give the furniture a lick and a polish and vacuum every two weeks and occasionally wash the windows. Since no one lived here, there was never any mess to clean up.

"I don't know," I said. "The entire situation is a little screwy."

"So you mentioned when you were showing me around."

I waited a beat. There didn't seem much point in keeping quiet about the details.

"I told you that Tessa Swarthout's stepmother died and Tessa and her sister left right after, abandoning all their possessions. Actually, the stepmother was murdered, probably by a burglar."

Ms. Steinberg's eyes went wide. "Well no wonder they didn't want to go on living here. I certainly wouldn't want to sleep in a house where there'd been a murder."

"It may be that the missing diaries contain information relating to the crime."

Laura Roth certainly thought they might be relevant. Even Detective Brightwell had entertained that possibility.

Mulling over what I'd told her, Ms. Steinberg leaned back in her chair. "All right. I'll ask my employees if they remember seeing books of any kind here, but I'd prefer not to tell them why you want to know. One of my best workers is highly suggestable. If she heard about the murdered stepmother, she'd convince herself that she *had* seen that poor woman's ghost."

"Thank you. Assuming I do inherit, I doubt I'll keep the property any longer than necessary before I put it on the market, but I'll be happy to renew your contract for as long as I am the owner."

Something in her satisfied smile made me think she shared Luke's opinion that I wouldn't find it easy to unload my white elephant. I wondered, briefly, where on earth that term had come from. Then I returned my attention to the printouts in front of me.

I skimmed the pages, uncertain what it was I was looking for. Whatever it was, I didn't find it. Time sheets meticulously recorded every visit to the Swarthout farm. An itemized expense list detailed the cost of cleaning supplies as well as the hourly wages of the cleaners.

My sigh sounded loud in the quiet kitchen. I looked up to find Ms. Steinberg watching me with a considering expression on her face.

"What?"

"In an old place like this one, there are probably all kinds of good hiding places for something the size of a small book."

"I don't know how big the diaries are. If they're more like journals, I could be looking for something as large as a ledger."

She dismissed that concern with a careless wave of one hand. "Have you checked in the rafters in the attic? That's where my brother used to hide his copies of *Playboy*."

"I'll keep your suggestion in mind." I'd read somewhere that searchers often fail to look above their heads, so she might be right, but at the same time I realized that my next sweep of the premises would probably be the last. I may be an optimist, but I'm also a realist. At some point, I'd have to accept that I was wasting my time looking for something that just wasn't there.

With startling abruptness, Ms. Steinberg sat up straighter. I am not exaggerating when I say that she looked like she'd just had the proverbial lightbulb turn on inside her head. "What about the inventory?" she asked.

"I beg your pardon?"

"The inventory. A list of all the items in the house when the stepmother died and how much they were worth." Her hands flew in time with her words as she grew more and more excited. "The authorities usually make an inventory of the deceased's possessions when there's a question about a will or an inquest into a person's death. Did you ask if there is one?"

I hadn't thought to, but I'd certainly remedy that oversight at my first opportunity.

She waved off my expressions of gratitude.

"I don't know that it will be much help, even if it exists. It would only enumerate what the stepmother owned, not the possessions belonging to the two sisters."

"Then I'd better hope it was Rosanna who kept the diaries."

Our business concluded, Ms. Steinberg wished me good luck finding them and promised to let me know if any of her ladies remembered seeing any books while they were cleaning.

I'll need luck, I thought when she'd gone. It was a pity that Leland Featherstone hadn't yet been old enough to practice law back when Rosanna was murdered. He'd probably still been a teenager at the time, but perhaps he could tell me who had originally handled the Swarthout estate for Tessa and Estelle, and if anyone had ordered an inventory to be taken.

Featherstone's name came first in the list of partners, so it was possible he was the firm's founder. Since I'd gotten the impression that he'd been Tessa's lawyer for a long time, I wondered if he'd taken over the client list of an older firm, one that was in business in the late 1950s.

The list of questions I wanted to ask Leland Featherstone, Esquire, just kept getting longer and longer.

Chapter Twenty-four

Another phone call to Featherstone, De Vane, Doherty, Sanchez, and Schiller yielded familiar results. Mr. Featherstone was in a conference and would have to get back to me. The earliest opening to meet with him in person was the following Wednesday, a full week away. I made the appointment and asked to be notified if he had any cancellations and could see me sooner.

After I disconnected, I wandered into the downstairs bedroom Tessa had used. Ms. Steinberg wasn't the first to voice the possibility that the diaries had been hidden. Luke had suggested pulling up floorboards to check beneath them. I'd been resisting doing something so drastic, but I'd reached the point where I couldn't afford to discount any theory.

I felt a little foolish circling the bed and pressing down hard with each step I took, but my effort to find a board that creaked or wobbled wasn't any more absurd than all the wall tapping I'd done with Luke and Ellen. Only later, at home, had I'd realized that in a farmhouse as old and uninsulated as this one, *all* the spaces inside the walls were hollow.

There wasn't much open flooring in Tessa's room. I considered moving the bed and bureau out into the hall, but they were both big, heavy pieces of furniture. I compromised by getting down on my hands and knees and running my fingers over as much as I could reach of the wooden surface beneath them. The floor felt gritty, but all the boards were tightly aligned. There wasn't enough room to insert so much as a fingernail between them.

I fared no better in the back room, the one Estelle had used during the season. Upstairs, I started in Rosanna's bedroom. I tapped and tugged and once again crawled under a bed to check the flooring. Nothing irregular leapt out at me.

Next came the corner room that contained the rest of Estelle's possessions. By the time I crossed the hall to her door, I was hot and tired and feeling more than a little pessimistic. Still, having come this far, I was determined to finish what I'd begun.

My expectations were not high. In the end, I almost missed the telltale creak. I stopped and shifted my weight, tentatively pushing down on the same spot a second time. Was I just imagining that one board had moved a little? I knelt and applied pressure with both hands. This time the floorboard wobbled *and* creaked.

"Don't get your hopes up," I muttered under my breath. "Just because you found a wonky section of flooring doesn't mean there's anything hidden beneath it."

The spot in question was located right in front of the nightstand next to the bed. It would have been a convenient place for Estelle to hide something she didn't want others to see. The floorboard and those next to it were among the shorter sections of wood, too, only seven or eight inches in length. It was impossible not to see the potential.

Encouraged, I pried at the seam with my fingers. That the board resisted wasn't too surprising. Whether it concealed a secret hiding place or not, it hadn't been lifted for decades.

Wishing I'd brought a crowbar, I kept clawing at it,

breaking two fingernails before the plank abruptly came free and sent me rocking back onto my heels. Setting the length of wood aside, I bent down and peered into the hollow space between the upstairs floor and the downstairs ceiling. It was a couple of inches deep, just the right size to hide a book, but it appeared to be empty.

Disappointment swamped me. If I'd been the weepy sort, I'd probably have burst into tears. Instead, I took a couple of deep breaths and then pried up the floorboards on either side of the opening.

More empty space taunted me. To be absolutely certain nothing was hidden under the floor, I'd have to stick my hand inside the hole and feel around in all directions. I might find a stash of diaries. I might also encounter something else, like a spider or mice droppings. Another snake seemed unlikely, but I dearly wished I'd thought to bring a pair of heavy work gloves with me from home.

"Stop shilly-shallying," I muttered under my breath.

Closing my eyes, I thrust my right hand into the opening and began to fish around. Moving my fingers forward and backward over the rough surface and then to the left and right of the opening, I encountered nothing worse than dirt and dust bunnies. I retracted my hand and fished in my pocket for a tissue to wipe my fingers.

Glaring at the hole, I flattened myself on the floor, took the flashlight I'd brought in from the car in my right hand, and inserted my arm as far as it would go. With my face thrust into the opening, I aimed the beam into the deepest recesses.

There was *something* there, but the anomaly was nearly swallowed up by shadows. I shifted position, let go of the flashlight, and stretched to extend my arm an inch or two farther into the narrow space. Even then my fingers barely grazed the object I was after. Holding my head at an awkward and rather painful angle, I tried again. My hand brushed against what I sincerely hoped was just a spider-web, then touched what I knew at once was the spine of a small book. Grabbing hold, I tugged it toward me. A moment later, I sat up with the prize firmly grasped in both hands.

It was no wonder I'd almost missed finding it. The leather-bound book wasn't very thick and it had a black cover. What puzzled me was that it had been concealed so far from the opening. Still seated on the floor, I judged the distance and realized that the spot where I'd found it was under the bed. It didn't take much of a leap of logic to surmise that there might be another loose floorboard in that location.

There was nothing for it but to move the furniture. After all, I'd only found *one* diary. There were supposed to be at least two.

I retrieved my flashlight, then shoved at the single bed until it was out of the way. As I'd hoped, I found more loose boards. I pried them up and aimed my light into the opening, but no matter how I contorted myself or where I directed the beam, I didn't see anything but empty space.

Methodically, I replaced the floorboards and returned the bed to its former position. Then I sat down on it and opened the diary.

On the flyleaf, written in a bold scrawl, were the words *Estelle Marie Swarthout, her book.* The first entry was dated three years before Rosanna's murder and recorded Estelle's opinion of the first rehearsal of a play in which she had a leading role. She included her impressions of her fellow cast members. Her comments were scathing. No one measured up to her exacting standards.

Rather than read every sentence, I flipped through the pages, stopping here and there to peruse a random paragraph. Estelle had recorded her opinions at length, and sometimes with considerable vitriol, but not with any regularity. She'd acted in at least two more plays and had strong opinions about them, too.

What I was reading was less a diary than a journal, not that most people make any distinction between the two. About halfway through the book, Rosanna's name caught my eye and I stopped to read what Estelle had written. It was obvious she didn't like her stepmother. Not at all. Among the words she used to describe her were *tightwad* and *controlling bitch*.

"Oh, look," I murmured. "A clue."

The more I read, the more I began to think that Estelle, alibi or no alibi, ought to be considered a likely suspect in her stepmother's murder. She'd certainly *wanted* the second Mrs. Swarthout dead! It was lucky for her that she'd hidden this little book so well. If the police had found it during their investigation of Rosanna's murder, they'd have arrested Estelle for the crime in a New York minute.

I paused to lean back against the headboard and consider that scenario. According to the newspaper accounts, Estelle and Tessa had gone to a movie together and come home to find Rosanna's body. If Estelle *had* killed Rosanna, Tessa must have lied to the police to protect her sister. That would have made Tessa an accessory after the fact, if not before.

Was that what she wanted revealed in print? Had she contrived a way for the whole story to come out after both she and her sister were safely out of reach of the criminal justice system?

What I couldn't fathom was why Tessa would make finding that truth, if it *was* the truth, so complicated. Why not just leave behind a letter to be opened following her death? She'd had no need to involve me, let alone leave me her house. Why insist that I be the one to find the diaries and publish them? And why diaries, plural? Where were the others?

You're jumping the gun, I warned myself. *This isn't a signed confession. Estelle wrote nasty things about a lot of the people she knew. Maybe she just used journaling to let off steam.*

An hour later, I'd skimmed all the entries but was no closer to finding answers. Estelle's diary did not contain elaborate plans for doing away with Rosanna. In fact, the last entry had been written a full month before her stepmother's death. Although I now knew a great deal about Estelle Swarthout's toxic personality, I had no proof she was a cold-blooded killer.

Slowly, my joints stiff from sitting in one position for such a long time, I eased off the bed and went back downstairs. It was already evening and once again I was dirty, tired, hot, sweaty, and hungry. It was time to go home, take a long soak in the bathtub, make myself a meal, preferably one heavy on comfort food, and cuddle with my cat.

Chapter Twenty-five

One of the things I purchased when I set up shop as a freelance editor was a printer that also scans and makes copies. My original plan was to copy the pages of Estelle's journal so that I could scribble notes on them before typing the edited version into a computer file. Instead, as soon as I got home, I scanned them and then made two printouts.

Once I'd backed up the scan, I contemplated the original, handwritten, leather-bound book. I'd need to read everything Estelle had written again, slowly and much more carefully, not only to check spelling and punctuation, but also to search for clues. There had to be a *reason* Tessa wanted it published, even if it wasn't connected to Rosanna's murder.

Preserving what Estelle had written, selfish and petty as those entries made her seem, must have been important to her sister. It wasn't up to me to question the terms of Tessa's will. I wouldn't quite call what I'd been asked to do a sacred trust, but since I'd accepted the task, I intended to do my best to live up to my responsibilities. The only thing I might be able to do to keep things in perspective was to write an introduction.

Another obligation had me picking up the phone and calling Detective Arthur Brightwell.

He listened to me ramble a bit before he informed me that he was already planning to be in Lenape Hollow the next day. Since he'd be at the police station all morning, he suggested we meet for lunch at Harriet's. He even offered to pay for my meal.

I accepted this unexpected invitation, but not without a few misgivings. It was distinctly out of character for Brightwell to be so agreeable.

He was already in the restaurant when I arrived. He'd claimed a table that sat a little apart from the others and thus offered a modicum of privacy. After we gave our orders—cheeseburger and fries for me and a club sandwich for him—he got right down to business.

"I hear you've been discovering quite a few things out at that farm of yours."

I took a sip of ice water and regarded him over the rim of the glass. "I told you about Estelle Swarthout's journal when we spoke on the phone."

"I'm not talking about the journal."

It took me a moment to catch his drift. "You mean the storage units in the barn? How did you hear about them?"

"How could I not?" His amusement was palpable and extremely annoying. "The drug-sniffing dogs work for the SO."

I knew those initials translated to "sheriff's office" and it was on the tip of my tongue to ask why local cops referred to *their* office as the PD—police *department*. Instead, I asked a serious, sensible, *relevant* question: "Should I be worried that there's a connection?"

"Between a cold case and whatever was going on in the barn? Doesn't seem likely. Sounds to me as if someone just took advantage of a piece of abandoned property in a remote location to set up a way station for stolen goods."

"That still took chutzpah."

"That or stupidity." He very nearly smiled. "Most criminals aren't the brightest bulbs, but sometimes they get lucky."

His very nonchalance made me want to argue with him. "This was a far cry from teenagers breaking into an abandoned house to party. Someone spent a lot of time, effort, and money to construct those storage units."

"It wouldn't surprise me to learn that local kids trespassed regularly over the years, if only to swim in the farm pond. Hunters, hikers, and ATV and snowmobile enthusiasts probably made use of the land, too. No one would have been there to stop them. But the thing is, those storage units *were* empty when you discovered them. They could have been built at any time in the past twenty or thirty years, and since they weren't full of contraband, there's no way to tell when they were last used."

"Do you think it likely whoever installed them will come back?" I hadn't been particularly concerned about the crooks returning, but now I had to wonder what would happen if they did.

The arrival of our food prevented him from responding. He dug in. I ate more slowly, once again wondering why Detective Brightwell had invited me to have lunch with him. He could just as easily have asked me to meet him in Detective Hazlett's office across the street. I didn't flatter myself that he wanted the pleasure of my company. The uncomfortable silence that had settled between us would have put paid to that theory even if common sense had not.

"So," Brightwell said after he polished off his sandwich. "You found Estelle Swarthout's diary?"

I fished the leather-bound volume out of my tote and passed it across the table. "This is the original, but I made a copy of the pages that you may take with you if you like."

"Am I going to find it useful in solving my cold case?" He flipped idly through the pages without showing much apparent interest.

"There's no need to be snarky." I narrowed my eyes at him. "And since when has it been *your* cold case?"

He shrugged and reached for his coffee mug. "I've taken an interest in it just lately, after a certain civilian brought it to my attention."

"And?"

"And there wasn't much to go on, even back then. A window in the kitchen door was broken, suggesting that's how a burglar got in. Mrs. Swarthout's body was found in the adjoining room. It looked as if she was trying to get to the phone to call for help."

"And the would-be thief followed her and stabbed her to death? Why not just run away?"

"Maybe she recognized him." He signaled to Harriet and ordered a slice of apple pie with vanilla ice cream on top. "You want dessert?"

I shook my head. "Where did the weapon come from?"

"It was one of her own kitchen knives."

I thought about that for a moment. "How many times was she stabbed?" The newspaper account hadn't supplied that detail.

"Are you sure you want all the gory details?"

"Humor me."

"Three."

Ada brought his pie. From the look on her face, she'd overheard enough of our conversation to realize we were discussing a crime. Avid curiosity warred with dismay on her expressive face. She knew way too much about my previous encounters with murder, and that they'd always ended up putting me in harm's way.

I couldn't see that happening this time. Darlene had

done searches for all the individuals named in newspaper accounts of the crime. She'd located most of them with the help of the Find a Grave website. I felt confident that whoever killed Rosanna was either long dead or in his dotage. There was no danger that he'd come after me.

"*Where* was she stabbed?" I asked as Brightwell forked up an enormous bite of the pie. "And I don't mean in what room."

He chewed and swallowed. "In the chest. The killer aimed for the heart."

"So she wasn't running away from the intruder. She was face-to-face with someone, possibly someone she knew."

His eyebrows shot up. He gave the book on the table between us a considering glance. "Exactly what did Estelle Swarthout write in there?"

"No confession, more's the pity." I picked up the original, returned it to my tote, and removed one of the two printouts I'd made of the scanned pages. "And neither is there a page labeled 'this is how I plan to kill my stepmother.' What is clear from her entries is that Estelle resented Rosanna, maybe even hated her. And if her sister was willing to lie for her, to give her an alibi . . ."

He continued to look skeptical, but he accepted the printout. It was more than an inch thick. I'd had to put a rubber band around the pages to keep them together.

"I'll give this a read," he promised, "but it sounds to me as if you're speculating on the basis of very little hard evidence. If everyone who ever resented a parent or stepparent resorted to violence, the crime rate would be a whole lot higher than it is. Most people work out their aggression by bitching about their relatives to sympathetic friends."

"Or writing down their complaints?"

"Or posting them on social media." He actually grinned. "So, generally speaking, it's more likely someone will tell the world how crazy Aunt Sally makes him, rather than punch out dear old auntie over the Thanksgiving turkey?"

He signaled for the check. "That's about the size of it. I'll grant you that most people *are* killed by their nearest and dearest, but a far greater percentage of families find more socially acceptable ways to settle their differences."

Chapter Twenty-six

I wanted to accept Detective Brightwell's logic, but I still had doubts. Preoccupied, I was already on my front porch, about to unlock the door, before I caught a flicker of movement out of the corner of my eye and realized I wasn't alone.

Key in hand, I whirled around and barely repressed a shriek when I recognized Bella Trent. She'd been waiting for me on my wicker sofa. I hadn't seen her sitting there and she nearly scared the daylights out of me when she stood up.

"It's about time you came home." She advanced a few steps in my direction, a determined look on her face.

I held my ground, but only with an effort. *Never let them see you sweat,* I reminded myself. The woman wasn't entirely rational, but she'd never physically harmed anyone. I hoped she wasn't planning to start with me.

"If I'd known I had company waiting," I said, lying through my teeth, "I would have been here sooner." *But not alone!*

I wondered if I could fish my cell phone out of my tote, turn it on, and manage to punch in a nine and two ones without her noticing. Somehow I doubted it.

"I want to talk to you," Bella said.

Since I wasn't about to invite her inside my house, I gestured for her to return to the sofa while I sat down in one of the matching wicker chairs. I didn't *think* Bella was dangerous, but I've been wrong about people before.

On closer inspection, she seemed calmer than she'd been the last time I'd seen her. Her voice lacked the shrillness it had in her phone messages. That her hands were twisted together in her lap was a sure sign of tension, but the outright aggression of our previous encounters seemed to be absent.

Optimist that I am, I thought she might be open to reason. "How can I help you?" I asked.

"You can stop pretending to be such an expert. How can you charge people money and still let mistakes slip through?"

I was unable to repress a sigh. "Bella," I said, leaning forward slightly so that our eyes met, "I am not Illyria Dubonnet's editor. Remember? I explained this to you before. She and I are old friends and she lets me read her manuscripts before she does the final revision. I'm what's called a beta reader. The only things I'm looking for are gaps in logic, or places where she inadvertently repeated herself, or really obvious gaffes."

"Like calling the heroine by the wrong name?"

Oops! "Sometimes, during the writing process, an author changes her mind about what a character is called, and even with 'find and replace' it's possible to miss changing all of the instances where the old name was used."

For once, I thought she was listening. Not only listening, but comprehending.

"But you *know* her? She's a *friend*?"

"Yes." As much as I might wish I'd closed that particular barn door, the horse had already escaped. There was no point in trying to deny my friendship with Lenora.

"I want to meet her," Bella said. *Big surprise!*

"That's not possible. I told you. She's traveling abroad. It may be months before she gets home."

"Where does she live?"

I shook my head. "I can't tell you that, Bella. She has a right to her privacy. I'm sure you can understand that. How could she write her wonderful books if she wasn't able to get away from the outside world?"

"But I'm her biggest fan." The whispered words reverberated with pain and grief. Her eyes swam with tears.

"Bella, if you love her work, you need to let her get on with it. Maybe you could send her a nice long letter to tell her how much her writing means to you. I know she lists a post office box as an address on her web page."

The violence with which she shook her head alarmed me. "No! You don't understand! I *have* to see her in person. I have to make her understand."

"Understand what?" I wasn't sure I wanted to hear her answer, but I couldn't stop myself from asking the question.

"That she has to get rid of that editor. The one who let those mistakes into her book." Swiping at the moisture on her cheeks, she narrowed her eyes at me. "If it wasn't you, then someone else is to blame."

Finally! A demand that was within the realm of possibilities.

"What a good idea," I said with patently false enthusiasm. "She can request a different copy editor for her next book. When you write to her, why don't you suggest just that? I'm sure she'll appreciate the input."

For a moment, Bella looked confused. Then her mouth squished into a pout that would have done a three-year-old proud. It looked ridiculous on the face of a grown women. "I need to tell her in person, and you *know* her."

And the merry-go-round takes another spin. It was obvious that sweet reason was not going to work on Illyria's biggest fan. Somewhat belatedly, it also dawned on me that I wasn't going to get rid of her until I gave in to her plea . . . or pretended to.

"I tell you what, Bella. When Illyria finally gets back from her travels, I'll talk to her about your concerns."

"Tell her I want to meet her face-to-face."

"That's going to have to be up to her, but I'll put in a good word for you."

"You'd better do more than that. You'd better convince her to agree."

The belligerence was back, and Bella was growing more agitated with every word she spoke, to the point where I didn't think it would be prudent to say anything to upset her further. Suggesting that she seek professional counseling was obviously out of the question. To be truthful, at that moment all I really wanted was to get away from her.

"I'll try my best," I promised, "but you'll have to be patient. She's not even in the country right now. Remember? I told you that before."

"I just want to meet her." With jerky movements, Bella got to her feet and walked away from me. I rose more slowly and stooped to pick up my tote, once again holding my house key at the ready. I froze when she reached the top of the porch steps and stopped. Slowly, she turned her head and glared at me over her shoulder.

"I'll be back," she promised.

Even Arnold Schwarzenegger couldn't have made that phrase sound more alarming.

Chapter Twenty-seven

Once I was safely inside the house, the first thing I noticed was that there was a new message on my answering machine. I hesitated before pushing PLAY. The last thing I needed to hear was another diatribe from Bella.

Instead, I got an earful from Darlene. The gist of it was that she needed a favor. A big one. Despite all I owe her, I almost turned her down. Then I reconsidered. Maybe spending an entire day doing something completely different was just what the doctor ordered. I was more than ready to be distracted from my concerns about the Swarthout farm. I could afford to take a mini-vacation—eight hours or so—away from editing manuscripts for my paying clients. And if I wasn't at home tomorrow, Bella wouldn't be able to nag me about setting up a meeting with her idol.

At eight the next morning, a Friday, I boarded a bus in the company of two other chaperones and the twenty youngsters, aged eight to twelve, who were enrolled in the library's summer reading program. The field trip had been arranged weeks before, and a photo essay about the event was scheduled to go into the library newsletter, the one I was supposed to be editing in my spare time. At the last minute, the library assistant who'd volunteered to take the pictures had been forced to bow out. She had a good excuse. She'd taken a bad fall and broken her ankle. That left me holding the bag . . . and the camera.

My fellow chaperones were Pam Ingram and Darlene herself. It wasn't until we reached our destination and were met in the parking lot by two horse-drawn wagons and a surrey, our transportation to the site of the living history center a half mile distant, that I wondered how my arthritic friend was going to manage the terrain.

"Not to worry," Darlene assured me. "They knew I was coming. That's why there's a second wagon, so they have room to transport my scooter up to the house. They've even offered to hoist me up to the second floor in the dumbwaiter, but I think I'll pass on that."

"Shouldn't there be an elevator? I thought the law—"

"There are exceptions for historic sites. The whole idea is to experience what living here would have been like in the eighteen nineties. The kids are really excited. Several of the books in their summer reading program are set in that era. One of the stories, about a city girl sent to live with her country cousins, takes place right here in Sullivan County."

"I didn't think kids their age were interested in history." The young teens I'd taught in Maine certainly hadn't been.

"Maybe it's a new trend."

"One can only hope."

It was at that point that a young man of college age approached us. He wore a linen shirt with an open collar and rolled up sleeves. His blue denim trousers were held up by brightly colored suspenders. They'd been hand-embroidered with an eclectic selection of flowers, some of which didn't resemble any species of plant life I'd ever seen in nature.

"They're called braces, not suspenders, ma'am," he corrected me when I admired this accessory. His eyes were bright with good humor behind wire rimmed glasses when he turned to Darlene. "I'm Clyde. I've already loaded that fancy contraption of yours into the wagon. Some kind of bicycle, is it? Are you going to need me to carry you to the surrey?"

"Just your arm will do." To judge by her wide grin, Darlene was enjoying Clyde's role-playing.

Personally, I'd have preferred to be swept off my feet. Whether they were due to workouts in a gym or from doing real chores on this reconstruction of a nineteenth-century farm, Clyde had muscles that looked equal to the task of hefting even what my late husband used to call a BMW—a "big Maine woman."

The ride lasted about ten minutes and ended at the site of a real nineteenth-century farm whose owners, like the Swarthouts, had taken in summer boarders. To accommodate even more paying guests, the Westbrook family had added a large, rectangular annex to the original building. As architecture, the result wasn't particularly pleasing, but the additional space would have done wonders for their bottom line.

Embracing my assignment, I took tons of pictures, starting with one of the costumed reenactor who greeted us in the kitchen of the house. She smiled throughout her presentation, despite the fact that she had to be sweltering in the dark blue, floor-length dress she wore. She explained that her clothes were too fancy for the everyday attire of a typical farmer's daughter, but that she about to leave to participate in a quilting bee at a neighbor's house.

Turning so we could admire the small bustle at the back, she went on to say that the dress was made of a fabric called cashmere and was trimmed in silk. She held up one arm so everyone could see that the three-quarter length sleeve was decorated with silk braid and had white lace at the cuffs. The hem of her skirt, which just cleared the ground, was adorned with two rows of the same silk braid. Sturdy ankle-high boots on her feet and a small cameo brooch worn at her throat completed the outfit.

"Would anyone like a drink of water?" she asked, and proceeded to demonstrate how to work the hand pump in the sink.

Since she had but one tin cup to offer us, no one took her up on her invitation. Belatedly, I understood why everyone in our party had been handed a bottle of water as we left the bus.

Two more reenactors appeared to split our group into three smaller ones. Pam went with the young people who were to start their tour at the schoolhouse and participate in a shortened version of a typical school day.

From reading the center's brochure, I knew it had opened in the 1990s, the brainchild of a professor at Sidwell, a tiny but prestigious liberal arts college in Strongtown, halfway between Kingston and Monticello and about an hour's drive from the site. He'd modeled his program on one developed decades earlier by the National Endowment for the Humanities. Since the farm buildings took up only a small portion of the two-hundred-acre site, a replica of a mid-nineteenth-century one-room schoolhouse had later been built in a far corner of the property. Visitors walked there in order to get a feel for the distance children once traveled to obtain an education.

Darlene's group remained in the house to learn about the chores done by the womenfolk in the family. I ended up herding seven noisy, hyper kids along the dirt path that led to the outbuildings and animal pens.

I have to admit it was an interesting experience, and it certainly offered plenty of opportunity to take pictures. I posed my young charges with Buck and Bill, the oxen used to pull a plow. We toured the barn, meeting horses and milk cows, peeked inside the pigsty and the chicken coop, and did our best to stay upwind of the fenced-in area that held the goats. We also visited a smokehouse and a wash-room—a special shed used for doing laundry—and ended our tour at a small structure that turned out to be a three-hole privy.

At first I thought it was a playhouse. The exterior was painted white and it had colorful red shingles on the roof. It stood about twenty yards from one corner of the annex, at the end of a flagstone walkway. Lilacs, noted for their strong scent, had been planted on both sides of the en-trance.

To render the outhouse usable by visitors to the center, minor compromises had been made with historical accu-racy. Personally, I'd have been happier if they'd hidden a row of Porta Potties behind a nearby stand of birch trees, but no one had asked my opinion.

Our entire group reassembled for lunch, which was served in the dining room in the annex. There was space for all of us to sit with plenty left over. According to the reenactor who served us, an older woman in a rust-colored dress with a big white apron over it, the Westbrooks could feed up to fifty people at a time.

"I should be able to manage on level ground with my scooter," Darlene said as we spooned up the most deli-cious homemade chicken soup I'd ever tasted. "I'm look-ing forward to seeing the animals and you're going to love the house tour."

"We're headed to the schoolhouse first."

"Then you'll have saved the best till last." She smiled to herself and resumed eating.

I sent her a questioning look. Something was up, but I didn't have a clue what it might be.

After my group spent an hour pretending to be nineteenth-century schoolchildren, with authentic lessons from that era given to them by a reenactor who introduced himself as their teacher, we returned to the farmhouse. By then I was close to my saturation point when it came to living history, but I pasted an expression of polite interest on my face to greet our tour guide. The woman who'd been our waitress at lunch began her presentation by demonstrating how housewives in the 1890s judged whether the temperature in an oven heated by a wood-burning stove was hot enough to bake bread. Several of my charges gasped when she thrust her bared arm inside.

As they had when the "farmer" described the perils of mowing hay with a scythe, the young people listened with rapt attention to a story about a long skirt set ablaze by a stray ember and another detailing the terrible burns a maidservant sustained when she carelessly tried to pick up a cookpot with her bare hands.

All children are bloodthirsty at a certain age. Some never grow out of it.

As the tour of the farmhouse commenced, I tuned out the narration, but I couldn't help but notice some of the little touches that had been added to make the place look authentic. A wooden darning egg lay on a side table, a sock with a hole in it positioned so that its purpose would be clear even to the most modern youngster. In the sitting room, an eclectic assortment of pictures hung on the walls, everything from prints and charcoal sketches to watercolor landscapes and portraits of family members. Scarcely an inch of what was behind them showed. Only here and there could I see that there were faded pink cabbage roses on the wallpaper. They looked remarkably similar to the ones decorating the front room at the Swarthout farm.

We trooped through the downstairs rooms in the main house and out into the annex by way of what our guide called the writing room. Summer boarders had availed themselves of the desk, paper, pen, and ink to write letters home. Casually abandoned on a chair was a Sears mail order catalog from 1893.

At the far end of the dining hall, a flight of stairs led up to the six bedrooms in the annex and, through a door and down two steps, back into the main house. The "bath room" turned out to be just that—a room in which one could take a bath. The dumbwaiter Darlene had mentioned was located nearby, since it was used to carry up buckets of hot water from the kitchen below.

"Before the annex was built in 1880," our guide informed us, "only the bedrooms in the main house were rented out. The family made room for paying guests by moving out of their own rooms. The women and girls slept in the attic during the summer months while the menfolk camped out in the barn loft."

A narrow stairwell much like the one at the Swarthout farm took us back down to the first floor.

"As I mentioned when we were in the bedrooms," our guide said, "there are no closets. We hang our clothes on wall pegs or in free-standing wardrobes. But the builders of this house disliked the idea of wasted space, so there is a closet of sorts under the stairs we just descended."

She led us around the corner and pointed to what at first appeared to be a blank wall. On closer inspection, one of the boys spotted a finger pull. My attention, which had been wandering, was suddenly riveted.

"Go ahead," the guide said. "Open it."

To the delight of the entire group, doing so revealed a compact storage area hidden behind the paneling. A few items of clothing hung from a bar that ran across the width of the opening while others were neatly folded on the shelf above it.

"It's a cabinet under the stairs," an eight-year-old girl exclaimed. "Just like in Harry Potter."

"It's a cupboard," the boy standing next to her said. "In the books it's called a *cupboard* under the stairs."

I didn't give a fig for Harry Potter. Darlene's smile finally made sense. She'd known I'd make the same connection she had between the Swarthout farm and this one. The two farm-boardinghouses weren't identical, but they had many similarities. I could hardly wait to get back to Swan's Crossing and find out if there was a cupboard under the Swarthout stairs.

Chapter Twenty-eight

Since it was nearly dark by the time we got back to Lenape Hollow from the field trip, I waited until the next morning to investigate. Ten a.m. Saturday found me confronting the blank wall that closed in the underside of the first floor stairwell of the Swarthout farmhouse. It wasn't paneled like the one at the living history center. Here the surface was solid wallboard—or is it drywall? I'm never sure of the correct term, even though I've looked it up more than once. Whatever it's called, it had been plastered over and painted an unappealing off-white that had dulled nearly to gray with the passage of time.

Feeling a trifle foolish, I ran my fingertips over every inch of the wall, searching for the slightest suggestion of a dip or bump. It was a futile effort. There was no hidden door. It had been a long shot. I'd known that from the start, but logic failed to diminish my sense of disappointment.

I had work waiting for me at home. For one thing I had to write up a piece on the field trip for the library newsletter and choose several of the best photos to go with it. I had a rapidly approaching deadline for that project and several regular editing jobs cued up, as well. Even so, I was reluctant to give up my search for more diaries. What if this house did have a secret storage cupboard, just not in the same place as on the Westbrook farm? The little closet-sized space that connected the back room to the middle room also contained a door leading to the basement and those stairs were located directly beneath the steps that ran from the first floor to the second.

A few minutes later, I stood on the landing looking down. The light from a single bare bulb gave me a clear view of the cellarway and the underside of those treads. Nothing had been closed in. There was no hiding place there.

Unwilling to give up, I descended into the cellar and looked *under* the steps, but once again I found only open, empty spaces. Frustrated, I returned to the landing and stamped my feet on the floor, not in a childish tantrum, although I felt like throwing one of those, but to make certain there were no loose boards. There weren't.

I even took a hard look at the ceiling. If there had been tiles, I'd have pushed them up to investigate the space above my head, but it was plaster, as were all the ceilings in the house. Unable to think of anywhere else to search, I called it a day and went home.

Chapter Twenty-nine

I spent the rest of the weekend putting the finishing touches on the library newsletter and editing Estelle's journal. If there were any further clues to be found, I missed them.

Sunday night was another hot, sticky one, making me grateful I had an air conditioner in my bedroom window. I wouldn't have survived a summer sleeping in the attic at Westbrook Farm.

We don't get a great many scorching days in the foothills of the Catskills, but there are enough of them with temperatures in the nineties to make sleep impossible without something to cool things down to tolerable levels at night. My ancestors were hardier individuals than I am. I like my modern creature comforts, and at my age I'm entitled to them.

I woke up on Monday morning well rested and determined to put a stop to the runaround Leland Featherstone had been giving me. I had an appointment with him in two days, but that was longer than I was willing to wait for answers.

It would be a stretch to claim I'd already fulfilled the condition Tessa had set in her will. Singular and plural aren't the same, so I still had at least one more diary to find. It stood to reason that Featherstone could help with that. He had to know more than he'd told me.

Even if the lawyer couldn't legally name names, I hoped he'd be willing to tell me if the farm was slated to go to an individual or an entity in the event of my failure. If Tessa's second choice was a charity or some other organization, especially one that would have little use for the place, I could safely abandon the theory that the residuary heir was someone who might have gone to the house and stolen one or more diaries to make certain I wouldn't find them.

At the law offices of Featherstone, De Vane, Doherty, Sanchez, and Schiller, the same receptionist who had been giving me the runaround on the phone once again informed me that her boss was not available. She appeared to be somewhere in her late twenties. In keeping with the conservative vibe of the law firm she worked for, she wore a tailored suit and had styled her hair in a way that added age, if not gravitas, to her features. Her nameplate read CHARLAINE GOLDING.

"That's a pretty name," I said. "Unusual."

"My mother named me after one of her favorite authors." Her cheeks went slightly pink at the admission.

"Let me guess—Charlaine Harris."

She nodded and looked pleased that I'd made the connection.

Having established a bond of sorts, I put as much friendliness as I could manage into my voice. "Tell me, Charlaine, is Mr. Featherstone really on the premises this morning? I mean, I'd understand if he didn't come in every day. He's getting on in years, after all."

Her gaze was wary but there was a hint of apology in her voice. "Well, yes. He is. All the partners and associates are here today. They're in a staff meeting, just as they are every Monday morning. Mr. Featherstone never misses one. It's just . . . well, I guess you've noticed that he's been avoiding taking your calls."

"Oh, I noticed, all right. That's why I'm prepared to wait right here until he's free, and this time I won't accept Mr. Coleman as a substitute. It's very important that I speak with Mr. Featherstone and only Mr. Featherstone."

She tugged nervously at a loose strand of hair, obviously regretting that she'd said as much as she had. "There's no telling how long the meeting will last, and he has a busy schedule for the rest of the day. Wouldn't it be better if you just came back on Wednesday, when you already have an appointment to meet with him?"

"I don't think so." The way things had been going, it seemed more than likely that Featherstone would wait until the last minute and then cancel.

I didn't blame Charlaine. Somewhere along the line it had probably been drilled into her that she should be pleasant to the general public at all times, but that it was also her job to protect her employers from unwanted visitors.

That said, I know that secretaries, receptionists, and clerks hold the real power in any office. It was a good bet that Charlaine knew much more about the lawyers she worked for than any of those men realized. If I took the right approach with her, who knew what interesting details she might let slip? The trick was to bide my time.

"I'll wait as long as necessary," I said, and took a seat.

I'd come prepared. Opening my tote, I had only to choose between a hardcover edition of the newest J. D. Robb thriller and my tablet, which contained hundreds of books, both fiction and nonfiction, many of which I had not yet read. I'd also packed a small bottle of water, a packet of crackers, and an apple.

The first hour passed fairly quickly. Ms. Robb is a superb storyteller.

At the ninety-minute mark, I got up to stretch and wandered back to the receptionist's desk. I bestowed my best grandmotherly smile on her. "Have you worked here long, dear?"

Charlaine smiled back. "Just over three years."

"Good benefits?"

"Not bad. And the partners are easy to get along with."

"What about the associates? I've met Jason Coleman."

Just the tiniest bit of pink crept into her cheeks. "He's very nice. Polite. I've worked in places where the bosses treat their office staff like dirt. I'm very fortunate to have been hired by Featherstone, De Vane, Doherty, Sanchez, and Schiller."

And you'd like to keep your job, I thought. *So you're leery of any questions that imply criticism of any of the lawyers working here.*

I can be flexible. I switched gears and instead asked about the history of the law firm. "Did Mr. Featherstone found it?"

"Oh, no. His *father* did."

"That must have been a long time ago."

"That's Conrad Featherstone's photo on the wall." She pointed to a large portrait hanging behind her desk. "He died in 1975."

Studying the photograph, I could see the family resemblance. "Was the firm called Featherstone and Featherstone back then, or maybe Featherstone and Son?" I winced as I proposed the latter. It sounded more like the name of a livery stable or a hardware store.

"To start with it was Featherstone, Darden, and Grenoble," Charlaine said.

Although this line of questioning didn't seem to be taking me anywhere useful, my curiosity bump is a big one. Out of sheer nosiness, I asked, "Who were Darden and Grenoble?"

"Mr. Darden was a pretty famous trial lawyer, but he died when he was only fifty."

"How sad. Did he leave heirs to follow in his footsteps?"

She shook her head. "The two remaining partners split his share of the firm."

"What happened to Grenoble?"

"He's dead, too." The pink came back into her cheeks.

"No heirs?"

"Well . . ."

I smiled encouragingly at her.

Charlaine lowered her voice. "Mr. Grenoble's share went to Mr. Conrad Featherstone, but it was understood that Mr. Featherstone would hire Mr. Grenoble's grandson as an associate as soon as he graduated from law school."

"And that would be?"

Her blush forewarned me of her answer: "Mr. Coleman. He doesn't make a big deal about it, of course, but it's pretty certain that he'll be made a partner before too much longer."

I was surprised he hadn't already been offered a partnership, but the more relevant point in Charlaine's story was that Leland Featherstone's father and Jason Coleman's maternal grandfather had been practicing law at the time of Rosanna Swarthout's murder.

I wasn't certain exactly what that signified, but I had a feeling it was important. I hoped it meant that good old Leland had access to Swarthout family papers from the time before Tessa owned the farm, documents like her father's will, and Rosanna's, and even, perhaps, an inventory of the contents of the house.

I returned to my chair and my book. I looked up only once while I waited, when I sensed someone watching me. Charlaine was busy with a phone call and I didn't see anyone else. I shrugged off the feeling. Either I'd imagined the sensation of being stared at or whoever had come out of one of the offices to take a look at me had gone away again before I lifted my head. Several hallways branched off from the reception area. Someone could have ducked down one of them and been out of sight in an instant.

Chapter Thirty

Another quarter of an hour passed before I was finally shown into Leland Featherstone's office.

"I'm rather busy today, Ms. Lincoln," he said without looking up from the papers on his desk. "Can we keep this short?"

He didn't invite me to sit but I took the client chair opposite him anyway. After I placed my tote carefully beside it, I fixed him with a hard stare. He didn't look at all well. His complexion was a pastier white than I remembered and his shoulders were hunched in a way that made me think he had a tension headache.

"You're a difficult man to get hold of, Mr. Featherstone. I find that surprising, given how considerate you were when we first met. Why, you even took time out of your busy day to personally escort me to the Swarthout farm."

Abandoning all pretense of work, he sat up straighter in his chair. His hands rested lightly on the edge of the desk. No nervous fiddling with paperclips for our Mr. Featherstone!

"What is it you want, Ms. Lincoln?"

"Answers. The fastest way to get rid of me is to provide them."

He gestured for me to proceed.

"Let me backtrack. You already know that the diaries I'm supposed to edit were not sitting right out in the open ready to be collected. When I had searched the entire house for them with no success, I began to wonder if someone had taken them, perhaps someone who would benefit by my failure to meet the conditions of Tessa's bequest. That's one reason I was anxious to speak with you. I want to know the identity of her residuary heir."

"You think that person stole the diaries?" His astonishment seemed genuine. "I think it highly unlikely."

"Why? Who inherits if I don't?"

"I'm not at—"

"—liberty to say," I finished for him. "Why not? Was *that* specified in Tessa's will?"

"No, but—"

"Is the other party also your client? If so, that strikes me as a potential conflict of interest, Mr. Featherstone."

"The person in question is not a client of this firm."

That was progress. We weren't talking about a corporation or a charity. "What makes you so certain this *person* wouldn't try to prevent me from finding the diaries?"

"The residuary heir is not even aware that he's in line to inherit."

He, I thought. *More progress.* "Does he have knowledge of the existence of the diaries? Or of the fact that I have a deadline to edit and publish them?"

"My young associate, Mr. Coleman, and I are the only people who are aware of your obligations. And anyone *you* may have told, of course." He sounded testy, and impatient to be rid of me, but I wasn't finished with him yet.

"Why did you try to hide the reason Tessa and Estelle left their home?"

"I hid nothing."

Definitely testy!

"You withheld information. You didn't say a word

about Rosanna Swarthout's murder, and you can't tell me you weren't aware of it. How old were you at the time? Eighteen? Nineteen?"

He frowned. "I don't see the relevance—"

"My point is that you must have known about the murder right after it happened, even if you weren't personally acquainted with the family. The story was in all the newspapers. It was probably a nine-days' wonder at the time."

His bushy white eyebrows all but knit themselves together as he glowered at me. I didn't blink. The staring contest continued for a solid minute—one of those minutes that feel like hours—before he apparently decided it would be easier to humor me than continue to stall.

"I believe I was about fifteen. Perhaps sixteen."

I did a quick mental calculation. I'd had him pegged at somewhere in his early eighties, but if he'd been no more than sixteen at the time of the murder, that made him a mere seventy-eight to my seventy-one. He hadn't aged nearly as well as I had.

"Were you personally acquainted with Rosanna Swarthout?" I asked.

"No, I was not."

"Did this law firm represent her?"

"My father dealt with the Swarthout family's legal business, but Rosanna died long before I passed the bar and joined the firm. I was never privy to the details."

"So he'd have handled Tessa's father's will as well as her stepmother's?"

"I assume so."

"Do you have copies? Was there an inventory made of the contents of the house during probate?"

He glowered at me. "I am not at liberty to share any such documents."

I can recognize a brick wall when I run into one. I changed tactics. "Had you met either Tessa or Estelle before their stepmother was murdered?"

Featherstone managed a sickly smile. "I believe you missed your calling, Ms. Lincoln. You would have had a successful career as a prosecutor."

"Thank you. I think. But compliments won't get you out of answering my question."

My *calling* had been to teach at the junior high school level. I fixed my patented teacher glare on him, the one guaranteed to wring a confession out of the most recalcitrant of fourteen-year-olds.

"I knew who they were," he admitted, "but what teenage boy pays any attention to a couple of middle-aged women? I was preoccupied with school and sports and girls my own age."

"Surely the murder of one of your father's clients must have caught your attention."

"I suppose it did, but you can scarcely expect me to remember much about it after all this time." He fell silent for a long moment. "I know your reputation, Ms. Lincoln, but I very much doubt you're going to solve Rosanna Swarthout's murder. You'd do better to focus on finding those diaries."

"As it happens, I've already found one of them, or rather I found a journal written by Estelle Swarthout. From the things she wrote, it's clear she did not get along with her stepmother."

This news left Featherstone gobsmacked. No other word can describe his reaction. I'd literally surprised the breath out of him. He excused himself and went into an adjoining half-bath. The sound of a faucet being turned on suggested that he needed a drink of water as well as a few seconds to collect himself. When he returned and resumed his seat, he looked steadier.

"I assume Estelle did not leave behind a written confession?" There was a strong undercurrent of sarcasm in his tone.

"Well, no, but—"

"When was this diary written?"

"The last entry was dated a month before the murder."

He looked thoughtful. "You say you've only located *one* diary?"

I nodded. "I'm still looking."

"Do you believe she wrote more at a later date?"

I hesitated. There had been blank pages at the end of the journal I'd found. Any others Estelle might have kept had most likely been written earlier, but I couldn't be sure of that.

"I have no idea."

Featherstone frowned. "Assuming you do find more, Ms. Lincoln, I'd advise you to be very careful in your editing. You don't want to go casting aspersions on innocent parties. From what little I can recall of the case, neither Tessa nor her sister were implicated in Rosanna Swarthout's murder."

"They alibied each other," I admitted, "but what if they were lying when they said they'd gone to the movies together?"

He scoffed at the idea. "Tessa and Estelle Swarthout were well-brought-up young ladies. Women of that generation simply did not commit murder, and Estelle would most certainly not have killed a member of her own family."

I found Leland Featherstone's statement surprisingly naïve for a lawyer. Surely he recalled what another well-brought-up young lady named Lizzie Borden allegedly did to *her* stepmother. True, Lizzie was acquitted and set free, but that didn't mean she wasn't guilty.

With the exception of the name of Tessa's residuary heir, I was no longer sure Featherstone knew more than he'd already revealed. His insincere smile and condescending tone of voice annoyed me, but they weren't proof he was hiding anything.

I stood and stooped to scoop up my tote. "I'll be going now. Thank you for your time."

He rose, ever the old-fashioned gentleman. Despite his age and the earlier suggestion of ill health, he held himself ramrod straight, shoulders squared, and offered me his hand. "Good day to you, Ms. Lincoln. I trust you'll notify me if you discover another diary."

"Count on it, Mr. Featherstone."

Our physical contact was limited to the merest brush of skin to skin, but even that much left me feeling chilled. His fingers were so cold they felt like icicles. If he didn't have some underlying illness, then my visit had shaken him more than he wanted to let on.

As I drove home from Monticello, I wondered just how involved Leland Featherstone's father had been with his clients. Was it possible Conrad had helped the Swarthout sisters cover up a crime? His son might not know all the details, but he might have his suspicions. If so, the last thing he'd ever do was share them with me.

Chapter Thirty-one

My visit to the lawyer had relieved my mind on one score. If the residuary heir was unaware that he was in line to inherit, it followed that he didn't know I had to find and edit two or more diaries before I could claim the property. That being the case, he couldn't have looked for, let alone found, another diary. At least one more existed and it was still somewhere in the house, just waiting to be discovered.

As for the cold case, it was more of a puzzle to be solved than a cause for immediate action. The remaining diary or diaries might or might not contain clues. I doubted they'd provide enough information for an arrest, even in the unlikely event that the killer was still alive.

The following morning, I edited a manuscript for a paying client and then proofread the text of Estelle's journal. After lunch, I intended to sit down with pen and paper and figure out the best way to proceed with the task Tessa Swarthout had set for me, but when I headed downstairs to make myself a sandwich, I found Calpurnia sitting in my tiny foyer and staring fixedly at the closed and locked front door. Instinctively, I spoke in a whisper.

"What is it, Cal? Is someone out there?"

My first thought was that a stray had come up onto the

porch. Dogs don't usually run loose in Lenape Hollow, but there are plenty of people who think it's cruel to confine their cats to the house. A strange animal in the vicinity would certainly account for my cat's odd behavior, although how she'd know one was there when there was no window in the door eluded me. I peered cautiously through the peephole. As far as I could tell, there was neither man nor beast on the other side.

I started to open the door to make certain of it, then hesitated. It was unusual for Calpurnia to go on alert. Like the miners who kept one eye on the canary in the coal mine, I was well aware that she could function as an efficient early-warning system. It was to my advantage to pay attention.

Slipping past Cal, I went into the living room and peeked around the edge of the drapes shielding the picture window. I didn't expect to see anything and had to suppress a gasp when I spotted Bella Trent. She was sitting in one of the wicker chairs on my front porch.

I stepped quickly back out of sight.

After a moment, I looked again. She hadn't seen me. Although she was facing me head-on, her eyes were closed, as if she'd fallen asleep waiting for me to show up. I had no idea how long she'd been there, but she'd had time to make herself comfortable. She'd borrowed one of the small, soft pillows piled at one end of the matching sofa and placed it between her head and the high back of her chair.

If she'd knocked or rung my doorbell, I hadn't heard the sound. As I often do when I want to concentrate on my work, I'd removed my hearing aids. Anything less than the fire alarm going off or a cat leaping into my lap would have failed to attract my attention.

Bella did not look as if she intended to leave anytime soon. This was a fine kettle of fish! Short of having the woman arrested for trespassing—a step I was loath to take since she wasn't a real threat, just an annoyance—I couldn't think of any way to get rid of her. Until she went away voluntarily, I was trapped in my own home.

"How do I get myself into these things?" I asked Calpurnia.

If I'd been smart in the beginning, I'd have denied being the Michelle Lincoln mentioned on Lenora's acknowledgments page. That could have saved me a whole lot of trouble.

Brooding, I went into the kitchen to make myself that sandwich. Calpurnia trailed after me, suddenly much more interested in begging for shreds of turkey than in guarding the house.

I'd finished eating but was still seated at the dinette table, sipping a second glass of lemonade and enjoying the light breeze coming in through the open windows, when something alien blighted my view of the backyard—Bella Trent.

Shading her eyes, she peered in through the screen.

I ducked.

A moment later, from a singularly ignominious position on the floor beneath the table, I stole a glance at the window. Bella was still there.

"Hello?" she called.

I didn't answer. I didn't think she'd seen me. I hoped she hadn't.

The shuffle of footsteps told me she was moving on, circling the house. When the knob on the back door rattled, I held my breath. I was *almost* certain it was locked.

The silence in the house was so complete that I could hear the seconds tick by on the kitchen clock. Calpurnia hopped up onto the chair I'd vacated and stared down at me, as if to ask what the heck was I doing there on the floor. I reached up to scratch behind her ears before I eased slowly to my feet.

Talk about a ridiculous overreaction!

Smiling at my own foolishness, I went from room to room, peeking out each window I came to in an attempt to spot Bella. When I saw no sign of her, I concluded that she'd given up and gone home.

Don't get cocky, I warned myself. *She may have left for now, but she's not going to stop bugging you.*

I doubted it would do any good to confront her and tell her to get lost.

It was then that a logical solution, albeit a temporary one, occurred to me. After considering the pros and cons, I made three phone calls, inviting Luke, Ellen, and Darlene to have supper with me that evening.

Chapter Thirty-two

I don't do fancy dinner parties. I started using our wedding china for every day about thirty years into my marriage and the only good silver I ever owned was inherited from my grandmother. It's still in its original box somewhere in the attic room I use for long-term storage.

That evening's meal was as simple as I could make it. I convinced Darlene's husband, Frank, to help Luke man the grill while Darlene, Ellen, and I put together shish kebobs with chunks of chicken and assorted veggies. Dessert came from Harriet's—one of Ada's Boston cream pies. We ate inside because it was too muggy to be comfortable outdoors. Besides, I had only cheap folding lawn chairs to offer for seating. I had been toying with the idea of buying a nice wooden picnic table, but that seemed extravagant for a person living alone.

It was a bit of a squeeze to fit the five of us around my dinette table. Ellen and Luke perched on the window seat flanked by Frank and Darlene while I sat with my back to the kitchen. The cat, hopeful tasty morsels would be dropped her way, was at my feet. I waited until we'd finished every last morsel of food before I cleared my throat and stood.

"I have an announcement to make," I said. "I've decided to move into Tessa's farmhouse so I can search for the rest of the diaries full-time. I only have a bit more than two weeks left to find at least one more, edit it, and post the contents online."

"What brought this on?" Darlene's voice was rife with suspicion.

"It seems a sensible thing to do."

"Why?" She knows me too well and wasn't to be put off with a vague answer.

"Aside from a fast-approaching deadline?" I shrugged. "This is just a good time for me to get away from Lenape Hollow for a bit." Turning from Darlene to Ellen, I added, "Bella Trent keeps turning up on my doorstep. Can you keep an eye on the house while I'm gone?"

In a heartbeat, my charming dinner guest was replaced by a no-nonsense officer of the law. "Has she threatened you?"

A look of alarm appeared on Darlene's face. "Mikki Lincoln, what have you been up to?"

With a sigh, I sat down again. Ellen's reaction forced me to give the others a capsule version of my interactions with Illyria Dubonnet's biggest fan. Even leaving out what Detective Hazlett had told me about Bella's prior run-ins with the law, the situation still sounded alarming.

"Can't you get a restraining order?" Darlene asked.

"I doubt Mikki has grounds for one," Ellen said. "Frankly, there's not much anyone can do unless and until Bella commits a crime."

"Trespassing," Frank suggested. "If she was in your backyard—"

"Do you remember old Mrs. Mintz? She used to own the house where the Frys live now," I added, since Frank was the only one who'd known me when she was our next-door neighbor. "She used to blow a gasket every time I cut across her yard to get to the field where we played softball. I refuse to turn into a modern-day Mrs. Mintz."

"But if this woman threatened you—"

"I'm pretty sure she's harmless, Darlene, nothing more than a nuisance, but ignoring her is becoming difficult. I'm hoping that if I go away for a while and there's no one here when she drops by, she'll be discouraged and give up trying to catch me at home."

"Admit it. You feel sorry for this Bella person." Darlene shook her head. "You always were a softy."

Luke held one hand so it shielded his mouth and spoke in a stage whisper. "Probably because Bella gets even more worked up over grammar mistakes than Mikki does."

"Ha ha." I made a face at him. "To be honest, I think she needs professional help, but I haven't a clue how to convince her to go into therapy."

"I'll ask around," Ellen offered. "Find out if Bella has family who can steer her toward counseling."

"Is introducing Bella to Ilona an option?" Darlene asked.

"Illyria," I corrected her. "And no. For one thing, Illyria Dubonnet doesn't really exist. It's a pseudonym and the persona that uses it on social media is . . . well, let's just say that the woman who actually writes the books doesn't bear much resemblance to the alter ego she created for herself."

Looking from face to face, each one filled with concern for my well-being, I realized I could trust the four of them with the truth. In fact, I owed it to them.

"You have to keep this to yourselves," I said, "but you've already met Illyria. She's my friend Lenora Barton, the one who visited me for a few days at the end of last summer."

"*She's* Illyria Dubonnet?" Darlene's eyes went wide with disbelief.

"In the flesh. You see the problem. Aside from the fact

that it would intrude on Lenora's privacy to spring Bella Trent on her, Bella herself wouldn't be happy with the outcome. She'd either be bitterly disappointed or think I was lying to her."

"Not to change the subject," Luke said, "but are you sure you'll be any safer staying at the farm?"

"Bella won't know to look for me there."

"I wasn't talking about Bella."

I made a face at him. "I don't think the people who built those storage units are likely to come back." At least I didn't have to explain that part of the story. I'd already told Darlene and Frank about my unexpected discovery in the Swarthout barn.

"Did you talk to the security company?" Ellen asked.

"I did. They missed the activity at the barn because the camera they installed was mounted there and aimed at the house." I didn't add that it hadn't been working anyway, or that Sure Thing Security had since removed it. I saw no point in giving my friends more cause to worry about me.

I started to clear the table. Everyone offered to pitch in, but when I shooed Luke and Frank out onto the porch with after-dinner drinks, they didn't put up much of a fight. Ellen, Darlene, and I made short work of the dishes. Calpurnia wound herself around my ankles until I convinced her that there were no tidbits left to beg for. With a haughty flip of her tail, she took herself off for a nap.

"Have you finished editing Estelle's diary?" Darlene asked as she dried a plate.

I handed her a saucer. "I have, but I still can't understand why her sister thought it should be published. What she wrote doesn't paint a very flattering picture of anyone in that household."

"Maybe Tessa wanted Estelle to have the fame she failed to achieve during her lifetime," Darlene suggested.

"What kind of fame was she after?" Ellen asked.

"She wanted to be an actress," I said. "She had leading roles in local productions and after Rosanna's death, she and Tessa headed for Hollywood."

"I tried to find some record of her online," Darlene put in, "but if she had a film or theater career after she left the farm, it wasn't enough of one to get into any online databases. Actors are usually pretty visible, even the old-timers, what with IMDb and all the rest. The only mention of her I found was the Social Security record of her death. She died decades earlier than her sister somewhere in New York State."

"Was there an obituary?" Ellen asked.

"Not that I could find. Not everyone has one, you know, especially when newspapers charge the family an arm and a leg to print it."

"What if she used another name professionally?" I suggested. "It's a little hard to envision Estelle Swarthout on a theater marquee. If I'd been in her shoes, I'd have changed it to something that sounded a little more glamorous."

"Possible," Darlene conceded, "but very few real names stay secret, especially those of people who are successful. I'll bet even your friend Lenora hasn't kept as tight a lid on her secret identity as she thinks. Did you know there are databases of pseudonyms?"

"There are databases for just about everything," Ellen agreed.

"The most likely explanation," Darlene continued, "is that Estelle moved away from the farm with Tessa and continued to live with her sister for the rest of her life."

"So the only records would have been in Tessa's name?"

"Right. That diary you found may be Estelle's only shot at immortality."

The party broke up shortly after we finished washing the dishes. Ellen had to be up at dawn to work the early shift and Darlene simply ran out of steam. She'd had a good day, using only her cane to get around, but she'd suffered a bout of insomnia the previous night. Despite a nap before coming over to my house, by seven thirty she was yawning, a sure sign she was in desperate need of sleep.

Luke lingered after the others had gone. By the glow of the porch light I could see that he had a worried expression on his face.

"What?"

"I'm not convinced that you'll be safe staying out at the farm on your own."

"I won't be completely alone. I'm taking Calpurnia with me."

"Your ferocious guard cat won't be much help against the person or persons unknown who were using your barn. What if they show up?"

"What if they do? They'll hardly stick around once they realize someone is living in the house."

He descended the porch steps, but at the bottom he stopped to look back over his shoulder. "I know you can take care of yourself, but it's sensible to take precautions. If only for my peace of mind, will you promise to phone me at least once a day?"

I rolled my eyes, but I had to admit the suggestion was a good one. "Fine. I'll call you every afternoon at five. Will that do?"

"I guess it will have to." He grinned and started to walk away, but he hadn't gone a half dozen steps before he stopped again. "Is it okay if I come by while you're staying there?"

"I don't need a babysitter, Luke."

"Perish the thought! I'm only interested in the pond."

"The pond?" I repeated, puzzled. "The pond at the farm?"

"That's the one. You know I'm just a country boy at heart. There's nothing I like better than to spend time at a good fishing hole on a hot summer's day."

"You are so full of it!"

With a wave and a laugh, he continued on his way.

Chapter Thirty-three

For my stay at the farm, I packed comfortable clothes and also loaded my trusty old walk-behind lawn mower and a Weedwacker into the trunk of my car. I tucked food and drinks, cat supplies, and several flashlights with extra batteries in around them. Once I'd secured Calpurnia in her carrier and in the passenger seat, I was ready to go.

"You'll like the farmhouse," I told her as I drove. "There are lots of places for you to explore. You might even catch a mouse or two."

Despite the housekeeping services Tessa had arranged, I'd come across evidence that the farm wasn't rodent-proof. No old house is, especially when it's located way out in the country.

It was late morning when we arrived, and not yet as hot as the weather forecasters were predicting it would be by midafternoon. I left the cat in the car while I unloaded the rest of what I'd brought. She didn't liked being abandoned for even that short time. When I finally lugged her carrier inside, I heard about it every step of the way. She was still complaining when I set it down on the kitchen floor.

"Give me another minute," I said. "I need to check the doors."

Naturally, I'd keep the front and side doors locked while

I was in the house, not only for my own protection, but also to prevent Calpurnia from escaping into the big bad world outside. I didn't want her going upstairs, either, so I wanted to make sure the stairwell was secure. She'd find enough to get into roaming free on just one floor.

After I arranged Cal's litter box beneath the pedestal sink in the downstairs bath, I turned her loose. At first, intent on giving me the cold shoulder, she refused to come out of the carrier. I kept an eye on her while I put away the groceries I'd brought with me. I'd plugged in the refrigerator on my last visit and it seemed to be functioning normally. That was a relief. If I'd had to rely on my cooler to keep food fresh, I'd have had to keep going out to buy ice.

The stove was another matter. The propane tanks that fueled it were long gone. Fortunately, I own a camp stove, one James and I kept to use during power outages. Together with a wood stove to keep us warm, and battery-powered lanterns for light, we'd even been able to stay in our home during the legendary ice storm of '98, when power throughout Maine went out for more than a week.

I unpacked my personal possessions in Tessa's old room. By then Cal had left her carrier and was busily exploring. I was already dressed in jeans and sturdy boots, so all I had to do before venturing outside was spray myself with bug repellent, slap on sunscreen, and don a floppy hat. After our visits to Sure Thing Security and Monticello Maids, Jason Coleman had offered to contact Tessa's lawn-care service for me, but they had yet to make an appearance. The overgrown front yard was an eyesore. If I had to look at it while I was in residence, I meant to do something to improve the view. I know it sounds strange, but I find mowing relaxing, as long as the lawn isn't too large.

The grass had grown so high that I didn't realize there was a bank of bright orange day lilies near the road until I almost mowed them down. Any "naturalized" flowers too low for me to see in time went the way of the grass, but on the bright side, I didn't disturb a single snake. When I finished with the lawn mower, I put the Weedwacker to good use.

Two hours later, dripping with sweat, I surveyed the result of my labors. The area immediately surrounding the house was by no means pretty, but the grass was now a reasonable height and the worst of the intruding underbrush had been hacked into submission.

Back inside, I treated myself to a cold drink and a bath. Like the refrigerator, the pump and water heater Tessa had left behind still worked reasonably well. I felt quite invigorated once I was clean and dressed in fresh, lightweight clothing. I slipped my bare feet into flip-flops and, still toweling my wet hair, went in search of my cat.

It was the gift Calpurnia had left for me that I found first. By stepping on it, naturally. The medium-size mouse Cal had deposited in the middle of the living room rug was quite dead.

At least it wasn't a snake.

Gingerly, I picked up her trophy by the tail and carried it to the front door. Checking first to make sure the cat wasn't lurking, waiting for her chance to make a dash for freedom, I stepped out onto the porch and flung the little corpse as far away from me as I could.

I spent the afternoon making yet another search of the downstairs rooms. Calpurnia helped. She attempted to climb into every opening big enough to hold her and a few that weren't before wandering off in search of more mice. Neither of us found what we were looking for.

The highlight of the day was my five o'clock phone call to Luke. Reminding me that he could easily take time away from his job—like me, he works for himself—he offered to drive to Swan's Crossing and help me search. I appreciated the thought, but turned him down. There was no sense in both of us wasting our time.

That night, tired out from all the exertion of the day, I opened both bedroom windows in the hope of catching a breeze and went to bed early. When I closed my eyes, I found myself wondering what it had been like to sleep in this room in the days when the Swarthouts took in boarders. Their guests, and maybe family, too, must have passed many a summer's evening sitting in Adirondack chairs on the wide wraparound porch just the other side of the walls of Tessa's old room. I could almost hear them talking in soft voices as the stars came out. Imagining the gentle, soothing rhythms of their speech, I drifted into sleep.

I was up bright and early the next morning, well rested and raring to go. First, of course, I had to feed the cat. While I was at it, I fired up the camp stove and fried a couple of eggs for myself. I'd found a working toaster and a coffeepot among the things Tessa and Estelle left behind, so all in all breakfast was quite satisfactory.

"I'm going upstairs today, Cal," I said. "It would probably be best if you stayed down here."

She still had her face buried in her food bowl when I left the kitchen, so I assumed it was safe to open the door to the stairwell. Wrong! It took me only seconds to pass through, climb the first few steps, and turn to tug the door closed behind me, but that was more than enough time for Calpurnia to streak past me. Since I'd made the mistake of leaving the door at the top of the stairs open on my last visit, she quickly disappeared into the hallway above.

"You'd better to be ready to come back downstairs when I am," I called after her.

I didn't relish the thought of trying to find her if she decided to hide. On the other hand, unless I immediately stumbled upon another diary, I'd be on the second floor for the rest of the day. At some point, Cal would show her furry little face and I'd be able to grab her.

I wished, not for the first time, that I knew how many diaries were left to find. One could be hidden in a relatively small space. A dozen would not be as easy to conceal.

Estelle's room was the logical place to start. I did everything short of ripping up the rest of the flooring but found nothing more exciting than dust bunnies, mouse droppings, and spiderwebs. Searching Rosanna's bedroom was equally unproductive, although I did pause to admire the dainty lingerie she'd favored.

I couldn't remember when silk slips trimmed with lace had gone out of fashion but I did recall wearing them under skirts and dresses. The ones that didn't bunch up had usually managed to show below my hems. Don't even get me started on the girdles that were required foundation garments in those days.

Looking down at myself, clad in worn cut-offs and a T-shirt, I had to chuckle. In the 1950s and even into the early 1960s, girls and women didn't have much choice. They were expected to wear skirts and blouses or dresses most of the time, even at home. Jeans were for horseback riding and not much else. Shorts were acceptable in the summer, but there had also been something called a skort that was a cross between shorts and a skirt. Much more respectable!

It was while I was searching the bedroom adjacent to Estelle's that I heard a faint scratching noise coming from the short, narrow hallway just outside the door. It didn't surprise me to discover that Calpurnia was the source of that sound, or that she was fixated on a section of baseboard on the opposite wall.

"Found another mouse, have you?" I asked.

She ignored me and continued to tap at the base of the paneling with one paw. The lighting was poor in this little side hall, so I turned on the flashlight I'd brought with me and shone it over the surface. Only then did it occur to me that the stairwell that led up to the attic was on the other side of that wall.

I hadn't looked up as I mounted the stairs between the first and second floors. As a general rule, people don't. They focus on what's straight ahead, or maybe glance to one side or behind them. Had there been empty space above my head, up to the underside of the attic steps, or had the Swarthouts, like the people who built the farmhouse at the living history center, found a way to make use of that space for storage?

I'd examined the wall beside the stairs on the first floor. I'd even checked the cellar stairs for a hidden cupboard. Why on earth hadn't I thought to check this section of wall at the same time?

"Early senility strikes again," I muttered under my breath.

When I aimed the flashlight at the paneled surface, I felt my heart start to beat a little faster. The spaces where the panels met were not of uniform width. In two places, about two feet apart, they were slightly larger.

Cal paused in her attempt to claw her way through the baseboard to send me a questioning look. When I knelt beside her and began to run my fingertips over the wall, I was afraid I was indulging in wistful thinking, but I kept at it until, at last, I found a tiny indentation in the surface. The finger pull was almost invisible, thanks to its tiny size and the lack of decent lighting in the narrow hallway.

I tugged gently. When nothing gave, I pulled harder. Abruptly, a section of wall perhaps four feet high and two feet wide popped out by a quarter of an inch and stuck. The opening hadn't exactly been hidden, but its outline *had* been obscured by the paneling.

Scarcely daring to breathe, I grabbed hold of the edge of the door, put my back into it, and pulled with all my might. It swung the rest of the way open with such suddenness that I fell back, landing hard on my posterior.

It's a good thing I'm well padded in that area. Undamaged, I shifted my position until I was kneeling and aimed the flashlight into the space under the stairs.

Unlike the cupboard at the living history center, this one had not been fitted out as a clothes closet. I stared in bewilderment at what I saw inside, unable at first to make sense of the strange collection of objects.

Calpurnia pushed past me, eager to investigate. There was plenty of room for her inside the storage area but it would have been a tight fit for me, with no room to stand upright. She sniffed curiously at each of the items picked out by the beam of my flashlight. A large, ornately carved wooden box sat on the floor in the center of the cupboard. A bronze candlestick with the stub of a white candle protruding from the top stood to one side of it. On the other side was a silver picture frame.

I reached for the latter and turned it around to reveal a black-and-white photograph of a woman. I had no difficulty recognizing her. I'd seen her before in the photo on the bureau in Tessa's bedroom. In that one, she'd been posed with Tessa and Estelle and I had no doubt that she was their mother.

With that realization came another: what I'd discovered was a shrine to her memory.

Chapter Thirty-four

My hands shook as I thrust my head and shoulders far enough inside the cupboard to grab hold of the wooden box. It was heavy and I was panting by the time I'd wrangled it into the hallway. Calpurnia watched the whole procedure with intense interest but didn't offer to help.

Eager as I was to see what was inside, I hesitated to open it then and there. The nearest ceiling light was several feet away and low wattage. I wouldn't be able to see much, even with the aid of my flashlight. Besides, if the box didn't contain another diary, I was just as happy to postpone finding that out.

For one awful moment, I wondered if what I'd discovered might be a funeral urn. Then I remembered that cremation wouldn't have been a popular choice at the time of the first Mrs. Swarthout's death. I knew the date from the entry in the family Bible. Thinking of that, I also recalled her first name—Nellie.

I stood, dusted myself off, closed the panel in the wall, tucked the flashlight into my back pocket, and used both hands to pick up the box. With my faithful cat trotting along at my heels, and occasionally running ahead to get underfoot, I carried it downstairs and into the kitchen.

When I'd placed my burden on the table, Cal hopped up to help me study it.

The box had a latch, but it wasn't locked. I hesitated. From its weight, there was something substantial inside, but it might not be what I was hoping for. Braced for another disappointment, I extended my hand, then hesitated.

Calpurnia nuzzled my outstretched fingers.

"Okay. Okay. I'm working up to it."

Cautiously, I lifted the lid. Right on top were two paper-bound composition books, the kind children used in school in the late nineteenth and early twentieth centuries. I let out the breath I hadn't realized I'd been holding and gingerly lifted out the first one. I opened it and looked at the inscription on the flyleaf.

"Nellie Swarthout," I read aloud. Just as her daughter had in the leather-bound journal she'd kept in the 1950s, Nellie had added, *Her book.* The first entry was dated June 5, 1915. Another entry in the family Bible came back to me. That was the date of Nellie's marriage to Tessa and Estelle's father.

The second composition book was also inscribed with Nellie's name. She'd left behind two diaries. And there it was—the answer to the question that had been bothering me from the moment I finished reading Estelle's journal: Why would Tessa want me to publish her sister's writings?

She *hadn't.*

Tessa might not even have known that Estelle kept a journal. It was what their mother had written that she'd wanted the world to read.

I smiled. Mystery solved. I allowed myself a few moments to savor my success before I turned my attention to what else was in the box.

It was a bulging scrapbook filled with photographs and clippings. I immediately envisioned adding illustrations to the published diaries, even though that would make much more work for me.

Before I investigated further, I fired up the camp stove and made myself a cup of green tea. Why tea? Coffee would have made me jittery and it hadn't occurred to me when I was packing that I might want anything stronger to drink. Although a fully stocked liquor cabinet has never been one of my requirements, I mix a mean rum and cola and on such a hot summer afternoon a cold beer would have gone down a treat.

From a practical standpoint, it was probably just as well I didn't have that option. I'd need a clear head when I read Nellie's diaries. Until I knew what she'd written, I couldn't be certain my discovery called for a celebratory glass of champagne. A medicinal shot of brandy might end up being more appropriate.

Calpurnia butted against my leg with enough force to make me look at her. Once she had my attention, she stared pointedly at her empty food bowl. I opened a can of cat food and dumped it in, but my thoughts were still on the task ahead of me. After setting my tea a safe distance from the contents of the box, I once again opened the first composition book and began to read.

Nellie had written in an easy-to-interpret if somewhat flowery cursive hand. The earliest entries were brief and focused on household matters. She devoted considerable space to the ins and outs of keeping a boardinghouse and the trials and tribulations of raising chickens for their eggs.

Although Nellie Swarthout said little about her pregnancy or the birth of her first child, the pages that followed gave glowing accounts of baby Tessa's marvelous achievements. I'm sure all that was fascinating to the new mom, but for me it fell into the category of TMI—too much information—and failed to hold my interest. When I caught myself skimming entries instead of reading them, I decided it was time for a break. I got up to stretch my legs and made a second cup of green tea to replace the one I'd let go cold.

Cal, who had been off who-knows-where doing who-knew-what, wandered back into the kitchen. She sent me an inquisitive look.

"This will never win an award as memoir of the year," I told her. Nellie's prose wasn't exactly riveting. To be honest, she'd led a rather dull life. "Still, I suppose it might be of interest to people who are already fascinated by local history."

I knew quite a few such persons, most of them associated with the Lenape Hollow Historical Society. Since Swan's Crossing is close enough to be considered a neighboring town, they'd be delighted with all the minuscule details of daily life at a farm/boardinghouse back in the day. So would the folks at that living history center I'd visited. Now that I thought about it, both places would probably end up offering copies of Nellie's book for sale on site and through their web pages.

"That will mean a little fame for me, too," I told the cat. "Not that I'm looking to make a name for myself."

It was time to get back to work.

Before plunging back in, I placed a lined tablet and a pen beside me so I could jot down notes to myself as I read. Most related to the editing I'd have to do. Nellie's spelling was creative, to say the least.

The second composition book contained more mind-numbing household details. Even the birth of a second daughter didn't do much to liven things up, but since Nellie often left lengthy gaps between entries, it didn't take long for Tessa to appear as a young teen. By then Nellie was making increasingly frequent mentions of "feeling poorly," but she didn't elaborate or list any specific symptoms.

I paused to consider the number of things that could kill

a person back in the 1920s but didn't come to any conclusions about what might have ailed her. What *was* clear was that George, Nellie's husband, wasn't a bit of help when it came to keeping house. He worked the land. Cleaning and cooking were women's work. Since his daughters were still too young to take over all of their mother's responsibilities, George Swarthout eventually broke down and hired a cook to look after the boarders who provided so much of the family's income.

Her name was Rosanna Mortimer.

"The plot thickens," I murmured.

Little did I realize how true that statement would prove. A few pages later, I stopped and reread what Nellie had written. Marking my place with one finger, I looked around for the cat and found her sleeping on the windowsill.

"Wake up, Cal. Listen to this."

She opened one eye.

I read aloud from the second diary: "I was desperately ill again today. I've seen the way she looks at my husband. If I die, she will persuade him to marry her. I feel certain of it, just as I feel certain she has already found a way to hasten my death."

That was Nellie's last entry.

Unable to sit still, I got up and began to pace. *This* was the story Tessa wanted the world to read. After seeing what their mother had written, her daughters must have been convinced that Rosanna had played a role in Nellie's death. I know I was.

Tessa had tasked me with editing the diaries because she wanted the charges made public. That much I could readily understand. What confused me was the timing.

When had Nellie's daughters found and read what was in these composition books? If it was soon after their mother's death, Tessa would have been in her teens and Estelle would have been even younger. Had they tried to tell their father of their suspicions? Had he dismissed their concerns as nonsense?

That was a scenario I could visualize, especially if George Swarthout was already under Rosanna's spell. According to the family Bible, he hadn't wasted any time marrying her!

What then? Even if he'd succeeded in convincing his daughters that they were wrong, they'd have been wary of their new stepmother. Was that why they'd hidden the diaries and the scrapbook, out of fear that Rosanna would try to erase every trace of her predecessor? After all, it was the portrait of wife number two that hung in the place of honor next to George Swarthout in the living room.

That two young girls might create a hidden shrine to their late mother made a certain amount of sense. What I had trouble understanding was why Tessa and Estelle would continue to live under the same roof as Rosanna for the better part of a decade after their father's death.

There had to be something in George's will to explain it. Had he put conditions on his daughters' inheritance? If he had, that might also explain why Tessa had kept and maintained the farm after abandoning it. In her shoes, I'd have sold it, especially if I needed money to live on in another location. Darlene and I had already speculated that George might have created some kind of trust, one that prevented his heirs from selling the property, but I couldn't be certain of that until I could get hold of a copy of his will.

When I sat down to reread Nellie's last entry, another possibility occurred to me. What if the sisters hadn't read what their mother wrote until years later, well after her death? That could explain why the three women had continued to live together for so long. At first, Tessa and Estelle hadn't suspected Rosanna of murdering their mother.

I frowned, spotting a major flaw in this theory. If they'd

been adults when they learned that Nellie believed Rosanna was—what? poisoning her?—why hadn't they gone to the police with their accusation, especially if their father was no longer alive by then and they had Nellie's writings as proof of their claim?

But *were* they proof? Probably not in the legal sense.

I couldn't help but wonder what two loving daughters might have done when they realized they would not be able to get justice by going through official channels, especially if they'd only just discovered Nellie's diaries and the accusation they contained. There was that gap at the end of Estelle's journal—a full month between her last entry and the date of Rosanna's murder. Was that significant? Could *that* have been when the two sisters belatedly discovered the truth about their mother's death? Instead of writing down her feelings and recording her plan for revenge, was it possible that Estelle had simply taken action?

It was an explanation that made a perverted kind of sense to me. Motivated by a desire to avenge Nellie, Estelle, or her sister, or the two of them acting together, might well have devised a plot to kill their evil stepmother.

My friends in law enforcement would call my conclusion way too speculative. They'd be right, but the more I thought about it, the more determined I became to learn more about what happened the night of Rosanna's murder. With that goal in mind, I fished my cell phone out of my tote bag and punched in Darlene's number.

Chapter Thirty-five

M y phone call to Darlene resulted in an invitation to have supper with her and Frank that evening. Although it was only three in the afternoon, I decided to leave for Lenape Hollow at once. Cal stayed behind in her role as guard cat. Even though I'd found the missing diaries, I intended to remain at the farm for a few more days. I wanted to give Bella Trent enough time to grow tired of pestering me to introduce her to Illyria Dubonnet.

I planned to make one stop on my way to Darlene's. The pages in Nellie's diaries weren't numbered, but there were fewer than a hundred in all. It wouldn't take long to make copies.

I could have gone home and used the scanner in my office, but with Bella on the loose I decided not to risk running into her. Instead, I headed for the Lenape Hollow Memorial Library where several copy machines are housed in an out-of-the-way corner of the main floor. I hoped to get in and out without being noticed, but I hadn't been in the building more than ten minutes before Pam Ingram accosted me.

It was obvious she had something on her mind, and it was a good bet, given that she was clutching a slip of paper tightly in one hand, that she'd come up with another item to add to the newsletter. Pam was easier to deal with than Bella, but I wasn't happy about being cornered. I kept making copies and tried to pretend I didn't notice her standing there.

"Tomorrow is the last day of July," Pam said, her tone accusatory. "Where is the August newsletter?"

"It will be available online and in print on the first of the month, as always."

Feeling just a teensy bit guilty, I made a mental note to send the electronic file to the local print shop, ASAP. They did the job for free and delivered the results to the library and I knew they'd appreciate a bit of lead time. It was my job to upload the pdf to the library website on the first of the month. I hadn't missed my deadline yet, but I would if I forgot about it again.

I turned to the next page in the diary, placed the composition book facedown on the glass, and pressed the button to make two copies, using a prepaid card to cover the cost. While the machine hummed and spit them out, I stole a glance at Pam.

"Problem?" I asked. In spite of my assurances, she looked worried.

"Is it too late to insert another announcement?"

"It's possible to make changes right up until the file goes to the printer, which will be about an hour from now. How much space do you need?"

"A full page would be nice."

"That won't be a problem." It's actually easier to add a whole page than it is to insert a smaller item into an existing page.

In many respects, it would be nice if life could be as simple as it was when I was young, but in general I can't complain about the benefits of modern technology. The word processing program on my laptop is vastly superior to any typewriter and I certainly don't miss having to rely on mimeographing or, even messier, a spirit duplicator, also called a Ditto machine, to produce a newsletter. When I was teaching, I spent many a day with stained fingers after printing multiple copies of worksheets for my students. Copiers, scanners, and printers are all huge advances in technology.

Pam thrust the paper she'd been carrying in my direction. I didn't take it. I had my hands full setting up the next page to be copied.

"Can you send me the details in an e-mail?" I asked. "Then I can cut and paste directly into the newsletter."

There's a little more to the process than that, but e-mails are easier to read than Pam's handwriting. Once she agreed to my suggestion, I thought she'd go away and allow me to finish and be on my way. Instead, she lingered.

"It's quite exciting, really," she said after a moment. "A mystery author is going to visit the library to give a talk and sign books."

"Really?" I didn't look up from the copier. "Which one?"

"What?"

"Who's the mystery writer?"

"No, not a mystery *writer*. A *mystery* author."

There *is* a distinction. One doesn't *author* books. But something in Pam's tone of voice told me I was still missing the point. "Is that a riddle?"

"No. It's a publicity stunt. Don't worry. The publicist who set it up is legitimate. She works for a major New York publisher." At my skeptical glance, she made a cross-my-heart gesture. "I verified her credentials, but I don't know anything about the author in question. *That's* the mystery. We won't know who our featured speaker is until he or she enters the library on the day of the event."

I finished copying the pages of the first of Nellie's diaries and reached for the second. "Doesn't that strike you as counterproductive? What's that old saying—don't buy a pig in a poke? You're asking people to give up an entire evening on the slight chance that the author in question is someone whose work they want to read. That the books are put out by a major New York publisher doesn't necessarily mean they're any good. I'll admit I haven't gone to all that many book signings, but when I have, the people attending were readers who were there because they'd already read and liked some of that author's earlier books." My lips twisted into a wry smile. "A talk and signing by the editor of some early-twentieth-century diaries, for example, wouldn't draw much of a crowd."

"Sheer curiosity will bring people in. You'll see. We'll talk it up to all our patrons. In addition to the announcement in the newsletter, we'll make posters and put them up all over town. Besides, I've been assured that this author's books are bestsellers."

That would hardly matter if Pam couldn't tell her patrons any of the titles ahead of time, but I kept my opinion to myself, along with a few salient facts I'd learned from my friend Lenora about how little it takes to become a "bestselling" author.

"I'll go write that e-mail," she said.

"Sounds like a plan." I went back to my copying.

Chapter Thirty-six

After I finished making copies, I sat in my car in the library parking lot with my laptop and took advantage of the WiFi hotspot to check my e-mail for Pam's message. In minutes, I'd put together the final version of the newsletter. As I fiddled with the font size and the margins, I marveled once again at the librarian's optimism. She'd be lucky to have a half dozen people show up to meet this "mystery author" and there would only be that many in the audience if all the officers and committee heads from the Friends of the Library felt obligated to attend.

Already thinking ahead to the next newsletter, I resolved to give a good portion of the space to the library's used book sale. An annual fall event, it was our best fundraiser, but it required quality donations as well as lots of buyers if it was to be a success.

There is a part of me that objects to encouraging people to buy secondhand books, for which their authors receive no royalties, but at least this way the proceeds go into a fund to buy new books for the collection. Authors *do* benefit from those sales.

With one pdf file of the newsletter winging its way to the online service that distributes it to subscribers and another copy sent to the printer, I uploaded the same material to the library website and set it to publish on the first of the month. When I was done, I felt quite virtuous. I'd finished the job a whole a day ahead of my deadline.

By then it was close to five o'clock and I knew Luke would worry if he didn't hear from me soon. If he drove to the farm and couldn't find me there, he'd probably panic. I retrieved my cell phone and punched in his number.

"Found them," I announced when he answered. "I'll tell you all about it later. I'm going to have supper with Darlene and Frank. Then I'll head back to Swan's Crossing for the night."

"No fair!" he complained. "I want to know more about the diaries now."

"This way you can enjoy the anticipation."

He laughed. "I'm coming by tomorrow," he warned me. "Early."

"Calpurnia will be delighted to see you." I disconnected, pulled out of the library lot, and drove the short distance to Darlene's house.

Supper was ready to go on the table by the time I arrived. As I do, they eat early. By unspoken mutual agreement, Darlene and I postponed any discussion of diaries, research, or murder until after the meal. By the time we headed for her second-floor lair, Frank was already settled in front of the television set in the living room to watch the Yankees. As a die-hard Red Sox fan—what else could I be when I'd lived in Maine for over fifty years?—I made a few wisecracks about the "evil empire" before I followed Darlene upstairs.

She'd used her chairlift, leaving me to make the climb weighed down with two heavy tote bags. I found her sitting in front of a computer monitor and keyboard that took up about a quarter of the surface of a long, narrow table. The remainder of the space is usually littered with scraps of fabric for one of Darlene's sewing projects, but for once they were nowhere in sight. She'd also shoved aside the containers that held pens, pencils, paperclips, and other office paraphernalia to make room to spread out the file folders from the library, including the one she'd brought to my house the other day. Dozens of sticky notes covered in her neat handwriting adorned every available surface.

"What did you bring?" she asked.

I extracted a sheaf of papers from one of my bags. The second copy I'd made of Nellie's diary was safely locked in the trunk of my car, next to the wooden box containing the original composition books. I'd removed the scrapbook I'd found with them, stuffing it into a second tote bag. I was looking forward to going over the contents with Darlene. So far I hadn't had time to give them more than a cursory once-over.

Darlene stared at the pages, a broad grin on her face. "You found the rest of the diaries!"

"I found the diaries Tessa wanted me to edit." Handing Darlene the copy, I retrieved a chair of the folding and uncomfortable variety from a closet and set it up next to her ergonomic and well-padded seat. "Funny thing is, they aren't Estelle's. These diaries were kept by Nellie Swarthout, Tessa and Estelle's mother."

"Have you read them yet?"

"I have." I gave her the capsule version of how and where I'd found the box and what the entries said.

"So Nellie was suspicious of Rosanna, and then she died. Huh."

"If Rosanna was brought in to cook because Nellie couldn't handle the work anymore, that suggests that Nellie was quite ill already. Back then, even if something like cancer or heart disease had been diagnosed, there were far fewer treatment options than there are today."

"Get sick and die," Darlene agreed. "But maybe Rosanna helped the process along, and not in a good, right-to-die way."

"We'll probably never know. There's no one left to authorize an exhumation of the body, and after all this time, any trace of poison has probably disappeared anyway."

Darlene made a moue of distaste. "Leave it to you to think of something like that!"

"Would you prefer to think Rosanna put a pillow over Nellie's face and smothered her?"

"I'd *prefer* to think the poor woman died of natural causes."

"Whatever happened to her, the upshot is that these have to be the diaries Tessa meant me to find and publish. I stopped at the library on my way here to make copies, one for me to take a red pencil to and the other for you to read at your leisure. I want to write some kind of introduction to go with the text. Right now I don't have a clue how much I should say about my suspicions."

"It's not like Rosanna's still around to sue you if you accuse her of murdering Nellie."

"That's true, but she can't defend herself, either, and it's possible that Nellie was just paranoid." I didn't believe that, but I was trying hard to be impartial. I wanted a second opinion before I rushed into print with wild accusations.

Darlene sent me a shrewd look. "Is that all that's bothering you?"

"Hardly. Do you think it's possible that one or both of the sisters might have avenged their mother's death by killing Rosanna?"

Blurted out like that, the idea sounded preposterous, but Darlene took me seriously. After a moment's thought, she came up with the same objection I had.

"If they read the diaries, why didn't they show them to their father, to stop him from marrying Rosanna? Even if there was no way to prove she'd harmed his wife, surely seeing what Nellie had written would have given him pause."

"My current theory is that Tessa and Estelle didn't read the diaries until much later. Maybe Nellie hid them. Or maybe their grief over her death kept them from going through her things until years afterward."

"But you're talking about *decades* later? Does that seem likely?"

"It could have happened that way." I heard the defensive note in my voice and winced.

Darlene frowned. "You say the cupboard under the stairs looked like it had been set up as a shrine to Nellie's memory?"

"Photograph. Candle. Nellie's journals, and this." I opened the second tote bag and removed Nellie's scrapbook. "I haven't had time to do more than glance at it. None of the photos are labeled, but the clippings all date from before Nellie's death. It's a good bet she's the one who kept it."

Darlene made room on the table to examine my prize, but her face wore a troubled frown.

"What?"

"There's something that doesn't make sense about your timeline. I can picture two young girls creating a secret shrine in a hidden cupboard, but I have trouble imagining a couple of middle-aged women doing the same thing."

"I was bothered by that, too, but there's no accounting for what people will do when they're in an emotional state of mind."

Darlene opened the scrapbook. "Maybe we're overthinking this. If they weren't overly fond of Rosanna, they could have hidden their mother's things right after their father remarried, but without reading all the way through her diaries first. Didn't you say most of the entries are pretty humdrum? Maybe they glanced at a few, found them dull, and didn't finish. Not then, anyway."

This logical explanation appealed to me. "If that's the case, it *could* have been decades before one of them discovered that damning passage about Rosanna."

"Too bad we'll never know for certain."

While we speculated, Darlene had begun to go through the scrapbook. The photographs it contained, many of them faded sepia prints, were for the most part shots of women in long dresses standing next to the farmhouse or men in the same location, posing with the game they'd shot during hunting season. The remaining pictures showed groupings of men, women, and children. One showed a woman in an ankle-length white dress lounging in a fancy hammock strung between two trees.

"Some of these folks were probably boarders rather than family," Darlene said, studying a page that featured several photos of groups of people enjoying themselves on the pond, a body of water that was much larger than I'd imagined it would be.

About halfway through the scrapbook, we came to a snapshot of a couple standing together in front of the porch at the Swarthout farm. "This might be George and Nellie, but it's hard to be sure."

We decided the two girls posing together in another photograph were Tessa and Estelle, but again it was difficult to be certain. The photographer had been an amateur. Details were blurry.

The clippings interspersed among the pictures weren't very useful. Nellie had been a sucker for bad poetry. Newspapers back in her day printed verses along with news and gossip. She had clipped and pasted dozens of these into her scrapbook.

"This is interesting," Darlene said, stopping to read one longer piece. "It's an account of the fiftieth wedding anniversary celebration of Tessa's grandparents, Myron, apparently known as Miles, and Pernolia Swarthout. Pernolia! What a name! Do you suppose that's a typo? Maybe it's supposed to be Pamela."

"Sadly, no. That same spelling appears in the family Bible." I glanced at the date and searched my memory. "I think Pernolia died the following year."

Ten minutes later, Darlene closed the scrapbook. "Well, that was fascinating, but not of much practical value. It's a pity no one wrote names below the photographs, but then, why would they? *They* knew who everyone was."

"I was hoping I might be able to use some of the photos to illustrate the diaries, but without identification, I don't suppose that makes much sense."

"Oh, I don't know. They were taken at the farm and you said most of what Nellie wrote about had to do with running the boardinghouse."

"I need more to go on." I gestured toward the file folders. "Have you found anything more in those? A copy of George Swarthout's will would be useful."

"No such luck. Wills and probate records from 1659 to 1999 are available on the genealogy site I use, but his wasn't there. Either he died without a will, or his assets at the time of his death were valued below the amount that requires probate. Have you asked Tessa's lawyer if he knows how the estate was left?"

"Mr. Featherstone hasn't exactly been cooperative. I asked. He didn't answer."

"Hmm."

I sent her a questioning look.

"Leland Featherstone, right?"

"Yes. Why?"

"I did come across one interesting coincidence." She riffled through the file folders until she found the same program she'd already shown me, the one listing Estelle Swarthout as the leading lady in an amateur production of *My Sister Eileen*.

"Take a look at the list of names on the stage crew."

"Leland Featherstone." I checked the date. "He was just a kid then."

"A teenager," Darlene corrected me.

"Funny he didn't mention that he worked on a show with Estelle."

"He was a lowly member of the backstage crew. She was the star and a lot older than he was." She shrugged. "It was a long time ago."

"If she had the lead in the production, she had to have made an impression on him, even if it was only as a diva to be avoided." To make sure I had my facts straight, I checked the date on the program. "It was only a few months after this that Rosanna was killed. You'd think he'd remember *that*."

Given his general reluctance to be forthcoming, I couldn't help but think he'd deliberately lied about how well he'd known Estelle Swarthout. Once again an ugly suspicion raised its head. Just how close had Conrad Featherstone been to the Swarthout family? A loyal son might well be tempted into deceit if that was the only way to protect his father's reputation.

Chapter Thirty-seven

A few hours later, back at the farm, I was sound asleep with Calpurnia curled up close to the small of my back. I don't know how much time passed before something caused me to jerk upright and dislodge her. Just that quickly, I was wide awake and she was on full alert.

Given that I wear hearing aids and take them out when I go to bed, it's rare that any nocturnal noise quieter than a violent thunderstorm interferes with my sleep. I fumbled on the nightstand for their case and the one holding my glasses. When I could hear and see at normal levels, I reached across the bed to twitch aside the curtain in front of the open window.

Beneath a waxing gibbous moon only a few days short of being at the full, I could see the overgrown field and the distant tree line. Nothing moved in that ghostly landscape.

Despite listening hard, I couldn't hear anything more ominous than the gentle rustle of the leaves of a nearby tree. A light breeze had come up while I'd been sleeping, enough to make the window curtain flutter after I dropped it back into place.

I was in Tessa's old room on the first floor. Since I was already awake, I got up to make use of the bathroom. I didn't bother turning on a light. I could find my way along

the hall by touch and moonlight provided adequate illumi-
nation in the bedroom and the bath. I was about to flush
when I heard what sounded like a shout.

I froze with my hand on the lever, listening hard. Even
with my head cocked, the rise and fall of voices barely
reached my ears. The speakers had to be some distance
from the house. I could only hear them because sound car-
ries well on a clear night with the wind behind it.

Moving quietly, I returned to the bedroom, donned my
robe and slippers, and collected my cell phone and my cat.
I tucked the phone into the pocket of my bathrobe and
carried Calpurnia slung over my shoulder with one hand
firmly planted on her backside as I made my way through
the living room. Once I reached the middle room, I leaned
over the easy chair and the little table that held the old-
fashioned, long-out-of-service telephone and peered through
the window.

I didn't see any vehicles in the driveway, but there was a
glimmer of light coming from somewhere farther back on
the property. When I moved to the rear window in the
kitchen to get a better view, I could hardly believe my eyes.
A truck was parked in front of the barn, its headlights illuminating a portion of the interior. Through the open
door—the small one that had been padlocked—I could
just make out two moving silhouettes.

Some people can punch numbers into their cell phones
one-handed. I'm not that coordinated, especially when my
fingers aren't quite steady. I had to shift the cat and hope
she wouldn't take off on me while I called for help.

The 911 dispatcher answered promptly. I tightened my
grip on Calpurnia while I gave her my location and tried
to explain the nature of my emergency. I guess "strange
men on the property" and "woman alone in the house"
were sufficient cause for alarm. She promised to send
someone ASAP.

While I waited, I stayed at my post at the window. How long it would take an officer to reach the farm was anybody's guess. Swan's Crossing has no police department of its own, so the sheriff's department is responsible for handling complaints. The nearest deputy could be anywhere in the county—five minutes away or thirty.

As I kept an eye on the barn, I tried to figure out what the men were doing. It didn't look as if they were unloading contraband. They hadn't carried anything in or out while I'd been watching. If the police arrived in time to arrest them, they could be charged with trespassing, but it would be even better to find evidence of what they were up to. Whatever it was, it had to be illegal.

Five minutes passed. Then ten. I didn't hear any sirens, but all of a sudden the men seemed to panic. They ran to their vehicle and it started to back away from the building even before I heard the truck doors slam shut.

"Drat," I muttered. "They're getting away."

I watched, helpless to stop them, as the truck slowed to execute a three-point turn in front of the garage. With its headlights illuminating that structure, the barn should have been swallowed up by darkness. Instead there was a dull, flickering red glow coming from inside. I bit back a gasp. No wonder those men were in a hurry to get away!

I hit REDIAL to place a second 911 call. This time my request for assistance was much more urgent.

"The barn is on fire," I told the dispatcher after I identified myself. "The nearest fire station is only a couple of miles away, at the center of Swan's Crossing. They need to get here as fast as possible."

That might not be very quickly. The fire department is manned by volunteers, and it was the middle of the night. It was anyone's guess if they'd arrive in time to save the building, let alone catch the arsonists.

The call took only seconds to complete. The truck was

still in the driveway, stopped just short of the house. I watched in bewilderment as one of the men got out of the passenger side and trotted back along the driveway to peer into the garage.

I swore under my breath. When they'd turned their vehicle around, the headlights must have picked out the bright green of the Ford Taurus parked inside. Now they knew that someone else was here at the Swarthout farm.

With a shout, the man turned and pounded up the outside stairs to the apartment above. A second man got out of the truck and followed him. A moment later, I heard wood splinter as they broke down the door.

Once they discovered that the apartment was empty, they'd either take off—the sensible thing to do, since they'd just set a building on fire—or they'd keep looking for the owner of the car, hoping to cover their tracks by eliminating a potential witness to their crime.

I didn't wait around to see if cooler heads would prevail. Moving as quickly as I dared in the semidarkness, I made my way back through the middle room and living room to the front hall.

Calpurnia chose that moment to decide she'd had enough of being carted around willy-nilly. She kicked and clawed in an attempt to make me release her. At the same time, a voice from the cell phone in my pocket implored me to "stay on the line."

I ignored both of them, spurred on to greater speed when I heard a distant shout.

The words were crystal clear: "Find her!"

As fast as I could, I headed for the one place in the house where my cat and I could hide without fear of discovery.

Chapter Thirty-eight

Even after shoving aside the candlestick and the framed photograph of Nellie Swarthout, I could barely squeeze both myself and Calpurnia into the cupboard under the stairs. Once I'd closed the hidden door behind me and squirmed around a bit, I ended up sitting on the floor with my head nearly touching my upraised knees. It was an awkward position, but I didn't have room to maneuver.

Determined to stay put until help arrived, I struggled to catch my breath while keeping hold of a squirming feline who seemed to have grown extra claws and added another five pounds in weight. The scratches she'd already given me stung.

Using one arm to press her close to my chest, I fumbled for the phone in my pocket with my free hand. I could hear the dispatcher's increasingly loud demands to know if I was still on the line.

"They're looking for me," I whispered. "I have to hang up."

As soon as I disconnected, I turned off the phone, fearing that if it rang, or even vibrated, it would give away my location.

Calm down, I ordered myself.

My heart pounded so loudly that it was nearly impossible to hear anything else, like the footsteps of those men or their voices.

Calpurnia continued to fight me. Even if I'd dared speak, there was no way I could explain to her that we had to be quiet. I tried stroking her with soothing motions. For my trouble, she bit me right on that tender spot at the base of the thumb. I could hardly blame her for the display of temper. She sensed my tension, but she had no way of knowing how dangerous our situation was.

When she growled low in her throat, I released her. She couldn't get out of the cupboard. I had to take the chance that, free to move about in the confined space, she wouldn't scratch at the door or make some other suspicious sound that would attract the attention of the . . . what? Thieves? Smugglers? Arsonists, certainly. And, quite possibly, men desperate enough to add murder to the list of their crimes.

My breathing was still ragged from the run up the stairs and the struggle to stuff myself into the cramped cupboard. I closed my eyes. I've never been claustrophobic, but in that moment I felt an overwhelming need to stretch out full length—the one thing impossible to do in such a confined space. That I had to remain immobile made me twitchy. When my left leg spasmed, I all but twisted myself into a pretzel trying to massage it without making any noise.

Help will arrive soon, I told myself. No more than a couple of minutes had passed since I reported the fire. I just had to be patient.

As my breathing and my heart rate steadied, I could hear faint sounds coming from the floor below. My eyes flew open. As I'd feared, after those men broke into the apartment and found it empty, they'd decided to search the house.

I listened harder, trying to judge if they'd found the room where I'd been sleeping. Once they saw that empty, rumpled bed, they'd be certain they'd been seen. They'd have to assume I'd already called 911. If they had half a brain between them, they'd give up the search and make a run for it before the cops arrived.

I couldn't understand why they were so intent on finding me in the first place. They'd set the fire and been heading out at a fast clip before they caught sight of my car. Why had that made them stop? It didn't make sense that they'd try to locate the owner. The rational response would be to assume that person was still blissfully asleep in the house. It wasn't as if I could identify them. If they'd just kept going, they'd be halfway to Monticello by now, free and clear.

More sounds reached me. Footsteps. A crash as something fell, or was flung to the floor.

Why didn't they just leave? Why risk getting caught to look for an unknown person who couldn't possibly have seen their faces and wouldn't be able to tell the authorities anything about the fire in the barn?

Then it hit me. They *weren't* looking for some random individual. They were looking for a woman. One of the men had shouted, quite clearly, "Find her."

Find *her*. Find *me*?

Maybe I'd misheard. The searchers might have realized they were looking for a woman after they saw my clothes in the bedroom, but they couldn't have known *before* they entered the house. Could they?

Did they know who they were looking for? Hardly anyone was aware I'd inherited the place and even fewer had been told that I'd temporarily moved in.

I sat very still, ears stretched, scarcely daring to breathe. I prayed for the distant wail of a siren, but the next sound to reach me came from much closer at hand. Someone opened the door at the foot of the stairwell and started to climb. He was just on the other side of the wall. I could feel the vibration of each heavy footfall.

When he spoke, it sounded as if he was standing right beside me. "She can't have gone far, and there's no way out from up here."

"We don't have time to mess around," a second man yelled up to him from the first floor. "Go get that can of kerosene from the truck and torch the house."

"With her in it?" the first man's voice went up an octave.

"With *you* in it if you don't snap to it."

The footsteps retreated downward. A moment later, the door at the bottom of the stairs was slammed shut.

Stunned, I felt frozen in place. This couldn't be happening. Why would anybody want to kill me? I was no threat to anyone.

I reached for the latch, then pulled back as if it was already red-hot.

What if this was a trick? Maybe they were trying to lure me into showing myself so they could . . . what? Kill me some other way than by burning me to death?

Anything was better than being roasted alive in a cupboard. I shifted until I was on my hands and knees.

"Don't scratch," I whispered to Calpurnia as I gathered her into my arms.

With extreme caution, I opened the door. Crawling out in total silence with a cat clutched to my chest was next to impossible. After the first second or two, I gave up trying to be quiet about it. Those men might still be downstairs, but I didn't sense the presence of anyone else on the second floor.

The short, narrow hallway was very dark. The only

light came from faint moonbeams filtering in through the window at the front of the house.

I sniffed the air. No smoke. Not yet. I hoped they'd been bluffing about setting the house on fire but I wasn't about to stick around to find out.

Shifting Calpurnia so that I was once again carrying her slung over my shoulder, I used my free hand to feel my way along the wall to the wide landing at the top of the stairwell. Even less light penetrated that far.

I discovered that the door was open when I stumbled through it and nearly took a header down the entire flight of steps. Twisting my body to avoid a fall, I lost my grip on Calpurnia. She squirmed out of my arms and took off.

The thought of losing my cat sent a new wave of panic through me. The compulsion to find her before I escaped from the house myself was unbearably strong. I'd taken a few steps away from the stairwell before I realized how futile the effort would be. She could be anywhere. I'd be a fool to risk losing my own life to save hers.

The sound of a siren, rapidly coming closer, decided me. I ran downstairs as fast as I could, lost precious seconds fumbling to release the deadbolt on the front door, and stumbled across the lawn to the driveway. By the time I got there, there was no sign of the bad guys. Two fire trucks were just turning in from the road. They headed straight for the blaze in the barn, speeding past me before I could redirect their attention to the house.

I couldn't blame them. The barn was fully engulfed in flames.

My heart in my throat, I turned to look behind me and breathed a sigh of relief when I didn't see any smoke or flames showing through the windows. That didn't mean there wasn't a fire inside, just that it hadn't yet had time to take hold. Frantically waving my arms, I ran after the fire trucks.

It seemed to take ages to reach them. By the time I was close enough to grab the nearest firefighter's arm, my legs felt as if they'd turned to rubber and I was wheezing like an old geezer with COPD.

"The house," I gasped. "They were going to set it on fire." I gulped in air polluted with smoke from the burning barn and started to cough, but I managed to add, "My cat is in there!"

He looked at me as if I'd lost my mind.

I repeated myself with greater urgency. The second time around the meaning of my words got through to him and he barked out orders to the other firemen, but it would take time to reposition one of the trucks and all the hoses were already out.

I turned and ran back the way I'd come. There was a fire extinguisher in the kitchen. Maybe I could get to it—

I was saved from this lunacy by the timely arrival of a sheriff's deputy. Since I was in the middle of the driveway, nearly level with the path to the side porch, he had to stop to avoid running me over. I changed course, staggering a little as I approached the patrol car.

"The men who set the barn on fire were going to torch the house, too," I blurted out.

"Calm down, ma'am. How do you know this?"

With an effort, I managed coherent sentences. "I overheard them. They had kerosene."

I swiveled my head to look at the house. There were still no flames showing, but I was frantic with fear that a fire had already taken hold somewhere it couldn't be seen. I turned and took two stumbling steps in that direction before the deputy caught me around the waist, lifted me off my feet, and put me down again flush with the side of his car.

"You don't understand! My cat is in there!" My voice rose to a wail.

"Stay here," he ordered, releasing me.

I obeyed only because he immediately took off toward the side porch, calling for backup on his portable radio as he ran.

One of the fire trucks from the barn rolled to a stop next to the police cruiser. Two firemen followed hard on the heels of the deputy as he took the porch steps two at a time. By the beam of his flashlight, I saw that in their hurry to leave, the arsonists had left the kitchen door wide open.

A moment later, the kitchen lights came on, swiftly followed by the lights in the middle room and living room. When I couldn't bear to watch through the windows any longer, I disobeyed orders and joined the firefighters in the kitchen.

The stench of kerosene made my nostrils sting and my eyes water.

"Careful," someone warned. "It's all over the floor."

It had been sloshed onto the kitchen cabinets, too.

One of the firefighters bent to pick something up off the linoleum. "Looks like they tossed a lit match, but it went out before it landed."

"Damn good thing," said the other fireman.

No smoke, I thought. *No fire.*

I headed for the front of the house, calling Calpurnia's name as I went.

The deputy waylaid me in the front hall. "Ma'am, you shouldn't be in here."

I ignored him and opened the door to the stairwell. "Calpurnia," I shouted. "Where are—"

I broke off when I caught sight of her. She was halfway up the steps, her tail fully fluffed. She looked as if she was about to bolt.

"It's okay, sweetie," I crooned. "The bad men are gone and we can go home now."

I took a step up. She retreated at speed.

It took me the better part of the next hour to coax her back into my arms. By then Detective Brightwell had arrived. I didn't ask how he knew about the fire or why he'd come out to the farm in the middle of the night. I was just glad to see a familiar face.

With Calpurnia safely confined in her carrier and the fire in the barn nearly out, I retreated into the downstairs bedroom to dress and pack. The nightgown, bathrobe, and slippers I'd been wearing throughout the crisis weren't fit to save. I bundled them into a plastic bag to take home and toss into the trash.

Brightwell was on his cell phone when I came out. A deputy helped me load Cal's carrier, my laptop and suitcase, and the box containing Nellie's diaries and scrapbook into the car. I was about to get in and head for Lenape Hollow when the detective emerged from the farmhouse.

"You look happy," I said when he joined me. I didn't think I'd ever seen Brightwell smile in quite that way before.

"It looks like we've caught your arsonists. A Fallsburgh police officer pulled over a pickup truck for speeding. When he started to get out of his cruiser, it took off again, but he'd already called in the license plate *and* taken note of the empty kerosene cans in the back. With a little help from neighboring towns, the truck was stopped and the two men inside are now in custody."

"I never saw their faces," I reminded him. "I can't identify them." I glanced toward the barn. It was a total loss.

"Chances are good that they left plenty of evidence behind in the house," Brightwell assured me. "The forensics guys will have a field day."

I managed a halfhearted cheer before I got into the car and drove myself home. I probably should have accepted the offer of one of the deputies to take me, but all I'd wanted by that point was solitude. I made the trip on autopilot. If I thought about anything at all between Swan's Crossing and Lenape Hollow, it was how much I needed to shut out the rest of the world and sleep for at least a week.

Chapter Thirty-nine

At noon the next day, I stumbled downstairs for coffee. I'd have hibernated longer if Calpurnia hadn't kept tapping me on the nose with her paw. After I fed her and myself, I felt half human again, but I was moving stiffly and was sore in places I'd forgotten I had.

I'd already overdone it, between the lawn work and the diary hunting. Add fighting to hold on to the cat, contorting myself into an unnatural position to fold myself into that hidey-hole, and a whole lot of running back and forth, and I had several sets of muscles that were no longer speaking to me. I wouldn't want to be eighteen again, but I do regret that I'm no longer as physically fit and resilient as I once was.

I'd just spoken to Luke on the phone, fortunately catching him before he heard about the fire from someone else, and was polishing off my second cup of coffee when Detective Brightwell rang my doorbell.

"I've come to take your formal statement," he announced.

"I can't tell you much more than I did last night," I warned him. "Coffee?"

Over steaming mugs of Breakfast Blend, I recounted the highlights of what had happened at the Swarthout farm. He recorded me and also took copious notes.

"So, you never saw their faces, but you did hear them speak. Do you think you'd recognize their voices if you heard them again?"

"I . . . don't know."

"Let's find out."

"You want me to talk to them?" I was appalled by the suggestion.

"That won't be necessary. I recorded their interrogations this morning. All you have to do is listen."

Although I felt ill at ease with the notion, I agreed. A few minutes later, I heard a gravelly voice declare, "I'm not talking without my mouthpiece."

Brightwell's voice came next: "Call your lawyer, then."

After a long silence, the suspect grudgingly admitted that he couldn't afford one.

Brightwell paused the playback.

I shook my head. "His voice isn't familiar." I managed a smile. "His language doesn't even sound like it's from the right century. Mouthpiece?"

"Not the brightest bulb. I think he'll crack, but for now I can't question him until a court-appointed attorney shows up and interviews his new client."

"If that man was in the house, he didn't speak. He has a rather distinctive voice. I'm sure I'd have remembered it." I hesitated. "Is being caught with empty kerosene cans enough to prove he and his pal were the arsonists?"

"We have a decent circumstantial case against both of them, plus the charges for speeding and resisting arrest. They aren't likely to get bail because they both have records. This guy did time for burglary and the other one was in jail for shoplifting. The problem is that, so far, we haven't found a fingerprint match for either of them in the house. Forensics is still working on other trace evidence, but a positive ID from you would certainly help get a conviction."

"They knew I was in the house." I sounded as shaky as I felt. "That's why they tried to set it on fire."

"Then they'll be charged with attempted murder as well as arson. Give a listen to the second man. If you recognize his voice, it will give me some leverage to convince him to rat out his partner."

Despite the warmth of the day, I shivered. As if she knew I could use comforting, Calpurnia appeared out of nowhere to place one paw on my thigh. I hoisted her into my lap and began to stroke her soft fur, a routine that soothed us both.

"Ready?" Brightwell asked.

"Not really, but I'd like to get it over with."

Like the first man, the second demanded to call his attorney. I tilted my head and closed my eyes. There was something about the cadence and timbre of his voice that stirred unpleasant emotions. My stomach roiled.

The speaker refused to answer questions, but he kept talking, taunting Brightwell. The longer he spoke, the more certain I became.

"That's the man who was coming up the stairs to look for me. The whiny one. He didn't like being told to set the house on fire with me in it." I grimaced, momentarily distracted from one bad memory by the equally unpalatable thought that cleaning up all that spilled kerosene was going to be a miserable job.

Brightwell stopped the playback. "What about the man giving him orders? Could it have been the other guy we arrested?"

I shook my head. "No. I'm certain it wasn't his voice I heard."

I considered what I'd seen from the kitchen window. Given the distance from the house and the poor quality of the light, I couldn't swear there had only been two men in the barn. I'd only seen two silhouettes and Detective

Brightwell had said that a pair of villains had been arrested, but what if there had been a third arsonist?

I asked Brightwell if that was possible.

"Did you see a vehicle other than the truck?" he asked.

"No. I'm probably wrong about there being more of them. Let me listen to that first guy again."

The second time around, the recorded voice still didn't ring any bells, but I picked up on something I hadn't noticed before.

"Is that usual for people accused of crimes?"

"Is what usual?"

"He wanted to call *his* mouthpiece. It sounds as if he had a specific lawyer in mind. Then . . . well, it's as if he thought better of that idea, so he asked for an attorney to be appointed for him instead."

"The court probably assigned him representation the last time he was in trouble with the law. Maybe he wanted the same guy again, then realized that if he hired him himself, he'd be the one paying the legal fees." Brightwell drank more of his coffee, watching me over the rim of the mug. "What are you thinking?"

"I'm not sure myself. Can you find out that lawyer's name? The one who defended him before?"

Brightwell went out on the front porch to make his call. I rinsed the coffee mugs, all the while trying to contain my impatience and rein in my notoriously overactive imagination. I was back in my chair at the dinette table by the time he returned.

"Oscar Sanchez." Brightwell slid into the chair opposite me.

"Of Featherstone, De Vane, Doherty, Sanchez, and Schiller?"

"The same. Do you want to tell me why you don't sound surprised?"

I took a deep breath. "It's probably just a coincidence,

but that's the law firm that also handles the Swarthout estate."

Interest flared in his eyes. "So someone working there would have known that no one lived at the farm, and a nice big abandoned barn was available for hiding something illegal."

"Exactly. Those storage units weren't built on a whim. Whoever put them there had to know that the location was remote and security was lousy. Until Tessa messed things up by dying and leaving her property to me, the people using the barn ran very little chance of getting caught."

"Which lawyer knew you'd found the storage units?"

"I told Jason Coleman, and he also knew I fired the security company. Leland Featherstone is the lawyer who handled Tessa's will, so I'm pretty sure Coleman would have reported my discovery to him. Anyone in the firm could have heard about it, and no one there knew I was planning to spend a couple of nights at the farm."

"I can almost follow the warped logic for burning down the barn," Brightwell said in a patient voice. "It was no longer safe to use and there was always a possibility that another search might turn up evidence that could identify them. But going after you and setting fire to the house still doesn't make sense."

It might, I thought, although I didn't yet have all the pieces of the puzzle. "I don't think I'm reaching to suspect there might be a connection to the law firm. Someone from there *has* to be involved. Even before those men came into the house, they knew they were looking for a woman."

In giving my statement, I'd repeated what I'd overheard word for word, but only now did I remember the panicked thoughts that had gone through my head while I was huddled in the cupboard under the stairs. I'd distinctly heard one of the men order the other—others?—to find *her*.

"When you don't know the gender of someone, the default pronouns are he and him, not she and her," I explained to Brightwell. "And the man on the stairs, the one whose voice I recognized, said '*she* can't have gone far' as he started to climb."

I closed my eyes, trying to play back the exact words the other man had used. I hadn't recognized his voice, but the phrase he'd used began to tug at my memory.

"We don't have time to mess around," I murmured.

My eyes flew open. For a moment I was speechless with astonishment.

"Go on." Brightwell was watching me like a hawk.

"There *was* a third man, and he was the one running the show. He's the one who told the others to find *her* and then, just before he ordered the man on your recording to torch the farmhouse with me in it, he said they didn't have time to mess around. Jason Coleman used that same expression the first time I met him."

Brightwell looked doubtful. "Why would Coleman, assuming it was him last night, take the drastic measure of trying to kill you? He's not some low IQ crook, prone to panic and irrational behavior. You said yourself it was too dark to see anyone's face, even in the moonlight."

"He couldn't know that for certain, and he and his henchmen had just set the barn on fire." I sent Brightwell a challenging look. "Do you have a better theory?"

"Not yet."

Brightwell's words sounded dismissive, but the grim expression on his face reassured me. He had every intention of taking a very close look at Jason Coleman.

Chapter Forty

Before Detective Brightwell left my house that Friday afternoon, he set a number of things in motion. First and foremost, he made me promise not to do anything foolish, like contacting Featherstone, De Vane, Doherty, Sanchez, and Schiller myself.

I don't think he trusted me to keep my word. Within an hour of his departure, Ellen Blume showed up on my doorstep. She was carrying an overnight bag and tried to feed me some cockamamie story about needing a place to stay for a few nights because her landlord was fumigating her apartment building. I pretended to believe her, although I knew perfectly well that if the tale were true, she'd have gone to her mother's house, which had a spare room, or to Luke's place, which didn't.

We let the fiction stand until Saturday morning, when she intercepted me on the way to collect my mail from the mailbox on the porch.

"I'll get it, Mikki." She blocked my way, almost stepping on Calpurnia to do so.

When she sidestepped to avoid Cal's tail, I got around her, reaching the door to the foyer ahead of her. "Even if Jason Coleman is crazy enough to make another attempt to kill me, he's not likely to do so in broad daylight."

Ellen's shoulders sagged. "I didn't think you bought my story."

"It was a nice try," I said consolingly.

After I turned off the security system, I went out onto the porch, collected two bills and a catalog from White Mountain Puzzles, and returned to the living room. Quite deliberately, I ignored the panel beside the door.

"You didn't reset the alarm."

"I don't always leave it on during the day."

"You know," Ellen said, "a little cooperation would be nice."

I punched in the code and headed for the living room. "A little information would be even nicer. Has Brightwell questioned Coleman?"

I settled down on the loveseat with the cat while Ellen took a nearby chair.

"I don't know, but I assume he's investigating. Brightwell likes to have all his ducks in a row before he confronts a suspect."

"And how long will it take to do a background check?" I wasn't prepared to remain under house arrest indefinitely.

"It will take as long as it takes. He has to make a case against Coleman or rule him out as a suspect. While he does that, he borrowed me from the PD and assigned me to keep an eye on you. It's a sensible precaution. If you want to kick me out of the house, that's your right, but if you do I'll have to sit out front in my car. Stakeouts are not only deathly dull, they're downright uncomfortable."

"That's right. Make me take pity on you."

"So I can stay?"

"You can stay. To be honest, I'm glad you're here. I'll sleep better with you in the house."

"Good. Now let's talk about something else."

"But there must be more you can tell me. What about

the two arsonists already in custody? Do you think there's any chance they'll be offered a plea bargain if they name names?"

Ellen rolled her eyes. To make clear she intended to change the subject, she picked up the catalog I'd tossed onto the end table and started to flip through it. "I used to love doing jigsaw puzzles. I didn't know you liked them too."

"Have you looked in the dining room lately?"

The jigsaw-puzzle table I'd brought with me from Maine was set up in one corner. Beckoning to her to follow me, I pointed out the fold-up legs, the tilt-top mechanism, the sorting drawers, and the cover that keeps the cat from scattering my work-in-progress.

"Lighthouses of the World" was just as I'd left it a week or two earlier. The border was in place and a few of the interior scenes were complete but it was largely unfinished.

Although Ellen and I passed a pleasant afternoon chatting over the puzzle table, that weekend was one of the longest of my life. Did I have second thoughts about my positive identification? Way too many of them. And although Detective Brightwell seemed inclined to believe me when I said Jason Coleman had been at the farm the night of the fire, he couldn't rush right out and arrest a prominent local attorney on my say-so alone. I'd been in a highly emotional state when I was hiding in that cupboard. If the only evidence against him was my belated recollection that the arsonist had used the same phrase I'd once heard from the lawyer's lips, Coleman's defense team would make mincemeat out of me in court.

Then again, if it *had* been Coleman, and if he still thought I might be able to place him at the scene of the crime, it was anybody's guess what he'd do next.

By mutual agreement, Ellen and I avoided all mention of murder, fires, and lawyers. As a result, I found out a great many things I hadn't known before about my cousin

Luke. At the same time, I got the distinct impression that Ellen was holding something back. I hoped she was just postponing making a certain announcement until she and Luke were together to tell me their future plans, but I had the oddest feeling that what she was keeping from me was something far different and probably much less pleasant.

Saturday night, I had a hard time falling asleep. I told myself that since no one had arrested Jason Coleman yet, he probably thought he'd gotten away without being recognized. He might still be worried about what his partners in crime would tell the police, but surely he no longer had any reason to come after me.

My subconscious wasn't convinced. I didn't get much rest that night.

On Sunday, I kept myself as busy as possible. I *did* still have editing to do. Ellen finished another puzzle and started a third from my hoard in the attic. I had kept some of my favorites from past years, on the theory I might want to put them together again one day.

I was just coming downstairs from my office when I heard Ellen yelp in dismay. I had a pretty good idea what had happened—the cat had taken a flying leap and landed in the middle of the puzzle table. Funny thing about that. The cover only works as a cat deterrent when it's in place. It doesn't do a thing to protect the puzzle when someone's actually working on it.

By Sunday night, I was too tired to stay awake and worry. I crashed as soon as my head hit the pillow. As a result, I woke up on Monday morning feeling refreshed. I was also so stir-crazy that it didn't bother me in the least to have Bella Trent turn up again.

Ellen caught sight of her about two seconds after I did. "Your stalker is back. I guess I'd better go have a word with her. Stay here."

Bella had parked on the street and was just getting out

of her car. While I watched from my front window, Ellen intercepted her. I couldn't hear what they said, but after a few moments, I saw Bella's face blossom into a radiant smile. Then she got into her car and drove away.

"Well?" I demanded when Ellen returned to the house.

"She won't bother you again."

"Uh-huh." I'd heard that before.

Ellen just shrugged. I peered at her more closely, noticing the dark circles under her eyes and the slump in her shoulders. I wondered if she'd slept at all since she'd moved in with me. If she took her assignment as my bodyguard seriously, she'd probably been forcing herself to stay awake.

"This is ridiculous," I said. "No one's after me. Go home and get some rest."

"I haven't been relieved."

"Then call Brightwell and find out what's going on. Maybe he's already arrested Jason Coleman."

"I do need to make a couple of phone calls." She glared at me. "Just don't take off while my back is turned."

"I wouldn't dream of it."

I didn't hesitate, however, to eavesdrop, positioning myself in front of the door to the utility room after she sought privacy in the adjacent dinette. To my surprise, it wasn't Detective Brightwell she contacted first.

"She was here again, Luke," Ellen said into her cell. "Despite her promise."

Does she mean Bella? I turned up the volume on my hearing aids and tilted my head to better hear Ellen's side of the conversation.

After a long pause, during which I presume Luke was speaking, she said, "Okay." Then she disconnected, leaving me in the dark as to what they were up to.

I was about to demand answers when I realized she was making a second call. This one *was* to the good detective. Listening in gained me nothing. He did most of the talking.

As soon as Ellen ended the call, she sought me out. "Good news, Mikki. Brightwell says you no longer need a bodyguard. He's going to meet with Jason Coleman this afternoon and he'll come talk to you again afterward."

Within an hour, Ellen had packed her overnight bag and left for home. I waved her off with a smile and a deep sense of relief. Her departure meant I was at liberty to proceed with a little plan of my own.

Chapter Forty-one

I was too impatient to wait for Brightwell to come to me. I'd done nothing but wait for something to happen for days. I changed into slightly more respectable clothing and drove to Monticello.

My timing was impeccable. I'd no sooner parked in the lot next to the redbrick law office than I spotted the good detective walking briskly toward the entrance. A uniformed officer accompanied him, suggesting that he might be planning to arrest Jason Coleman on the spot. One could only hope.

I got out of my car and followed them inside. I was in time to hear the receptionist tell Brightwell that Mr. Coleman was expecting him and point the way to Coleman's office. When Charlaine glanced my way, I put my finger to my lips to warn her not to call attention to me. Then I trotted after the two officers.

Jason Coleman's secretary had been absent from his outer office on my previous visit. Now a nicely dressed, middle-aged woman stood guard over her boss's inner sanctum. I couldn't see her face clearly with Brightwell and the deputy standing in front of her desk, but she must have caught sight of me the moment I appeared in the doorway.

"You can go right on in, Detective Brightwell," she said, before turning her attention to me to ask, "How can I help you, ma'am?"

I winced.

Brightwell glared. "Ms. Lincoln. Why am I not surprised?"

"Good afternoon, Detective Brightwell. I thought I—"

"You thought wrong. Wait here." With that, he stalked into Coleman's office, closing the door behind him.

That he also left the deputy behind puzzled me, but I knew better than to think a uniformed officer would answer my questions. I shifted my focus to the secretary. According to the nameplate on her desk, she was Laura Koenig.

I pasted a pleasant smile on my face and planted myself in front of her. "Ms. Koenig, I'm Michelle Lincoln. I wonder if—"

"I know who you are, Ms. Lincoln." She sounded resigned.

Caught off guard, I blinked at her in stupefaction for a moment before her identity belatedly registered. "Koenig?" I asked. "I could have sworn you introduced yourself to me as Laura Roth."

"Roth is my maiden name."

"Ah." Then a second penny dropped. I remembered my impression that someone had ducked out of sight just as I looked up from my book. "Were you the one watching me when I was here the other day?"

She sighed. "I didn't want to take the chance that you'd mention my ill-advised visit to the Swarthout farm. It could have cost me my job."

My eyebrows shot up. "I don't see why it would. You were concerned about your parents' reputations. That was a perfectly legitimate reason to be interested in what I might find there."

"My employers don't know who my parents were and I'd like to keep it that way."

I glanced around. Brightwell was still closeted with Coleman. The deputy had taken up a post by the door to the hall, effectively blocking anyone else from entering . . . or from overhearing my conversation with Laura Roth Koenig.

"I won't rat you out, but I'm curious to know how you ended up here, of all places, and how you found out that there were diaries hidden in the farmhouse."

Her eyes widened. "You found them?"

"I found the ones Tessa wanted published, but they were written by Tessa's mother, decades before Rosanna Swarthout was murdered."

Her carefully made-up face fell. "Damn."

I felt sorry for her. Darlene had found no further mention of the Roths in her research and Estelle's journal hadn't even mentioned the tenants in the apartment above the garage. Charles and Nina Roth might have been questioned about the crime, but I had difficulty believing they were ever serious suspects. I couldn't understand why they'd let the investigation cast such a pall over the rest of their lives and allowed it to blight their daughter's, too.

Laura was the picture of dejection as she sat at her desk. She'd wanted so badly to find solid evidence that would exonerate her parents. I sympathized. If I'd had proof of my theory about Estelle's role in her stepmother's death, I'd have shared it with her, but I didn't. Instead I asked how she'd discovered the conditions in Tessa's will. My best guess was that, as a secretary at the law firm, she'd been the one to type it up.

I was wrong.

"It was by accident," she said. "I saw a note Mr. Coleman had written to himself. Please don't tell him. He'll be furious if he thinks I was snooping. I wasn't. Truly."

"Relax. I don't want to get you into any trouble." I frowned. "I thought it was Leland Featherstone who was Tessa's attorney."

"Mr. Coleman handled Ms. Swarthout's legal affairs for the last couple of years, but when she decided to make a new will, Mr. Featherstone dealt with her himself."

Something in her tone of voice tipped me off. "You don't care much for Jason Coleman, do you?"

"It's not my place to approve or disapprove."

Letting that slide for the moment, I leaned closer, resting my palms on her desk and speaking in a low voice. Even so, I had a feeling the deputy was listening to every word and no doubt committing them to memory.

"Did you apply for a job here so you could find out more about the Swarthouts? I know Mr. Featherstone's father was the family lawyer at the time of the murder."

Color blossomed on her cheeks. "That was the idea in the beginning, but it turned out there was nothing to find. There *are* no old records relating to the Swarthout family. They must have been lost or discarded when Conrad Featherstone retired."

"Yet you stayed on."

She gave a wry little laugh. "Why not? The pay is good and I am trained as a legal secretary. I'd had a couple of other jobs before I heard about the opening here."

"Have you always worked for Jason Coleman?"

"Not at first. I started out as secretary to Mr. De Vane, but when Mr. Coleman joined the firm, I was assigned to him." She hesitated. "Mr. Featherstone thought it would be a good idea for him to have the assistance of someone with my experience."

I moved a little closer, resting one hip on the side of her desk and putting my right hand on her shoulder. "What makes you so uncomfortable about him, Laura? What's he done?"

"I . . . I think he takes advantage of some of his elderly clients." Alarm flashed in her eyes. "I shouldn't have said that. It's not my place."

Now we're getting somewhere!

"Did he take advantage of Tessa Swarthout?"

"I don't know, but I can tell you that he searched the Swarthout farmhouse before Mr. Featherstone took you out there."

"The house? How do you know?" I'd been told that he'd walked through the fields and down to the pond, but no one had told me he'd gone inside.

"Mr. Coleman makes to-do lists. That was the note I saw. By accident, I swear."

"Go on."

"It had several items on it. The first was *walk property lines.*"

I nodded. "Mr. Featherstone told him to do that."

"Number two and three were *search house for Tessa Swarthout's diaries* and *destroy diaries.* As soon as I realized there *were* diaries, all I could think was that they might contain something that would clear my parents' names."

"He didn't find them." It was not a question.

She shook her head. "He came back from his visit to the farm in a foul temper. The door to his office was closed, but I could hear him pacing and muttering to himself. It was after he left for the day that I picked up a crumpled piece of paper I found on the floor and read the four items on his list."

"Four? What was the last one?"

"*Clear out barn.*"

Chapter Forty-two

When I burst into Jason Coleman's office, dragging Laura after me, the lawyer was seated at his desk, fingers steepled and a smug smile on his face. Detective Brightwell sat in the client chair, apparently content to listen. They both looked up in annoyance at the intrusion.

Coleman's gaze went first to me, then to the deputy in uniform who'd followed us in. He dismissed his secretary's presence. I presume he thought she was trying to stop me from interrupting. He started to stand, but before he was fully upright or had a chance to order me to leave, Brightwell spoke up.

"Let her in, Davis. And you stay, too."

"Yes sir," the deputy said.

Coleman subsided. "Have a seat, Ms. Lincoln." He made a vague gesture toward the remaining client chair. "You may go, Laura."

"I don't think so. Ms. Koenig has pertinent information to share."

If I'd been in Coleman's shoes, I'd have been worried. He put up a brave front, but his voice wasn't entirely steady. "What's going on here?"

I sat down facing the lawyer, but I addressed the detective. "Did you ask him where he was on Friday night between midnight and two in the morning?"

"Mr. Coleman tells me he was asleep. At home. In his own bed. Alone."

Coleman's laugh sounded forced. "Where else would I be at that time of night?"

"Leaving fingerprints all over my house in Swan's Crossing?" I suggested.

Out of the corner of my eye I caught Brightwell's wince, but he didn't intervene. I wished I knew how much he'd told Coleman, but it was too late to backtrack.

"Are you talking about the Swarthout farm?" Coleman sputtered. "Of course my fingerprints are there. I was in that house on several occasions, on business for Mr. Featherstone."

"According to him, he asked you to walk around the perimeter of the property. He didn't tell you to go inside the house."

"I wanted to be thorough. See here—what's this all about? If you're accusing me of something, spit it out."

"Laura," I said. "Please tell the detective what was in the note you found."

"I really don't think—"

Laura interrupted her boss to rattle off the four items on his to-do list.

"Interesting," Brightwell commented.

"I did nothing illegal." Coleman's long, narrow face was flushed and the gray eyes I'd once characterized as mild were hard and cold as chips of ice.

"Maybe not illegal, but definitely unethical," I said. "You wanted to find the diaries before I did to make sure I wouldn't inherit. Why?"

A voice spoke from the doorway before Coleman could come up with an answer. "Under the terms of Tessa Swarthout's will, Jason Coleman inherits her estate if you fail to comply with her conditions."

Leland Featherstone braced one hand on the doorframe, looking like a man who'd just received a bad shock. However much he'd overheard had obviously come as a revelation. He wasn't just upset. He was angry.

I wasn't too steady myself. The announcement that *Coleman* was Tessa's residuary heir left me reeling. I glared at him. "Is that the reason you wanted me dead? So you'd be sure to end up owning the Swarthout farm?" I had to clasp my hands tightly together in my lap to stop them from trembling.

Brightwell stood. "Jason Coleman, I'm arresting you on suspicion of arson and attempted murder." While Featherstone, Laura, and I stood by, he read the lawyer his rights and turned him over to the deputy to be transported to the county jail.

"This is preposterous," Coleman blustered as he was led away. "You have no case."

"Take my advice," Featherstone said. "Don't say another word without your lawyer present. I'll send Doherty. He's had the most experience with criminal trials."

To my surprise, Brightwell did not immediately follow his prisoner. "I'd like a word with you, sir," he said to Leland Featherstone.

The senior partner had recovered his aplomb. His bushy white eyebrows drew together in a thunderous expression. He sent the detective a long, considering look that suggested this wasn't the first time they'd encountered each other in an adversarial situation.

"Why don't we move this discussion to the conference room?" he suggested. "I'm sure the ladies will be more comfortable there."

"That's not necessary, sir. You and I can discuss this one-on-one."

"The ladies," I interrupted, "have a vested interest in what you two have to say." I certainly did, and from the worried expression on Laura's face, she was still afraid she was in danger of losing her job. I meant to make sure that didn't happen.

Chapter Forty-three

The conference room was a large, brightly lit space furnished with an oval table and comfortably padded chairs. We'd barely seated ourselves before Featherstone's secretary appeared to distribute coffee and pastries.

Brightwell waited until she left to address the senior partner. "You already know, as legal representative of the Swarthout estate, on Friday night, someone burned down the barn at the Swarthout farm and tried to set fire to the house. Ms. Lincoln was staying there at the time and was fortunate not to have been trapped inside. Two of the men involved in the arson have been caught and questioned. Acting on orders from a third individual, they had been using that barn to store stolen goods."

He stopped speaking when the lawyer gave a start of surprise.

"Coleman never told you about the storage units, did he?" I asked.

"Explain!"

Featherstone snapped out the order and I obeyed, sketching out the highlights of my discovery, the search by drug-sniffing dogs, and my subsequent decision, with Coleman's agreement, to fire Sure Thing Security.

"I knew none of this." Featherstone's voice wasn't quite

steady. He sent me an apologetic look before addressing Detective Brightwell. "I gather you were about to tell me that the third arsonist was Jason Coleman?"

"It appears he was at the farm that night and that he was the one who ordered the house to be torched when he realized that Ms. Lincoln might have recognized him. We found his fingerprints at the scene."

"Where?" I interrupted.

"On the stairwell door leading to the second floor," Brightwell said.

"Then I'm surprised you hadn't already arrested him before I burst in on you."

"I was about to," Brightwell said in a mild voice. He turned back to Leland Featherstone. "Were you aware that Mr. Coleman has a gambling problem?"

Sorrow warred with anger on Featherstone's deeply lined face. "I knew he got into a little trouble in college, but his grandfather was an honorable man. I hoped Jason would take after him."

"You authorized him to deal with important clients." Brightwell gave him a name that was unfamiliar to me but clearly struck a nerve with the lawyer.

The color of Featherstone's skin went from pasty white to gray in a heartbeat. Shoulders that were already stooped with age sagged alarmingly. Just as I was about to ask if he was okay, he rallied. "What did he do?"

"About a year after Mr. Coleman started working here, a very valuable diamond necklace went missing from her home. The thief was never caught and the necklace was never recovered. Our best guess is that it was broken up and the stones sold separately."

"If you're suggesting—"

"We can't prove he stole it, but it was shortly after that when Coleman had dealings with two men who'd earlier been defended by another lawyer from this firm. That, we *can* prove. We're still looking into credit card and phone records but the paper trail is pretty clear. I wouldn't be surprised if we eventually get a confession from one, if not both, of the arsonists. Criminals tend to become very cooperative once they realize that telling us everything they know will lead to a lighter sentence."

"What does the barn on the Swarthout farm have to do with this?" Featherstone asked.

"We're fairly certain Coleman is the one who repaired it and installed storage units where the horse stalls used to be. It looks as if his success in stealing the necklace inspired him to continue to use that same method to finance his gambling habit. He appears to have arranged a series of burglaries. Your firm represents a good many wealthy clients and has social contacts with others. Stolen items were stored in the barn until the heat died down enough for them to be safely fenced."

Featherstone looked shell-shocked. After a long silence, he cleared his throat and began to speak in a low, rigidly controlled voice.

"The Swarthouts were longtime clients. My father was Tessa's father's lawyer. Back then, young Coleman's grandfather was a partner in this firm. That's why he was hired and why he seemed a logical choice to take over Tessa's business affairs." He studiously avoided looking at me. "She didn't have any relatives left to inherit. When she insisted on naming her lawyer as her residuary heir, I assumed it was simply because she'd taken a liking to him. I never suspected that he might have used undue influence, and I swear I never told him he was a beneficiary in her will. That provision wouldn't have gone into effect unless Ms. Lincoln failed to find the diaries." He sighed heavily. "He *did* know the conditions she set for her to inherit. I don't suppose it would have been difficult for him to get a look at the will itself."

"So," Brightwell interjected. "he took the precaution of clearing out whatever was in the barn once he knew Ms. Lincoln would be taking a look at the property. If she hadn't found the empty storage units and made a fuss about them, he'd probably have waited to see if she located the diaries before doing anything else. Instead, he panicked."

"But the police had already been there," I objected. "They found nothing. Oh!"

"What?" Brightwell asked.

"I don't think I told him that I called the police, or that they searched the barn. But if he was worried about evidence he might have left behind, why didn't he set fire to the barn as soon as he knew I'd discovered the storage units?"

"It would have taken him a few days to organize things."

Featherstone, hunched over his coffee, spoke more to himself than to us. "He'd never have been caught if he had just been patient. All he had to do was wait a few more weeks. When no more diaries surfaced, he'd have inherited. The barn and its secrets would have been his to do with as he pleased."

I cleared my throat. "That's not quite true. You see, it wasn't Estelle's journal that Tessa wanted published. I finally found the diaries she meant to preserve. They were written by her mother. I'll have them edited and online well before the deadline."

Featherstone's head jerked up and he stared at me. "They're *Nellie* Swarthout's diaries?" A note of incredulity had crept into his voice.

"Yes, and there are two of them, so the search is over. I inherit."

"Did Coleman know you found them?" Brightwell interrupted.

I shook my head. "I hadn't gotten around to telling anyone here at the law firm."

"They . . . they must be quite old," Featherstone mused. "Written long before the house was closed up."

I confirmed this and told him how I'd come to discover the hidden cupboard and its contents. "I'm surprised Tessa and Estelle didn't arrange to have someone retrieve them," I added. "I can understand why they couldn't bear to go back into the house themselves after Rosanna's murder, but those diaries and the scrapbook that was stored with them must have had sentimental value for them both."

"I have no answer for you," Featherstone said. "I wasn't even aware there *were* diaries until Tessa had me put that provision in her will. I asked her who wrote them, but she wouldn't say. I doubt Coleman knew any more about them than I did." He swung his head around to pin Laura with a hard stare. "Did he?"

Looking like a scared rabbit, she shook her head. She hadn't said a word since we entered the conference room.

Featherstone gave a dry, rattling laugh. "Don't worry, Ms. Koenig. You did the right thing by coming forward. I'll see to it that you have a new assignment and a bonus, too. We can't have crooks like Jason Coleman working for Featherstone, De Vane, Doherty, Sanchez, and Schiller."

He attempted a smile, but it didn't reach his eyes. Leland Featherstone seemed to have aged a decade in the last hour.

Chapter Forty-four

The rest of that week and another weekend passed without any further contact with either Leland Featherstone or Detective Brightwell. Since the original event—an abandoned barn catching fire and burning to the ground—had only rated a single paragraph in the local paper, no reporters showed up on my doorstep to dog me for a story. Jason Coleman's arrest had been duly recorded in the police log, but that too went almost unnoticed by the press. Either they had more important stories to cover, or the attorneys at Featherstone, De Vane, Doherty, Sanchez, and Schiller had called in favors to keep the law firm's name out of the news. Whatever the reason, I was perfectly happy to remain anonymous.

Along with my regular work, I edited Nellie's diaries and learned how to configure them to turn them into electronic books on various platforms. I didn't expect anyone to actually buy one, but Tessa's instructions had been quite specific. I was also to post pdf versions on social media sites and use print on demand to produce paper copies that might, or might not, be offered for sale in local historical society gift shops.

Writing an introduction to go with the material was time-consuming. Adding one wasn't required, but it felt wrong to send Nellie's words out into the world without any context. The tricky part was deciding how much Swarthout family history to reveal.

Proofreading was a bear. By the time I was ready to do the final pass on a printout on Monday morning, just five days short of my deadline, I was so familiar with the text that I had no choice but to read it aloud to make sure no pesky typos had managed to sneak in. I am not fond of the sound of my own voice. As for Calpurnia, she sent me one disgruntled look when I started to declaim and headed for the hills.

To say I was relieved to be interrupted by a ringing phone would be an understatement. Since the caller ID told me it was Darlene on the other end of the line, I popped my hearing aids back in and hit the button to engage the speaker. I can hear better that way, since the alternative is to take out one hearing aid and hope the person calling will speak clearly, loudly, and distinctly. Leaving the hearing aid in while pressing the receiver against that ear isn't an option. The batteries react with a deafening squeal.

As soon as I heard what Darlene had called to tell me, I did a little happy dance. She'd acquired a copy of George Swarthout's will.

"That's great," I said. "What does it say?"

"I'll give you the details when I get there."

"Can't you just give me the CliffsNotes version over the phone?" Yes, I am aware of the irony in asking that question. Luke had said practically the same thing to me when I'd put off giving him the latest details of my adventures at the Swarthout farm.

Darlene's response also paralleled mine: "Nope. See you in a few." Then she hung up on me.

True to her word, Darlene arrived a short time later. By then I had coffee waiting. As I'd hoped, she brought muffins, homemade and freshly baked. As soon as we sat down at the dinette table, she fished an envelope out of her purse and placed it on the surface between us.

"You were right," she announced. "George Swarthout set up a trust. He was a typical chauvinist patriarch who didn't think females capable of managing money or property by themselves. He took it upon himself to do it for them from beyond the grave."

I gave the envelope a dubious look. "Is that legal?"

"Apparently, and trusts are hard to break without going to court. I imagine his womenfolk didn't fight the terms because they'd have had a difficult time coming up with the cash to pay a lawyer. Everything was tied up in the trust."

"Catch-22." I opened the envelope, drew out a certified copy of George Swarthout's will, and began to read.

I'm no expert when it comes to interpreting legalese, but the basics didn't seem all that complicated. George had left the family farm to his widow for her lifetime. After Rosanna's death, his two daughters inherited jointly, but the provisions didn't stop there. On the death of one of the sisters, everything went to the other. That surviving daughter was still not permitted to sell the land. The property and the trust remained intact until after *her* death.

More than ever before, I was glad I'd been born in the era during which the women's movement succeeded in making things better for wives and daughters.

I skimmed to the end, and found it got worse. Fifty percent of whatever money George had when he died had been earmarked for upkeep of the property. The other fifty percent was to be doled out to Rosanna, Tessa, and Estelle in small increments as an allowance.

"Did he leave much of a fortune?" I asked.

"That's not clear," Darlene admitted. "I wasn't able to find an inventory, but I have a feeling the farm's income was barely sufficient to support the three of them. Why else would they continue to take in boarders?"

"And rent out the apartment over the garage," I added. I'd already brought her up to date on what I'd learned about the Roths.

"The mindset of people back in the fifties makes me angry every time I think about it," Darlene said. "A few women managed to make careers for themselves, but most just stayed home and let their fathers or husbands make all the decisions for them."

"Exactly what I was thinking." I bit rather savagely into a muffin. "After reading Estelle's journal, I didn't like her much, but I had to feel sorry for her. As much as she wanted an acting career, the deck was stacked against her. Thanks to her father, she didn't have enough money for trips to the city for auditions, let alone headshots or acting lessons, or even appropriate clothing."

"You're assuming she really did have talent," Darlene said. "She was a big fish in a little puddle here in Sullivan County, but starring in amateur productions put on by a rural drama society wouldn't have meant much to a Broadway producer."

"True, and I suppose the same applies to Hollywood." I sighed. "By the time Rosanna died, Estelle must have been too old to find work there as anything but a character actress."

"Do you think she managed even that much?"

"The first address I have for Tessa after they left the farm is in California," I reminded her, "but you're probably right and Estelle found out the hard way that it was too late to have the career she wanted." Sipping coffee, I considered her situation in light of George's will. "With Rosanna gone, Tessa and Estelle would have split fifty percent of their father's money two ways instead of three."

"It would have still been tough going for two single

women in those days," Darlene said. "They couldn't get credit cards or take out loans, or—"

"You're missing my point. George's will gives them a solid motive to have murdered their stepmother."

"Maybe. Maybe not." Darlene polished off the last of the muffins.

I frowned and finished my coffee. It irked me more than I liked to admit that I might never know for certain who had killed Rosanna Swarthout or why Tessa and Estelle had so completely abandoned the only home they'd ever known.

Chapter Forty-five

Late that same Monday, Detective Brightwell phoned me. I listened in amazement as he informed me that Jason Coleman had confessed, confirming that his gambling problem had led him to steal from his law firm's clients and to take advantage of his position of trust with Tessa Swarthout.

"He claims the fire in the barn wasn't his idea," Brightwell said, "and insists he didn't know anyone was inside the farmhouse when his associates decided to torch it."

"I know what I heard him say. I'll testify to that." Coleman deserved a long prison sentence and I was ready to do my bit to see that he got it.

"Good. That's good." There was a long pause.

"What?"

"Coleman said something odd to his attorney before he formally agreed to cooperate. It doesn't seem to have any connection to the charges against him, but it might be of interest to you. When he said it, Coleman sounded—" Brightwell hesitated, as if he was searching for the right word. "I don't know. Sulky?"

"Petulant?" I suggested.

He laughed. "Like a kid ratting out a playmate on the grounds that the other child did it first. What he said was that Leland Featherstone went out to the Swarthout farm-house before Coleman did and, I assume, *before* he notified you about your inheritance. Any idea why Coleman would be miffed about that?"

"Maybe he thought Featherstone had discovered his operation in the barn and was willing to overlook it?"

"Until you came along? I suppose that makes as much sense as anything else."

After Detective Brightwell gave me a few particulars about what to expect when the case came to trial, I thanked him for the update and disconnected. Curled up on the loveseat with Calpurnia on my lap, I tried to think why Featherstone had gone out to the farm. At his age and in obvious ill health, it hadn't even made sense for him to accompany me out there. Had he been looking for the diaries? Any reason why he should, other than to turn them over to me, eluded me. Coleman had been the only one with a motive to find and destroy them. Until Featherstone helped Tessa make her will, he hadn't even known there *were* diaries.

"To give him the benefit of the doubt," I said to Calpurnia, "he might have yielded to simple curiosity." That was certainly something I could understand.

I got up and made myself a cup of green tea, still mulling over the lawyer's behavior. I carried it upstairs to my office, scowling as I settled into the chair by the window.

Why had Coleman been bothered by Featherstone's trip to the farm? Did he know something I didn't? His grandfather had been partners with Featherstone's father at the time of Rosanna's murder. Had *he* known something significant about the case? Something he had told his grandson?

Cal padded into the room and sent me one of those contemptuous looks only cats can manage. I stared at her. She was right. Sometimes humans make things much too complicated. But as I sipped my tea I continued to think about Leland Featherstone, I remembered how surprised he'd been to learn the diaries had been written by Nellie Swarthout. He'd expected me to tell him I'd found another of Estelle's journals.

Back when I'd announced that I'd located the record Estelle *had* kept, I hadn't thought Featherstone's reaction particularly strange. I'd already begun to suspect that he wasn't well, and at his age, any number of things could have sent him scurrying into his private restroom to regain his composure. Now, though, I had to wonder if he'd been alarmed by what I'd discovered. He'd only relaxed after I told him that Estelle's entries stopped a month before Rosanna's murder.

He'd insisted he'd barely known her, and I'd believed him even after Darlene discovered his name as a member of the stage crew on a production Estelle had headlined. There had been no mention of him, or his father, in the pages of her journal.

Or had there?

I paused with my cup halfway to my lips. Was it possible I'd overlooked one? There were several passages where Estelle had referred only to "that bitch" or "Mr. Smarty Pants" or "the diva who upstaged me"—she hadn't always named names. Had Conrad Featherstone been mentioned in her journal, after all?

Call me naïve, but it took me multiple readings to find the significant sentences. When I finally did, I couldn't believe I'd missed their importance. I guess my mind just doesn't naturally descend into the gutter.

"Listen to this," I said, waking Calpurnia to read aloud. "Indulged in a delicious treat backstage after rehearsal. It's been a long time since I tasted fresh fruit. That it's forbidden made it all the more pleasurable."

I didn't think she was talking about apples.

"Am I just being a dirty old lady?" I asked the cat.

She didn't bother to answer me. It didn't matter. I was ninety-nine percent certain I was right and that Estelle Swarthout, by then in her late thirties, had initiated a sexual encounter with Leland Featherstone, aged between fifteen and sixteen and working on the stage crew for an amateur production of *My Sister Eileen.*

He *had* been searching for the diaries mentioned in Tessa's will. He thought they might have been written by Estelle and he'd been afraid of what she might have said about him. He'd hoped to destroy any record of their fling.

"Like anyone would care," I muttered.

Such liaisons—an older, sexually experienced woman seducing an underage teenage boy—aren't exactly unheard of. These days, Estelle might have been arrested for statutory rape, if the wrong person found out, but back in the 1950s? Hardly! Even as late as the mid-1990s, as I discovered when I was working on a project for the historical society, such things went on and no one raised a fuss.

Mr. Featherstone doesn't have to worry, I thought as I put the journal away and got ready for bed. *I'm not about to expose his dirty little secret.*

I took off my glasses, removed my hearing aids, and turned out the light on the bedside table, ready to settle in for the night.

Sixty seconds later, I sat bolt upright again. The section of my brain that stores random knowledge had reminded me of another case of an older woman preying on teenage boys. In that instance, seduction had led to murder.

Pam Smart was a schoolteacher in neighboring New Hampshire when I lived in Maine. After granting sexual favors to two of her students, she persuaded them to kill her husband. When the sordid details eventually came out, all three were arrested, tried, and convicted. She's still in prison.

I lay there in the dark, wondering how strong Estelle Swarthout's influence over Leland Featherstone had been. I'd considered the possibility that the father had helped Estelle cover up a crime. I hadn't envisioned a scenario in which she persuaded the son to kill her stepmother. If she'd convinced someone else to commit the crime, that certainly explained how she'd been able to provide herself with such an excellent alibi.

"Sheer speculation," I said aloud. "Your imagination has really run away with you this time, Mikki Lincoln!"

I forced myself to lie back down and close my eyes, but I didn't sleep much that night. My thoughts kept circling back to Leland Featherstone and Estelle. Try as I might, I could no longer convince myself of his innocence. That the respected senior partner at Featherstone, De Vane, Doherty, Sanchez, and Schiller had once been an infatuated teenager led me to believe that he might also have been capable of stabbing Rosanna Swarthout to death with a kitchen knife.

Chapter Forty-six

There was only one way to find out if my theory was correct. The next morning, I drove to the offices of Featherstone, De Vane, Doherty, Sanchez, and Schiller intending to show Leland Featherstone the program Darlene had found in the library file. She'd given me the folders to return. Fortunately, I hadn't yet done so. I felt certain that by watching Featherstone's face when he recognized it, if he recognized it, I'd be able to tell just how deeply he'd been involved with Estelle Swarthout.

If he didn't react, I'd still have a way to ease into asking more questions. I wasn't sure how far I could go in that direction. How *does* one quiz a man his age about an indiscretion that took place when he was a teenager? Aside from the delicate nature of the inquiry, I didn't want to come right out and accuse him of being Estelle's lover, let alone of murder. More than once, I almost turned around and went home, but my need to know the truth was too strong to allow me to retreat.

Charlaine, the law firm's ever-vigilant receptionist, lifted her head from the paperwork in front of her when I entered. "I'm afraid Mr. Featherstone has a very busy schedule today," she said in a listless voice. "Perhaps you could make an appointment for later in the week?"

"It's very important that I talk to him. I don't need more than a few minutes of his time."

She sighed. "I'll ask."

When she picked up the phone to talk to Featherstone, I couldn't help but notice that she was in desperate need of a manicure. Most of her subtly painted fingernails were still intact, but one or two showed signs of having been chewed.

On closer inspection, I saw other marks of distress. A long strand of dark brown hair had come loose from her French twist to trail listlessly across the high collar of her blouse and the blouse itself was somewhat rumpled. I'd wondered once before if she had a personal interest in Jason Coleman. Now I felt certain of it, and very sorry for her, although she was certainly better off without a crook like him in her life.

Charlaine disconnected after a brief conversation conducted in a voice too soft for me to overhear. "I'm sorry, Ms. Lincoln, but Mr. Featherstone is tied up in a meeting."

"I'll wait until he's free."

"It's scheduled to last all day."

She'd had practice lying for her bosses, but that didn't mean she was good at it, or that she liked that part of her job. I was tempted to barge past her and force my way into Featherstone's office, but that would only get me tossed out on my ear, probably by that same very large, very determined security guard who'd been on the verge of ejecting me on an earlier visit.

"Tell Mr. Featherstone I've found another diary," I said. "This one was written in the nineteen fifties."

When she'd relayed my message, a look of surprise came over her face. "He'll see you now. I'll have to take you to his office. His secretary would normally come get you but she's out sick today."

I started to tell her I could find my own way before be-latedly realizing that if Featherstone had done what I feared he had, and thought I had proof of it, I might be wise not to walk into the lion's den without backup.

"Do me a favor?" I asked in a whisper as our feet sank silently into the plush carpeting of the hallway. "Leave the door open a crack and stay near enough to hear what Mr. Featherstone and I say to each other."

Her eyes widened. She understood that I was asking her to bear witness to our conversation. Considering what had come to light about Jason Coleman's criminal activities, she had to be wondering if other members of the law firm, even the head honcho, were as honest as she'd once be-lieved them to be.

In Featherstone's outer office, I stopped her by placing one hand on her forearm. "It's important, Charlaine, or I wouldn't ask."

"Okay. I can sit at Mindy's desk." She rapped lightly on the door before opening it. "Ms. Lincoln, Mr. Feather-stone."

When she backed out of my way, I entered. I didn't dare look around to make sure she'd followed my instructions, but I didn't hear the click of the door closing. Mentally crossing my fingers that she was seated near enough to catch every word we exchanged, I advanced toward the massive desk behind which Featherstone sheltered.

"What's this about another diary?" He sounded testy.

"As you know, Nellie Swarthout wasn't the only one in the family who recorded her thoughts and activities. Es-telle also kept a journal."

"So you mentioned on a previous occasion. Have you found another?"

"Yes." Sitting across from him, I met his eyes, hoping he couldn't tell I was lying.

"And?" His face gave nothing away.

"She mentioned you."

His eyes narrowed, bringing his bushy eyebrows so close together that they almost touched. A bit of color flared beneath the normal pasty white of his complexion. "I'm sure you're mistaken. I barely knew the woman."

"In the late nineteen fifties, you and she belonged to the same local drama society." I produced the program and slapped it down on the desk in front of him.

After a cursory glance, he ignored it. Leaning back in his desk chair, he regarded me with cool indifference. "That was a long time ago. I seem to recall that Estelle Swarthout took leading roles in several productions put on by our local drama club, and I occasionally helped out backstage for some of them, but I doubt she noticed me."

"She did more than notice you and you noticed her right back. She was a good-looking woman. You were a teenage boy." I held his gaze, unblinking. "I taught teenagers for decades. Then and now, they're ruled by their hormones."

Featherstone came up out of his chair and rounded the desk with more speed than I'd have expected from a man of his age. "What are you insinuating? What did Estelle write in her damned journal?" He halted in front of my chair and leaned in, placing one hand on each side of me to box me in. "Why did you come here?"

"Back off."

He didn't budge.

"Let's talk about this like reasonable adults, shall we, Mr. Featherstone? After all, the events in question took place a very long time ago."

I didn't mention that there is no statute of limitations on murder. We were both well aware of that fact.

He straightened, but continued to loom over me. I tried

to scoot the chair farther away from him, but it was heavy and the carpeting was plush. I didn't get very far. I was beginning to think that lying about the existence of a second diary and its contents might not have been the smartest way to proceed.

Since it was too late for me to change course, I continued to lie through my teeth. "Estelle made plans and recruited someone no one would suspect to help her. It's still remarkable that the two of you got away with it."

"You don't know what you're talking about."

If he'd said *he* didn't know what I was talking about, I might have been more inclined to believe him. Pronouns are important. His word choice and the way he was breathing heavily and clenching his fists convinced me that I had indeed discovered the identity of Rosanna's murderer. Why else would he be so agitated?

"You must have been disappointed afterward," I said, "when Estelle withdrew her favors. Or did she convince you that it was too dangerous to continue your liaison?"

"There was no liaison," he said through gritted teeth.

"One-night stand? I suppose Estelle was the type who'd prefer that—less emotional attachment on her part."

"How dare you insult that poor woman!"

That brought me up short. *Poor woman?*

"You *pity* her?"

"Of course I do. I did."

He turned away from me, moving toward the window with tottering steps. He stood there, swaying slightly, his back to me as he stared out at the parking lot. I doubted he saw the cars or any of the nearby buildings. His mind was clearly focused on the past.

"What happened to her after she left the farm?" I asked. "Why didn't she pursue the career she wanted so badly?"

When he finally answered me, his voice was choked

with emotion. "She had a complete mental breakdown after the murder. She was the one who refused to return home or let anyone else go in to collect their possessions. Tessa relied on my father to find a place for them to live. Estelle was bedridden for weeks. She never fully recovered, not even after Tessa took her to California in the hope she really could find work as an actress."

He rested his forehead against the windowpane. It took him several moments to regain control of himself, but when he did, he seemed to realize that he might have revealed too much.

"My father was the Swarthout family lawyer," he said in an obvious attempt at damage control. "That's the only reason I know anything about the situation."

"Did your father also persuade the police not to investigate too thoroughly?"

The lawyer gave a short, humorless bark of laughter. "How would I know? I keep telling you—I was just a kid at the time."

When he turned to face me, I got hastily to my feet.

He made no move in my direction. I couldn't guess what he was thinking, but when he spoke, his voice was harsh and overly loud.

"If Estelle wrote anything about me in her diaries, she was delusional. She was a very disturbed woman. She was brilliant onstage, but she didn't deal well with reality."

"You sound as if you knew her rather better than you've admitted." Even knowing the risk, I couldn't stop myself from blurting out another question. "What did she promise you in return for killing her stepmother?"

His cry of agony was the most terrifying sound I've ever heard. He took a step toward me, hands outstretched as if to throttle me.

I backed away from him, prepared to make a run for it,

but in the next second Featherstone dropped like a rock. He fell to the plush carpet, clutching at his chest and gasping for breath.

Charlaine appeared in the doorway, took one look at her boss, and reached for the phone. It was a good thing she'd been eavesdropping. I was so shocked by the sudden turn of events that I couldn't have managed to punch in 911, let alone make a coherent request for an ambulance.

Chapter Forty-seven

Three days later, on Friday, the day before the deadline Tessa had set, I launched Nellie's diaries into the world. I was already in my robe and slippers, having fixed myself a grilled cheese sandwich and a bowl of tomato soup for my supper—that was all I felt like eating—when my doorbell rang.

My first thought was that someone was bringing me bad news about Leland Featherstone. As of a few hours earlier, when I'd last checked with Detective Brightwell, Featherstone was still in intensive care, his prognosis uncertain.

I'd never imagined that confronting him would cause a heart attack, although in retrospect I should have considered that possibility. With the benefit of hindsight, I recognized signs that he had a dicey heart, but I'd been so intent on proving my theory that I'd blatantly ignored them.

If it turned out he was guilty of Rosanna's death, I wanted him arrested and tried for that crime, but I'd never intended for him to end up dead.

"When will I learn?" I'd asked Calpurnia when I returned home from Monticello that day. "Solving murders should be left to the police."

Except, of course, that the police would never have interpreted that passage in Estelle's journal the way I had. Circumstantial evidence it might be, and pretty weak besides, but together with what Featherstone had told me before he collapsed, it had been enough to convince me that Estelle Swarthout had seduced her underage lover into killing her stepmother.

I opened the door to find Luke and Ellen standing on my front porch. My cousin frowned when he saw what I was wearing.

"Are you sick?"

"I'm just having an early night." His exasperated sigh put me on the defensive. "Is there some reason why I shouldn't?"

"Yes, there is. Have you forgotten? This is the evening that mystery author is appearing at the library. I thought we could all go together."

"I'm not—"

"Aren't you curious to find out who it is?"

"Not really. No."

"But you *have* to come." Ellen sounded extraordinarily insistent.

I couldn't understand why she was so upset with my decision to stay home. It was just a lecture and book signing. I eyed her with sudden suspicion. "What aren't you telling me?"

"You'll have to come with us to find out." Luke took me by the shoulders, turned me around, and gave me a gentle push in the direction of the stairs. "Go change into something suitable for meeting a famous author. Who knows? He or she could turn out to be one of your favorites."

Muttering under my breath about pushy people, I started to climb. If I stayed in, the evening was likely to turn into a pity party full of self-recrimination, and since they were giving me no choice, I decided to welcome the distraction.

Ten minutes later, looking reasonably respectable, I rejoined them downstairs. They were sitting close together on the living room loveseat with Calpurnia sprawled across both their laps. Luke jumped up as soon as he heard my footsteps.

"Ready to go? Great. We want to get good seats."

I had to chuckle at that. Lenape Hollow is a great little town, but it isn't known for having huge numbers of avid readers. This "mystery author" would be lucky if there were a dozen people in the audience. Even if the event had been advertised with a name attached, I doubted the turnout would be much better. Maybe Stephen King or Nora Roberts or the author of the latest tell-all memoir out of Washington or Hollywood could attract a bigger crowd, but anyone less famous? Not a chance.

The number of cars parked on the street and in the lot behind the building came as a pleasant surprise. Maybe more people than I'd realized read the library newsletter. I didn't think Pam had done much else by way of advance publicity. Then again, I hadn't been paying a lot of attention. I'd had other things on my mind.

Inside, at least two dozen people milled about. All of them, it seemed, had been sufficiently intrigued by the "mystery" angle to show up.

When I spotted Bella Trent among them, I quickly changed direction, determined to stay as far away from that annoying woman as possible. Ellen saw her, too, and steered us toward a trio of seats on the opposite side of the room. They were in the second row with an excellent view of the empty podium and the decorative screen set up behind it.

Another quarter of an hour passed before a smiling Pam Ingram made her way to the front of the assembly. Her face flushed with excitement, she waited until everyone quieted down before she spoke.

"Ladies and gentlemen, it is with great pleasure that I introduce our speaker for the evening, the wonderfully tal-

ented, world-famous writer of historical romances, Ms. Illyria Dubonnet."

I think I gasped aloud, although the applause from the
crowd drowned out the sound. I'm pretty sure my mouth
dropped open. I know my eyes widened in astonishment
when a complete stranger emerged from behind the screen.

Then I looked again, and "Illyria" winked at me.

The *eyes* belonged to my old friend Lenora Barton, but
the rest of her was unrecognizable. Makeup, a wig, and
certain . . . enhancements to her rather pedestrian figure,
had turned her into the very image of what a successful,
bestselling romance writer *ought* to look like. She was im-
peccably turned out in a pale blue pantsuit that clung in a
subtly flattering way to her newly acquired figure. The
wig wasn't some brassy "big hair" do, but rather an age-
appropriate confection somewhere between white and
gray. The makeup, on closer inspection, only seemed lav-
ishly applied because I was accustomed to seeing her without any at all.

Lenora threw herself into the role with an enthusiasm
that had me goggling at her throughout the talk. For a
woman who had always claimed she was happiest staying
out of the spotlight, she had come out of her shell with a
vengeance.

By the time the question and answer period arrived, my
astonishment had been transformed into admiration.
Years of teaching had given Lenora the ability to listen to
questions and respond to them in an easy manner that
made everyone feel comfortable. For the most part, her
replies were truthful. Fortunately, no one asked her if Illyria Dubonnet was a pseudonym.

At the end of the Q&A session, Pam removed the screen
to reveal two chairs placed behind a sales table piled high
with Illyria Dubonnet novels. Lenora chatted with her
fans and autographed copies of her books while Pam sat

beside her making change from a cash box and accepting checks. She even had a device attached to her iPad that enabled her to take credit cards.

I felt a moment's trepidation when Bella Trent approached her idol, but I needn't have worried. She fawned over "Illyria" but she was so in awe of her that she could barely speak coherently. Lenora dealt with her with aplomb, treating her as she would a shy student having difficulty with an assignment.

Frowning, I turned to glare at Ellen and Luke. "Bella *knew* who the mystery author was going to be. *You* knew."

"Luke arranged it all." Ellen beamed with pride. "He came up with the perfect solution to your problem with Illyria's biggest fan."

Looking sheepish, Luke shrugged. "I was concerned about the way Bella was behaving. She was *stalking* you, Mikki. So I got in touch with your friend Lenora, planning to ask if she had any suggestions."

"And?"

"And, as it happened, my timing was perfect. She hadn't gotten around to telling you yet, but since she retired from teaching in June, she's been working on a plan with her publisher and a publicist to go on a book tour."

"But she's always refused to do one before."

"Exactly. She's been a mystery author in more ways than one. That means there's a huge demand on the part of her readers to meet her in person. Her visit here is a sort of test run, but she's already booked in a dozen cities, starting on the release date of her next novel."

For as long as I'd known her, Lenora had turned down requests to give talks or do signings. She wouldn't even attend any of the conventions organized by fans of the genre. Phone interviews, blogs, and other social media advertising, things she could do from the comfort of her own home and without revealing what she looked like, had been the only exception to her publicity blackout. She'd never Skyped or used Zoom.

Her choice had made sense to me. Between her teaching career and the long hours she devoted to researching and writing her novels, she hadn't had a lot of time for that sort of promotion. Besides, she'd always said she wasn't convinced that personal appearances helped sell books. After all, her novels regularly topped the charts without them.

Then, too, keeping a low profile had avoided potential backlash from parents and school board members, who might have objected to having someone who wrote graphic love scenes in a position to influence the minds of young children. At a guess, it had been Lenora's retirement from teaching that prompted her to create this new persona and go public.

It was obvious she was enjoying herself, and she'd certainly made her self-styled "biggest fan" happy. When the evening came to an end, Bella was grinning from ear to ear as she watched "Illyria" depart in a chauffeur-driven limo.

"Lenora will meet us back at your house in an hour," Luke whispered in my ear. "She's just going to the motel to remove her disguise and collect her luggage."

Chapter Forty-eight

"Are you sure you know what you're doing?" I asked Lenora when she'd stored her belongings in my guest room and rejoined me in the living room.

Luke and Ellen were in the kitchen, fixing drinks and fetching the tray of snacks they'd managed to sneak into my refrigerator while I was changing my clothes to go to the library. I scooped Calpurnia up off the loveseat and plunked myself down with the cat on my lap. Lenora sank into the nearest armchair, grinning almost as broadly as Bella had been.

"Surprised you didn't I?" she asked. "You never know about the quiet ones."

"I know *you*. A *tour*." I barely refrained from adding, "Are you *crazy*?"

"It will be an adventure," she insisted, "and if I decide I don't like it, I can always fake a nervous breakdown and go back into hiding."

"Are you so certain you'd be faking?"

"O ye of little faith! So far, I'm enjoying myself immensely."

I couldn't help but smile back at her. If she truly enjoyed getting out and meeting her public, then more power to her. At least she no longer had to worry about what the local board of education might think of her double life. Retirement definitely has its benefits.

"Did you see how happy that one woman was just to have met me?" she asked. "I had no idea a reader could be so enthusiastic."

"That's one word for it." The wry twist to my lips must have given my feelings away. Or perhaps it was the note of sarcasm in my voice.

"What?"

"Obviously my dear cousin didn't tell you the whole story when he asked if you'd make an appearance in Lenape Hollow." I started with my first meeting with Bella and by the time Luke and Ellen arrived with our modest repast I'd brought Lenora up to date on what her biggest fan was really like.

"Poor Mikki. You've had a time of it, haven't you?" Her amusement spilled over into outright laughter. No sympathy there!

"You don't know the half of it," Luke muttered.

"Hush," I told him.

"I think I'll write Bella a note," Lenora said. "I'll make it clear to her that you were not responsible for those errors in my text, and that she's not to bother you in the future. I'll send her an advance reading copy of the new one to sweeten the pot. Autographed, of course." She took a sip of the drink Luke handed her before sending a questioning look in his direction. "I don't know the half of it, you said? Who's going to fill me in on the other fifty percent?"

"It's a long story," I warned her.

"I'm not going anywhere."

"It starts way back in the nineteen fifties."

An hour later, I'd finished recounting all the events connected to Tessa's house. By then we'd made serious inroads into the food and I'd finished one rum and cola and half of a second.

Ellen had excused herself to take a phone call halfway through the recitation. She returned in time to add her two cents. "There's been a development. Leland Featherstone made a deathbed confession. You were right about everything, Mikki. He did kill Rosanna Swarthout."

"He's *dead*?"

"Actually, no, but he *thought* he was dying. That's why he wanted to clear his conscience. As soon as he finished giving Detective Brightwell all the details, his condition began to improve."

"It really is a shame that I don't write thrillers," Lenora said. "That's such a nice, twisty plot."

"Too twisty," I complained.

Lenora wasn't listening. "I wonder . . . with a little tweaking, it might just work as romantic suspense. Set in the more distant past, of course. Perhaps during the Regency period."

"You're welcome to recycle any of the details you like." I knew I didn't have to worry that she'd write me into the story. There couldn't possibly be a market for septuagenarian heroines in the historical romance genre. "I'm just happy to be able to go back to my normal, humdrum existence, with nothing more complicated to deal with than putting together the next library newsletter."

I don't understand why they all thought that statement was funny.

"What are you going to do with the farm?" Lenora asked when she stopped chuckling.

"Sell it. If I can. There's certainly no point in hanging on to it."

Luke cleared his throat.

I glanced at him. Ellen was perched on the arm of his chair and they were holding hands. For the first time, I noticed that one of her fingers, normally bare of jewelry, sported a ring of the diamond variety.

"When did *that* happen?" Embarrassed to have blurted

out such a thing, I quickly added, "Congratulations, you two. I'm delighted."

"Now that we've decided to get married," Luke said, "we want to buy the Swarthout farm from you. We plan to fix it up and live there after the wedding."

I guess I'm just an old softie. I was so choked up with happiness that for a moment I couldn't manage a single word. Instead I unceremoniously dumped Calpurnia onto the floor and went to engulf the two lovebirds in a bear hug.

"Of course I'll sell it to you," I assured them.

Cal, affronted by such cavalier treatment, took her time about settling into my lap again after I returned to the loveseat. Eventually, when I'd been stroking her long enough, she began to purr.

With that steady vibration under my palm, the sound underscoring congenial conversation with some of my nearest and dearest, I felt quite content myself. I had no pressing deadlines hanging over my head and no mysteries left to solve. The closest thing to an obligation in my immediate future was writing the ad for the library's annual used book sale, an event that always went off without a hitch.

I had no reason to think that this year would be any different.

A Random Selection from "The Write Right Wright's Language and Grammar Tips" by Mikki Lincoln

What's wrong with this sentence from a review? *Marla Coburg sets her Corrie Blankenship series in the rural Maine village of Hyssop Falls, where she owns a yarn shop.* Answer: The pronoun *she* refers to the author, since the Corrie Blankenship series would be *it*. Since it's the character, not the author, who owns the yarn shop, this isn't only incorrect, it's needlessly confusing.

Here's another sentence that doesn't say what the reviewer meant it to: *In the Corrie Blankenship series by Marla Coburg, the heroine is busy running her yarn shop while not solving murders.* This means the opposite of what it was meant to say. Apparently Corrie is *not* solving murders. If the sentence had been *the heroine runs a yarn shop when she's not busy solving murders*, the meaning would have been clear.

Did you notice that man across the street painting—with the beard? Apparently he prefers using his beard to a paintbrush. Messy!

A one-man show, by definition, cannot be *in concert*.

Be careful not to confuse the adjectives *ascetic* and *aesthetic*. *Ascetic* means "austere." *Aesthetic* means "artistic" or "having a sense of the beautiful."

Discrete and *discreet* are not the same. *Discrete* means "distinct." *Discreet* means "prudent" or "modest."

You may be given permission to fly a friend's airplane, but *can* you? If you don't have a pilot's license, I'd advise against it.

You lay your gloves on the table but you lie in your bed. We won't get into the old joke about laying linoleum.

You pay someone a compliment, but send them a present with your complements.

Although some dictionaries now allow it (see "Is Irregardless a Real Word? at www.Merriam-Webster.com), many purists insist that it's just plain wrong, as well as unnecessary, to add that *ir* to regardless. You go to the baseball game, *regardless* of the weather.

Refer to a person as who, not that. *She's the one who went to the game*, not *She's the one that went.*

The abbreviation *i.e.* means "in other words" and should be followed by further explanation. The abbreviation *e.g.* means "for example" and should be followed by one or more examples.

When you say you mean something literally, it means you are *not* exaggerating. You say it figuratively if you are using similes or metaphors.

A recent television ad touting a dealership's contributions to a charity claimed it was "donating a portion of every car sold." This makes one wonder what the charity will do with a hubcap or a hood ornament.

A breath is what you take. Breathe is what you do.

Pronunciation of place names can vary greatly. The correct pronunciation is the one used by the people who live there. If you are in Vienna, Maine, for example, that *i* is long. Similarly, Maine people pronounce Madrid with the accent on the first syllable and Avon with the accent on the second. Calais is pronounced *callus*. Residents of Lenape Hollow, New York, named after the Native American tribe that populated the area in pre-Revolutionary War days, also go their own way. They put the accent on the first syllable of Lenape rather than the second.